STEAM UNION

Book Two of The Hayle Coven Destinies

PATTI LARSEN

ONE

I shifted uncomfortably in the wobbly folding chair, doing my best to keep the polite smile on my face though my lips and cheeks ached from it. Shenka hustled around the basement making last-minute adjustments, and I wished she'd just come sit down next to me already.

Bad enough I had over fifty witches staring at me, waiting for me to say something. I could use the support.

The space was better lit than usual, my chair on the edge of the pentagram, witches from covens all around North America crowded into the area in a rough circle, packed in layers of bodies. My toe scuffed over the painted white line, eyes roving over the old lamps Shenka dug out of the mess and set up to cast pale yellow light around the basement. We usually made due with the single bulb over the center of the room, and I found I kind of missed the shadows. This much brilliance seemed to dim the wonder I always held for this place, making it feel chintzy, somehow, almost like a carnival sideshow instead of the base of my family's magic.

So many memories down here. They crowded around me almost as much as the anxious, waiting witches. Of discomfort, unhappiness at first, sneaking my nutjob grandmother sweets to keep her quiet during coven rituals, welcoming Dad from his home plane, Demonicon, to ours. The anguish of forcing myself to use magic as a teenager though it often made me ill. Uncovering the truth of who I was, taking over my coven after freeing Gram's power from where she'd hidden it inside me.

The years pressed down on my shoulders, made me feel old suddenly. A funny concept for a woman who would supposedly live forever. I had no idea what old really was. And yet, sitting here with my hands fidgeting in my lap, tension mounting with the scrutiny of my witch peers, I felt every single second of my existence like a weight on my heart.

I knew why they were here, in Wilding Springs, in my basement. Why all the coven leaders—or, the majority of them, anyway—and their seconds perched with eager worry, arriving in pairs and quartets without notice until my basement was flooded with them and their nervous magic.

Thank goodness for Shenka. As she finally settled

beside me, her own smile easy, more practiced than mine, I reached out and squeezed her hand in thanks before drawing a breath to speak. No idea what I was going to say. But I had to say something.

"I can guess why you've come." They bobbed their heads at me, pressure of their intense focus increasing. I shifted under the stress and went on. "Our people have suffered terrible losses and we're still afraid."

"We have the right to be." Karyn Barrett, new leader of the Barrett coven, nodded sharply, her dark hair in a tight ponytail, her thick, blonde bangs wavering over her hazel eyes. The first time we'd met had been under terrible circumstances, at the Stronghold, just after Lula and Phon Kennecott helped rescue what remained of her coven. "And no offense to the new Council, but we're not seeing a whole lot of progress to guarantee our safety."

Murmurs and more nods.

You need to cut this off at the pass. A silver ball of fluff wound his way through the chairs, accepting affectionate pats and full body strokes before coming to my side. The big Persian leaped into my lap, curling his thick tail around his paws, amber eyes scanning the crowd. *The last thing we need is someone suggesting mutiny against the Council.*

I know that, I sent, testy with Sassafras. The demon in the body of the cat purred softly, easing my tension a hair.

And I know you do, he sent, much more gently. *This is a tricky bit of business, Syd.*

Tell me about it. "I know the Council is working hard to find ways to protect us," I said out loud to the waiting witches. "But Liander Belaisle and his Brotherhood have gone underground again. We all know how hard it is to uncover sorcerers when they don't want to be found."

After the havoc he'd wreaked against our territory, killing off over a third of the witch population and stealing not only their family power, but that of the Council, Belaisle had more than enough to answer for. And that was just this time around. I had older hurts to lay at his feet.

"So they say," Tallah Hensley spoke up. Shenka's sister was thinner than the last time I saw her, leaned out face hardened, posture stiff. My second twitched next to me. Shenka had only just returned to my side after spending four weeks assisting her sister in rebuilding the Hensley coven in California. The last fourteen days Shenka had been home felt like walking on eggshells with her, but I hardly blamed her. We were all pushed to our limits these days.

"I have our Council Leader's personal assurance," I said. "She's working without rest to find ways to ensure our safety and that of our families."

"If only Miriam had been Council Leader when this all fell apart." Dagney Rhodes choked a soft sob into the handful of tissues she clutched to her lips.

"It never would have happened in the first place," Paula Santos snapped at her, olive skin tight in anger. These were all new faces, their names coming to me slowly. I knew their mothers and grandmothers far better. But those women I'd once called my peers were dead and gone, lost to the takeover of our territory by the Brotherhood six weeks ago.

Six weeks. I still couldn't believe it had only been so long.

More mutterings, some of agreement, though Tallah spoke up again.

"Miriam Hayle is an excellent leader," she said, sounding like she didn't mean a word. "But, she herself has been thralled, under the influence of the Brotherhood. At this point, frankly, she just can't be trusted."

I wanted to slap her. How dare she attack my mother like that? But I held back, drew on the strength of my vampire essence for calm while my demon paced and snarled. The hitchhikers I carried in my head, their power mingling with mine, were a source of great comfort to me, now more than ever. The younger me would have lost her temper, flown off the handle, started a fight I'd win if it killed someone. But, thanks to Shenka, motherhood and my alter egos, I'd managed to mellow just a little bit. Enough I simply glared at Tallah instead of showing her just what I thought of her opinion.

Because, the truth was—and it hurt, oh, did it hurt—the Hensley leader was right.

Damn it.

"Our covens are depleted," Karyn said, young face pinched and aged beyond her twenty-four years. I'd gotten to know her a little, liked her a lot. She had a good head on her shoulders. I was more likely to listen to her than Tallah at this moment and gave her my full attention. "It will take generations to rebuild our numbers. But even if we were to replace every single witch we've lost, we're still at a terrible disadvantage." She swallowed hard, hands twisting in her lap. The scent of fear filled the room, a sharp tang of physical anxiety. "We're vulnerable and we know it, now."

I agreed with that much. Without sorcery to counter sorcery, the other paranormal races didn't stand a chance. The first magic could only be fought with more of the same. Which was why Belaisle and his Brotherhood managed to not only sway the old Council Leader, Erica Plower, into signing a treaty that gave them power over the territory, but to do as much damage as they did in such a short time.

"I'm sorry we just showed up." Karyn looked guilty, then, glancing sideways at the unrepentant Tallah. Was I going to have to keep an eye on Shenka's sister? The rage in her seemed to grow by the minute. And while I liked

Tallah, had called her an ally in the past, she and I had fought over Shenka's choice to be my second and had butted heads over other issues that kept us from being true friends. The loss of the bulk of her coven to the Brotherhood hit her hard, clearly. Still, that was no excuse to abandon good judgment.

I nodded to Karyn, let it go. I was glad Quaid was out, frankly, that Dad had the kids at Harvard with Mom. This little impromptu meeting wasn't sanctioned by the Council and was making me more nervous by the minute. But what was I supposed to do when they just popped up out of nowhere in the arms of ex-Enforcers, returned to their families in disgrace, and dropped themselves in my lap?

"I understand your concerns," I said, reaching for all the diplomacy I'd absorbed from the responsible people in my life over the years.

"Do you?" Tallah was shaking a bit, jaw tight. "You didn't lose one witch, did you?"

They watched me with hurt, fearful eyes. What was I supposed to say? "We were fortunate. And grateful."

"We're not blaming you for anything, Syd." Karyn shot Tallah a glance and the Hensley leader looked away. "Please, understand that. In fact, we're happy at least one family survived intact. And that you were there to save us."

I'd spent most of my life railing against the closed-minded arrogance and head-in-the-sand attitude of witches. Her unexpected announcement made me pause and blush. But Karyn wasn't done.

"We came here outside the knowledge of the North American Witches Council for a reason." A small smile warmed her face, took away the taut bleakness. "We need your help."

I couldn't protect them all, if that was what they wanted.

Pay attention, Sassafras snapped in my head. *This is important.*

Dagney Rhodes pushed her blonde hair behind one ear, round cheeks pink with a flush of emotion. "We know discord is the last thing we need right now." At least someone understood it. We had to work together, to trust each other. Our separate ways, the privacy witches clung to, the secrecy, had to stop. At least to the point we could go to each other with problems and ask for help without losing face. "But our numbers are so reduced." The Rhodes coven had once been over two hundred witches, now down to just over twenty. I knew personally. I saved them from the Brotherhood the same day their beloved leader, Violet, was killed. "And we are helpless if the Brotherhood returns to finish us off."

"We're proposing a second layer of connection," Karyn said. "A shadow council to watchdog the NAWC. And we want you to lead it."

TWO

I gaped at her, unable to breathe or think for a long moment. Sassafras's power prodded me gently back into motion.

There is an opportunity here, he sent.

You're kidding me, I snapped back. *Sass, this is a terrible idea. Mom would have a fit.*

I take it you do intend to inform Miriam of everything that's occurred here, and will occur in the future? His sarcasm cut through the last of my shock.

You want me to say yes and then spy on them for Mom. How despicable. I shuddered at the thought. *Better to shut this down now and walk away.*

If you don't accept they will simply act without you, Sass sent. *And you know it.*

I looked around at the determined faces staring at me. They'd already talked this through before bringing it to me, that much was obvious. I was the last stage in their plan.

"Mom needs to know about this," I said. "I won't keep it from her."

Tallah drew a sharp breath to retort, but Karyn beat her to it.

"We are well aware of your relationship to our Council Leader," she said, softening her words with another smile. She seemed to relax a little, a good sign in my estimation. "But we ask you, if you agree to lead us, to keep this secret just for a little while." She shrugged, lips twisting wryly. "We understand the irony of wanting no more secrets, and yet asking for this to remain hidden. But, Syd, you have to realize how afraid we are. And how important it is for us to find ways to stay safe outside a Council that has proven several times in the last decade they are susceptible to influence by the Brotherhood."

Okay, fair enough. From the takeover by Batsheva Moromond to Mom's thralling and now Erica's betrayal... they had a point.

Just lie, Sass said with bland abruptness. *And we'll tell Miriam later.*

"We don't plan to keep this a secret forever," Dagney said, leaning forward. "In fact, we intend to contact Femke Svennson and inform her of our plans. And suggest each territory Council enact a shadow program to watchdog their members. Like a failsafe system." She sat back again, shaking her head. "Too much power in the hands of too few. And the covens left out of the major decisions, all because we've been stubborn and proud." Her dark eyes shone with tears. "It's ironic, isn't it, the Brotherhood set us up for failure so long ago, and the repercussions are still hitting us now?"

It was the sorcerer sect that drove witches and other paranormal races underground, hiding from normals, their control of the Catholic church in the Dark Ages fueling the fear of magic in the hearts of those who didn't control any of their own. Dagney was right. Doing so made witches afraid to trust each other, to trust anyone. And drove wedges between covens, kept them apart and afraid of detection, instead of working together for a better future for all paranormals.

It had to stop. And if they were going to talk to Femke... the new World Paranormal Leader would at least listen, I knew that much. Though if I agreed to lead this shadow council, that meant I'd be the one passing on the request. And Femke and I, once solid friends, had fallen out over the last six weeks. I knew she blamed me for forcing her to accept her new role, for then being pressured to give up her leadership of the European Council and fully embrace her current job. I remained angry with her for conspiring to put my mother back on the North American Leader's seat, especially when Mom's first order had been to have her former best friend and second, Erica, burned at the stake.

Galleytrot, the black hound of the Wild Hunt, saved Mom that command. But while Erica was gone with Gwynn ap Nudd in her new form as a hound herself, I still rankled that the baby Council with Femke as their advisor put my mother in that terrible position in the first place.

"The bottom line," Karyn said with great intensity, her blue family magic coiling around her feet, stirring the power of my own coven in sympathy, "is that we only trust you, Syd. You've consistently had our backs, though we never really knew or understood it." Many of the leaders shifted, embarrassment wafting from them. "You gave of yourself without support, often in the face of opposition of those you sought to help. We want you to know we get it now." Nods, mutters of thanks. "And we want you to help us help ourselves."

"We're not asking you to save us," Dagney said, glancing around at the open, worried faces around her. "We're asking you to teach us."

So young. And eager, despite their collective fear. For a moment my heart lifted. Maybe this was a good idea. A new generation of youthful leaders, ready, willing and able to do whatever it took to ensure their safety, open to new things, to progress and change. It was a hell of a way to reorder the way of witchdom, but sometimes I just had to take the silver linings the Universe offered me and say thank you.

As if reading my mind, Karyn spoke again. "The old ways put us in jeopardy," she said. "And while we loved our leaders, we see the future, where we are heading if we don't act." A ripple of fear rose from them all, waves of emotion raising gooseflesh on my arms. "None of us want to be caught like this again."

"And while we're encouraged by the WPC's formation," Tallah said, voice harsher than her counterparts, "no one is fooling themselves here." She gestured around her, to the grim faces watching me. "We know if something like this happens again, we're on our own."

I wanted to protest, but she was correct. Sadly.

Accept, Sass sent. *And give them what they need.* His mental tone was subdued, soft. *And they* do *need this, Syd. To function. Can't you feel it? Some of them are barely holding it together.*

I did feel it, the desperation running under their fear, the terrible depression like a black mist hovering at their feet.

They need you. My vampire's mental voice was almost curious.

I turned my head, met Shenka's eyes.

Please, her mind whispered. *Help them.*

I drew a sharp breath. "I'm not the kind of leader you should be coveting." I'd already convinced myself of that.

No way would I be the right choice. I'd turned down the WPC leadership and was ready to do the same for the NAWC. Why should this be any different?

"We're not looking for a bureaucrat," Karyn said. "Or a diplomat. We want someone who we know will act in our best interest when required. And you've proven over and over you're that person, Syd, even when you've been forced to act alone because no one would stand with you." She lurched to her feet, the rest of them joining her a heartbeat later. I choked on the heavy air in my lungs as she went on, voice vibrating with emotion. "I'm here to tell you now, the Barrett coven will never abandon you again."

No mutters, this time. Pledges of allegiance from all of the coven leaders in the room, spoken in layered, shaking voices. My mind spun away from the emotional moment, looking for something to latch onto to prevent me from sobbing openly at their allegiance. Settled on the understandable realization the Dumont family wasn't in attendance. Like that was a shocker. Andre Dumont and I weren't exactly buddies. In fact, if he was still alive, I'd be surprised. After abusing and almost killing my werefriend, Charlotte, he deserved the slow, rotting death she'd inflicted upon him.

Just funny where my mind went when I was faced with something so huge I wanted to cry.

Syd. Sass's mind hugged mine, his furry head

swiveling around, amber eyes glowing up at me. *Say something, silly.*

I stood slowly, lifting him into my arms, bowed my head.

"Thank you," I said, cleared my throat around the tightness there, not entirely defeated by my thoughts of Andre and his coven. "I accept."

Their relief cleared the oppression in the room so fast I felt light headed, almost giddy. Grim expressions changed to hope, some laughter and smiles washing away the darkness. Sass hit it on the head. They needed this more than they needed anything. More than a new NAWC, more than comforting words from my mother. They wanted the chance to fight back and to do it as one, as part of a greater whole. I couldn't turn down the chance to make that happen after fighting so long to see this exact result come to being.

I waited for them to move through their flood of emotions before pulsing the room with magic to get their attention.

"First order of business," I said. "If you want to be safe from the Brotherhood, you have to fight sorcery with sorcery."

"We'd heard you've been waking power in your family." Tallah sounded almost jealous. Shenka must have told her and from the slightly guilty twitch of my second's eyes, I was right.

"Something all of you need to do," I said. "That way, if the Brotherhood returns," I refused to say "when", though that seemed much more likely, "you will be able to stand against them."

Nods of enthusiasm and another wash of excitement. This was what progress felt like. I just hoped we could maintain momentum and not fall back into old habits.

Cynical much?

"We don't want to become our enemy." Paula's shining, dark hair shivered, brown eyes huge.

"I can assure you," I said as their hesitation returned, "that won't be the case. You're all familiar with the Steam Union?"

A low level of animosity ran through the room.

"They left us helpless when the Brotherhood attacked." Karyn hugged herself, leaned away from me.

"No one knew what was happening." It was hard to be gentle, but I managed and their worry eased. "And they had their own battle to win, betrayed from within their own ranks." I didn't bring up the fact their leader, Eva Southway, had allowed that attack simply by being greedy and accepting every sorcerer—Brotherhood all— into her order after the fall of Liander Belaisle. "I promise the Steam Union members I recommend to help you will do everything they can to teach you how to use your sorcery." Now, to recruit some. Since Eva wasn't my biggest fan and seemed to have fallen off her rocker, I wasn't sure how I'd go about it. Though my grandmother, Ethpeal, and her husband, Demetrius Strong, were both in the Steam Union. Along with outcast Pier Southway for help, I was sure I'd find a way to make this work.

That was, if Eva didn't implode her own people in the meantime.

I'd have to worry about logistics later. For now, I had the coven leaders relaxing again, their optimism hugging me tight.

A moment later, Karyn's physical arms were around me, Sassafras purring enthusiasm between us.

"Thank you," she said, pulling away, blinking back tears that glistened on her eyelashes. "We knew you wouldn't let us down."

I stepped away, smiling and nodding as the leaders left, whisked away by the drawn faced and silent ex-Enforcers who had brought them to me. I knew a few of them by name only, had met them in the past. Though in some cases not their fault, the bulk of the Enforcer order had been disbanded, rather than charged with crimes against other witches for their role in the Brotherhood takeover. Since they had only stood back and allowed the new law to send witches to their deaths at the hands of the Brotherhood—unforgivable in my estimation, regardless—they had instead been sent home to their covens to bolster numbers. It was clear from their attitudes they would never forgive themselves for following orders.

The bitter, furious part of me hoped it hurt forever.

As the last of them left, I found myself standing in the back yard of my house, bare feet on the soft grass, wondering what the hell I'd just gotten myself into.

THREE

I finally returned inside, light from the kitchen drawing me onward. Shenka shuffled some dishes into the sink, Sassafras perched on the table, watching her with the end of his tail twitching.

"Well," I said with forced enthusiasm. "That was something."

Shenka's shoulders jerked, but she didn't turn around. I let her be, sinking into a chair at the table, reaching out to stroke Sass's fur.

"Your plan is a good one," Sass said.

"Thanks for that, oh high and mighty cat." It was meant as a joke, but he didn't laugh and neither did I. Shenka continued to ignore us, but before I could reach out to her to find out what was wrong, Sass went on.

"Where, pray tell, do you plan on finding enough sorcerers to train all of those covens?" His eyes flared with demon magic, ears flattening.

"I'm working on it." I sighed and sat forward, face in my hands, elbows on the table. "The main Steam Union is off the playlist, I guess." Since Eva kicked me out the last time I saw her… thing was, it was her own fault as far as I was concerned. The Steam Union fell apart because she willingly allowed former Brotherhood members to join her ranks. End of story. When I defeated Belaisle all those years ago and his organization fell apart, I had a sinking feeling the Brotherhood had another plan up their sleeves. When Belaisle resurfaced and attacked our covens, his people woke from their sleep in the Steam Union and did some damage of their own.

If Eva blamed me for that, she had another thing coming.

"I'll talk to Gram and Demetrius," I said. "And Piers, when he gets in touch again." I missed my sorcerer friend. His sister, Clover, had come for him weeks ago, begged him to help her sway their mother. I'd had a few sniffs from him since, but nothing tangible. And while I was willing to help, Piers had his own issues to deal with that had nothing to do with me.

Maybe it was time to change that. I could always try to go through Piers's girlfriend, Zoe Helios. The young Oracle who saved my family by warning me the Brotherhood were about to attack had lost her ability to see the future. But she still had solid sway over Piers. I was happy to see he'd finally found a great match and liked her very much.

But her loss of foresight led me down a far different and even more troubling line of thought. Into the fate of the Universe, the loss of visions by the Fates themselves and a huge, looming mess I just couldn't get into right now.

Focus. Gotcha.

"I need to talk to Mom." This time, Shenka spun around, hands covered in suds, dark eyes snapping anger.

"You can't!" She almost shouted at me, her voice wobbling. "Tallah said you'd betray them, but I didn't believe her." Shenka sagged, turned away.

"You're kidding me, right?" I didn't want to be angry with her, but damn it, this wasn't some game we were playing. "Shenka, do you really think it's a good idea to keep this a secret from Mom? After everything we've been through?" She shuddered, wouldn't meet my eyes. "I'm happy to help them now that they are willing to accept help. But Mom needs to be in on this and you know it."

Gently, Sass sent. *She's been troubled since she returned from California. There is more to her hurt than we're hearing or seeing.*

I let out a long breath. "Shenka." I stood up, went to her, pulled her around. She still wouldn't meet my gaze, lower lip caught so tight between her teeth the dark, glowing skin looked ashen. "You know I would never do anything to put anyone in danger. I'm the one who fights all she can to do the opposite. Right?"

She nodded briefly, without comment.

"Okay," I said, letting her go, crossing my arms over my chest and leaning against the counter. "You tell me what I should do."

She finally met my eyes, hers wide and moist. Her glossy black hair shivered as she shook her head ever so slightly.

"Oh, Syd," she whispered. "I don't know." And ran from the room, sobbing.

Okay then.

Sassafras hopped down from the table. "I'll go talk to her," he said. "You get in touch with Miriam and fill her in."

I watched his fluffy butt sashay out of the room, tail up and quivering like a furry flag. My mood darkened just enough I'd lost the optimism I felt at the support of the covens. I didn't ask for this, didn't want it. But I was stuck.

Might as well make Mom's night right along with mine.

The moment I reached for my mother, another mind touched me, drawing my attention.

Syd. Trill Zornov's magic used to feel clean, the purity of her maji creation power a breath of fresh air. But, thanks to her new friends she'd somehow managed to muddy it up with sorcery, eliminating her need for her partnership with her little brother, Owen. And worse, I worried there was something terrible going on with her, tied to her power and the people she kept company with these days.

We hadn't parted on good terms last time. I'd basically kicked her and her buddies out of the Stronghold when I found out what she'd done to her magic. But she was my friend, and I refused to just wash my hands of her, especially if she was reaching out first.

Trill. I hugged her with power and she gratefully hugged me back. *Coming over?* Face-to-face I might be able to fish more information from her.

No need, she sent. *Just checking in.*

Her reticence to talk in person made me nervous. And though it probably wasn't necessary, I wanted to see her face and feel her power at the same time, just to make sure she wasn't hiding anything from me. Paranoid? You betcha.

It'll only take you a minute, I half joked. *Too busy to see your old friend?* I winced inwardly, knowing how much I sucked at subtle.

She hesitated before sending the affirmative through her magic. *Back yard.*

I retraced my steps, the push of her energy cutting through the wards enough warning she beat me there. The family magic stirred, though it let her through. It, too, was uncomfortable with what she'd become.

Or, correction. What she was becoming. She felt different, still, as though the sorcery inside her smothered her creative power. But she smiled at me, hands in the back pockets of her jeans, long, dark hair in a loose braid over one shoulder. She'd been an angry, frustrated and intense young woman when I met her. Reminded me a lot of me, quite frankly. Trill had matured into a beautiful, though troubled, woman and I wished I'd found more time to spend with her. Maybe I could have kept her from taking this road she seemed to be barreling down with no brakes.

I approached her, hugged her for real, but Trill's embrace only lasted a moment before she let me go and backed up. The contact was enough for me to feel the rigid tension in her muscles, for my power to do a quick inventory of hers. She must have known I was snooping because she frowned and looked down, one hand sweeping back her bangs as she shuffled her boots on the grass.

"Nice to see you," I said, keeping my tone casual.

She shook her head, a flash of anger passing over her face. "Don't patronize me," she said. "Or handle me. I'm not a child anymore, Syd."

I nodded, crossed my arms over my chest. "I know," I said. "But you're kind of acting like one, Trill."

Her jaw clamped tight before loosening, sadness

passing over her entire body like a flood of grief. "I shouldn't be here," she whispered. "But I had to talk to you." Her dark eyes met mine, desperate need in them so intense I swayed toward her. "You need to believe me. No matter what happens. I'm on your side."

And yet, her words made me very nervous. "Just the fact you're saying that to me," I said, "makes me doubt, Trill." I dropped my arms to my sides, held out both hands. "Talk to me."

She stepped back a pace as though I'd threatened her. "Things are changing, so much is happening." Her hands clutched at her temples, pulling loose strands from her braid to dangle their loneliness over her face. "I have to act. But everything I do, Syd, is for the good of all."

"You're trying pretty hard to convince me," I said, power reaching for her as my own anxiety rose up and tried to choke me. Whatever she was into, it had to be bad. "Or are you trying to convince yourself?" I had to pin her down, make her tell me what was going on. But my power slid over hers and she dodged me as easily as if I'd been a normal.

"I wish you hadn't done that," she said, a tear tracking down her cheek. "I trusted you."

"No," I said, sorrow making it hard to speak. "You didn't. Or it wouldn't have been necessary."

We stood there a long moment, staring at each other while I gathered my magic to subdue her. Something was horribly wrong. And I couldn't just let her go.

Darkness burst into life, four tunnels of power opening beside Trill. The family magic crackled in protest, but I quieted it as Cable Noonan and the rest of his people stepped through. The young blood maji leader glared at me before hooking his hand around Trill's upper arm.

"We have to go." His dark eyes never met mine, thick, black beard making him seem older though I could tell from the feel of him he was close to Trill's early twenties.

"Get your hands off her." I startled myself with my powerful reaction as his grip tightened around her.

"Syd, it's okay." She let him manhandle her, a faint smirk on his face as she relented.

"No," I said, glaring right at him, hating his casual arrogance, the way his black motorcycle jacket creaked, the coldness of his gaze. "It's not, Trill. One word and I kick his ass."

"Please, don't worry about me." She took a voluntary step back with him, heading for the darkness hovering in my back yard. "I'll see you soon."

I hesitated too long. They were already moving and, knowing I'd lost my chance, I could only watch with growing worry as Cable pulled Trill into one of the tunnels and they disappeared.

But not before her eyes met mine, begging me to

understand.

I just hoped the next time I saw her we were still on the same side after all.

FOUR

Again I stood in the back yard, pondering the state of things, when two small bundles of giggling came running across the grass. They hurtled themselves at me while the tall, handsome man who escorted them laughed into the cool evening, a shaggy, giant hound with red fire in his eyes following close behind.

I scooped my daughter into my arms, kissing Ethie's tanned cheek soundly. Her blue eyes glittered with good humor, dark hair falling in perfect waves around her lovely face. She was the picture of a Hayle witch, with her father's darker skin and strong jaw. But there was no doubt in anyone's mind she was my daughter.

"Mom." She poked my nose with one finger. "Sorry we're late."

I kissed her again, set her down and replaced her with

her shyly smiling brother. Gabriel was getting so heavy, but I refused to stop picking him up just yet. At seven he looked more and more like his lost father, Liam O'Dane, than ever before. Some days seeing his handsome face made the loss of my first husband easier. I still had a part of Liam with me. But there were other times, like now in the dark mood I was in, his resemblance only brought up sadness.

He must have sensed it, because he kissed me gently and patted my cheek.

"Love you, Mom," he said.

I kissed him back, lips pressing to his forehead as I swung him back and forth in my arms.

"My sweets," I whispered. "Love you, too."

My father, formerly Teris Haralthazar, Ruler of Demonicon, now mortal Harry Hayle, bent and hugged me, Gabriel between us, Ethie sandwiching herself in our legs.

"Miriam wanted to have dinner," he said in his deep voice. I nodded, shrugged.

"No worries," I said. "We had a busy night." For a moment I considered filling in Dad about the shadow council, let him dump it in her lap, but figured Mom should hear it from me directly. I bounced Gabriel before setting him down, arms aching from his weight. "How was school?"

"Awesomesauce!" Ethie giggled at the word, covering

her mouth with both hands. She might only have been six, but she had the oldest soul I knew. Considering she carried some of the power of her great-grandmother, Ethpeal, as well as her name, I wasn't surprised at all. Her new favorite word—one she'd heard me say once and latched onto like it was the best thing ever—rang from her little lips like a battle cry. She spun in a circle, pink dress flaring out around her knees. "Nana taught us how to make fire dance."

Mom was training the two of them, thank the elements. Knowing I'd be a terrible teacher helped in the decision, though I felt bad she'd offered before the crap hit the fan. Mom had enough on her plate, running the new Council, but she insisted when I tried to renege.

"The time with your kids," she told me with tears in her eyes, "is the only joy I get. Don't take that away from me."

And so every morning Dad picked them up and whisked them off to Harvard. His ability to travel the veil hadn't left him when we'd destroyed his effigy, giving him the freedom to move about freely. Which meant I could leave the kids in his capable hands and not worry about them.

"That's cool," I said. "You can tell me all about it once you're in your PJ's and under the covers."

Ethie groaned, but Gabriel took her hand firmly in his and smiled up at me, leading his sister away. She stomped all the way to the door, head down, face scrunched in irritation. I barely held in my laughter, Dad's lips twitching, until the pair was safely inside.

Dad's snort released my amusement and we laughed together for a moment.

"I hate to say it," he told me with a grin of pure evil, "but I think she's actually worse than you were. If that's possible."

I smacked his arm. "Thanks, Dad."

He hugged me, chin resting on the top of my head. "Love you, cupcake."

Sigh.

When he let me go I didn't even bother commenting. He'd been calling me that since I was a little girl and no amount of chastising would make him stop. Ever. Besides, though I'd never admit it to him, I'd grown to love his term of endearment.

He joined me in the kitchen, the two of us barely sitting down when the shields in the back yard quivered one more time and the familiar, chocolaty power of my husband registered in the family magic. Quaid sauntered in a moment later with a hearty shoulder clasp for Dad. He crossed to me, bending to kiss me, the heat of his skin warming me up and making me feel instantly better.

Our lips weren't connected nearly long enough, though. He sank into the chair beside me with a tired sigh, one big hand running over his face. He'd developed a few lines on his forehead, barely noticeable, but there. Seeing him age, even that little bit, always made me nervous. We were both twenty-nine, but I'd stay like this forever while Quaid…

Yeah, not going to think about that, thanks.

"Long day?" He'd been gone since before breakfast, spending the majority of his time at Harvard, too, though for different reasons. His reinstatement into the Enforcer order had been on purpose. I knew Mom was grooming him, with the help of her present Leader, Varity Rhodes, to take over the Enforcer leadership as soon as possible. That meant a crash course in being the boss man. I didn't envy him and worried sometimes, though if anyone could handle it, it was Quaid.

He grinned at me. "I'm having the most fun of my life," he said, dark eyes sparkling, the scruff on his cheeks making him look so delicious I wished Dad wasn't here. My husband's hand squeezed my knee, fingers drifting up my thigh under the table, out of my father's view. I shivered slightly at his touch and the glittering in his eyes. "So, yeah. Long day. But it's worth it."

Seeing him this way made me so happy. Quaid gave up his place as an Enforcer to marry me, and I could only guess at the massive sacrifice he'd had to make. When Mom and I told him he was welcome, that the laws had been changed, the boy in him—a boy I'd only seen once or twice, one who had been beaten and kicked and almost broken—showed up in his hoot of joy.

We'd celebrated. And celebrated. I blushed, thinking about it. Maybe I could convince him an encore was in order...

"How are the new headquarters treating you?" Dad's grin told me he knew he was breaking my focus, and I blushed all over again.

"Not bad." Quaid sat back, shrugging his wide shoulders inside his black t-shirt. His dark curls fell to the collar, longer than he'd worn it in ages and my fingers itched to run through those shining strands, to caress the hot skin of the back of his neck.

Down, girl.

Quaid shifted in his seat, hand climbing further up my leg as he went on.

"It's not the Stronghold," he said. "But I think we'll manage just fine."

The former home of the North American Enforcer order was also the center of the Universe and the focus of my other problem. None of us realized just how important it was until it was too late. That it housed the broken body of Creator, nine parts scattered around the Universe. It wasn't until the heart was stolen, the Stronghold's personality silenced with its theft, that my drach friend, Max, and I figured out what was going on.

A huge mess waited to tear the Universe apart, and Liander Belaisle was right in the middle of it. Not content any longer to rule this plane, he'd tied himself to Dark Brother, Creator's sibling in the other Universe, and was attempting to steal the pieces of Creator. For what ultimate purpose we could only make educated guesses. But that theft, we believed, was the source of the loss of the Fate's ability to see the future.

Bad to worse. While I struggled to balance the fate of the Universe with the safety of witches here on this plane.

"I know Varity has been after Miriam to just promote you," Dad said.

Quaid fell suddenly silent, head dropping, a tiny frown pulling his dark brows together. His hand retreated from my leg, a forced smile coming to his face as he rubbed his thighs aggressively.

"She has," he said. And that was all.

Which immediately made my witchy—and wifey— senses fire off on all rockets.

Dad left a few minutes later. I hugged him and let him go, watching him cross the yard to the house next door. It was nice not to have normal neighbors anymore, with my mom and dad—at least when she was able—just across the grass.

I turned and went back inside, climbing the stairs to the kid's rooms. I peeked in on Ethie, finding Quaid tucking her in. She was already asleep, dark hair spread over her pillow, one hand curled up against her cheek like the petals of a precious flower. Sassafras perched next to her, his furry tail brushing over her shoulder. I kissed my sleeping daughter and left Quaid to finish up before going to Gabriel's room.

He was sitting up, looking down at his hands where green sparks danced and turned like tiny fireflies. I crossed to him, sank to the side of the bed. His hands closed convulsively over the sparks, killing them, as his serious face turned up toward mine.

I could tell there was something bothering him right away. His empathy came from his father, as deep seated as Liam's had been, the Sidhe in him doing nothing to cut his emotional sensitivity.

"Mom," he said. "All the bad stuff that happened, all the witches that died. Was that my fault?"

He said what? "Who told you that?" I leaned in, protective mother mode on full blast.

"It doesn't matter," he said, sighing. "It's true, then."

I cupped his chin in one hand, forced him to look up at me. The green sparks he'd played with now lit his hazel eyes.

"Listen to me," I said. "None of this is your fault, my fault, anyone's. But Liander Belaisle. You understand, Gabriel?"

He didn't argue with a gesture, but his expression didn't change.

"I know what I did when I was young was a bad thing." He said the words as though he'd rehearsed them.

35

"I've heard the talk, Mom. About what Ameline made me do. The Gateway to the other Universe. Everyone thinks that was the start of all the trouble."

I laughed. I couldn't help it. Gabriel's determination to take on the world's problems faded in confusion as I shook my head, still chuckling.

"Sweets," I said. "I can promise you, trouble started long before you were born. And only weak minds look for someone to blame when they could be focusing on a solution."

Gabriel nodded, relaxing a little. "But I did make a mess," he said.

"You did." I stroked his hair back from his forehead, the soft freckles on his nose wrinkling at the gesture. "But that wasn't your fault, either. Fate made sure you were there, that I was there. And Ameline." My former nemesis, Ameline Benoit, under the influence of Fate, stole my son and aged him faster than normal, using him to open the gateway. "And we're dealing with it. Gabriel, we all make mistakes. But what you did wasn't a mistake. It was necessary."

I think I got through to him. He smiled at me, hugged me hard. He smelled of the earth and fabric softener and my arms clutched him tight, a sob held firmly in my chest. He didn't need to see me break down at the reminder of how much he was like his father.

And how much I missed Liam still.

"I remember her, you know." Gabriel's whisper was muffled against my shirt. I released him, let him fall back into his headboard. "Ameline." There was no fear on his face or in his power, but there was sadness. "She wasn't a very nice person, Mom."

I had no idea he still carried memories of her. He'd never mentioned it. And now, knowing what I did about her, that her soul remained trapped in the maji chamber under the vampire mansion not so far from here... maybe there was a way to ease his conscience further.

Was I really considering bringing my son to see the woman who almost killed me?

"Sometimes I think I'm missing something important," he said. "When I'm with Nana and she's teaching me to use my power. I know more than she does." He shivered. "Mom, I can see everything when I really want to."

I had no idea what that meant, but I was afraid for him suddenly, wanted to wrap him up in magic and protect him forever. My demon rumbled her concern, Shaylee's earth power sharp. But my vampire sighed and spoke.

He must make his own way, she sent. *As you did. And we will be here for him. But if he fails or succeeds, that is out of our control.*

Gabriel settled down as my mind churned, snuggling under his covers. He sighed softly, eyes closing, drifting off to sleep while I hovered over my precious son and wondered what to do.

A wet nose pressed into my hand, the giant bulk of the black hound, Galleytrot, settling next to me. His heavy head landed in my lap as he joined me in staring at Gabriel.

"He is special," the dog rumbled, the sound of a thunderstorm approaching. "And has his own destiny to fulfill, Syd, I have no doubt of that."

"You'll watch over him?" I wanted to cry, felt tears leaking from the corners of my eyes. I pressed one hand over my mouth to hold in my sadness.

"Always," Galleytrot said. "As will you. But he is the child of two Universes, now, Syd. And I fear that means we may not be able to protect him from what is to come."

I'd been feeling the same way for a while now. Bad enough he was growing up. Whatever the Universe had in store for my son, if it was anything like what I'd faced, I could only worry and hope I'd given him the tools he needed to make the right choices.

I sat there a long time with the giant hound's head on my knees, willing Gabriel to be safe and small and sweet forever, knowing this was a battle I would never win.

FIVE

By the time I slipped into our bedroom, Quaid was already sliding under the covers. I had yet to tell him about my day, or he me about his, but from the weary look on his face I knew it would have to wait.

Still, the issue of Gabriel was too troubling to let go. I hopped up onto the bed, hands toying with the hem of the sheets as Quaid sighed and settled into his pillow, bare arm dark against the cotton.

"Gabriel seems to think the loss of witches was his fault." Anger roared suddenly now I was out of my son's gentle influence. "Who the hell would tell him that?"

Quaid's dark eyes blinked slowly. "You know witches," he said, sounding sleepy. Too sleepy for my liking. This was our son we were talking about. "They like to blame, speculate, pass rumors. He must have overheard some busybodies looking for a target. It's nothing, Syd."

"Nothing?" My brow tightened, hands fisting around the sheet. "He's seven, Quaid. He doesn't need that kind of pressure on him." I thought of what he'd said, how he could see everything if he tried. What did that mean? Anxiety bloomed along with my anger, the perfect one-two combination to render me an insomniac.

"He's a sensitive kid," Quaid said, yawning into one fist before closing his eyes. "He'll be fine, don't worry about it."

I prodded him sharply with one finger. "Not good enough," I snapped.

Quaid's eyes opened, his own anger flaring. "I'll talk to him tomorrow, okay? He's smart, Syd. He'll get it. But he has to learn to stand up for himself and not take things personally."

He did not just say that to me.

I opened my mouth to start a fight—knowing it would start a fight—only to have Quaid roll over and turn his back to me.

"Give it a rest, babe, would you?" Quaid sighed again. "I'm wiped. We'll talk about this in the morning."

Good thing I loved his Enforcer ass. Or he'd be out in the front yard with all his crap looking for a new place to live.

It took me a long time to get to sleep, as I expected,

the soft snoring Quaid settled into just adding to my irritation. But, I finally drifted off, though when I woke, groggy and cranky, he was already gone. A quick power sweep of the house just made me angry all over again. Quaid had already left for the day.

So much for helping me with Liam.

Syd. *Gabriel.*

Right.

I stomped down to the kitchen, realizing the kids were gone, too. I must have slept in. The coffee pot was almost empty, adding to my annoyance, and I grumbled and complained softly to myself as I made a fresh batch. Where was Shenka? She usually took care of it.

Whiner.

By the time I settled down at the table with a pair of partially burnt toast slathered in peanut butter and a piping cup of coffee, my mood had deteriorated into sullen funk. So, when Shenka finally swept into the kitchen, a frown on her face at the mess by the toaster, I latched onto her.

"Can you believe he just left this morning?" She was always good for a bitch fest with me when I needed one. Not often, I wasn't that kind of person, really. But every once in a while it felt good to vent with her. "He promised he'd talk to Gabriel with me and instead he just vanished."

Shenka didn't reply, pouring her own cup of coffee.

Her hands shook slightly, but I didn't comment, just sank deeper into my angst. If talking about Quaid didn't get her going, I'd have to shift complaints.

"I wish we could just find the next damned piece of Creator already." Weeks. It had been weeks. And not a sniff of luck. For all I knew, Belaisle had the others already and we were screwed. Man, I was in the worst mood ever.

"I'm sorry you're having such a hard time." Shenka's tone said just the opposite. Her testiness came through loud and clear.

I glared at her over the lip of my mug. "Thanks a whole lot, Shenka."

She tossed her dark hair, instantly contrite. "I'm sorry," she said, though her tension screamed otherwise. "I've just been so busy with the new coven members." Ever since the Brotherhood retreated, we'd been accepting refugees from fallen covens into our family. We'd grown almost double in the last six weeks. My bad mood vanished in my own rush of guilt.

"No, I'm sorry," I said, sitting up straighter. "You've been handling everything. Can I help?"

For a moment, her face softened and she smiled at me. The old Shenka I adored was home, with me again, and everything was all right. Then, her eyes tightened just before she turned away. "I can handle it," she said. "I'm your second, after all." Was that bitterness? Where was it coming from? I stood up, went to her, but her bright, brittle smile told me she didn't want to talk about it. "I'll do my job and you take care of the big stuff." Definitely a bite to her words. "As usual."

Before I could ask her what the hell her problem was, she stomped from the kitchen, leaving her coffee steaming on the counter. I stared down into the creamy liquid, alternating between irritation and sadness. Things had been strained between us since she came back from California. What had Tallah said to her? Or, was Shenka just tired of being second in our crazy family?

"It's not always about you, you know." I spun to find Sassafras cleaning one front paw from his perch in the center of the kitchen table. "There's been a lot of upheaval, Syd. Things will smooth out again. You just need to be patient."

I flopped down into my chair, no longer hungry for my crispy toast. "I know that," I said.

"I don't think you do." The silver Persian swatted at me before resuming his grooming. "Let her deal with her issues. On her own terms."

I sighed out the last of my bad mood. "And I should deal with mine, is that it, fuzzy butt?"

Sassafras just glared with his amber eyes. I leaned in, ran one finger down his furry tail.

"Okay," I said. "I get it." He hopped down from the table as I stood and headed for the basement door, coffee cup in hand. "Just, keep an eye on her for me, would you?"

Sass nodded, slipping past me down the stairs as I began my descent. "Always."

With that assurance, I let go of my worries about my son, my husband, my best friend and family. Had to. I had bigger issues to tackle this morning. And a pair of Universes to save all over again.

The concrete floor was rough under my bare feet, but ignored it as I settled into the power in the basement. I'd had to embed it all over again after we returned to the house when the Brotherhood threat was chased off. For a while, this place felt like a normal's home, not like the place I spent the last thirteen years. Amazing how emotional it made me. It was, after all, just a building of wood and stone.

But it was home. With the family magic returned to it, it had that solid, dependable feeling about it even more than ever.

Sassafras came to a halt in the middle of the basement, his tail flicking over the center of the pentagram. "Have you spoken to your mother yet?"

Damn. Oops. "I'll get to it," I said, sinking into a lotus position behind him. He turned slowly to face me, his cat brow arched, fire flaring in his eyes. "I promise. Was a little busy last night."

Sassafras shrugged. "And Femke?"

I didn't want to talk about it. "Stop being so bossy," I said.

"You two have been cool and cordial with each other for weeks now," he said. "Don't think I haven't noticed the brief times you've been in touch. When are you going to bend that proud neck of yours, Syd? Femke is your friend."

Grumble, mumble. "She could apologize first."

Sassafras sighed. "I am the last person to criticize you for standing your ground," he said. "But when it comes at the cost of a valuable ally and personal relationship, I don't mind telling you I think you're daft."

He was right. Sass was always right. Hated that.

"I really thought we would have patched things up by now." The hurt I felt at our being at odds surfaced in a way that surprised me. I didn't realize it bothered me as much as it did.

"Except you're both proud, powerful women who can't be seen to show weakness," he said. "Bad enough Femke chose to step down as European Leader." I hardly blamed her. Juggling two Councils would have driven anyone to drink. But I got his point. "It's time to reach out and mend this fence, Syd. Before it goes too far."

"Fine." I prodded his round belly with one finger, determined to change the subject. "How is your sorcery training going?"

I'm sure he saw right through my attempt, but from

the flare of excitement in his magic and the way his tail quivered like it did when he was happy told me he was giving me this out because it meant talking about his favorite topic.

Himself.

"Splendid, if I do say so," he purred, whiskers spreading out as his ears curved sharply forward, pushed in nose wiggling ever so slightly. "Demetrius is doing a bang-up job teaching the family, you know. He's all kinds of clever. Who would have thought?"

I knew what Sass meant. The first time we met Gram's husband, Demetrius Strong was the leader of the Chosen of the Light, a sect of sorcerers and witches who followed the old ways, thought all magic was evil. He'd even tried to burn me at the stake, once. It wasn't until years later I discovered not only did he know Gram from their youth, but he was actually one of the good guys, a Steam Union sorcerer tortured and turned by Liander Belaisle. It was Demetrius who helped me defeat Belaisle at the Stronghold, regaining his sanity and his health with the victory. I'd grown to adore him even when he was broken and crazy, used to Gram's nuthouse routine from my childhood. But I loved him even more now he was whole. His patience and kindness never ceased to amaze me and I couldn't have been happier for Gram she finally got to marry her one true love.

"I wish there were a hundred of him and Gram," I

said. "I'd send them out to all the covens." Waking sorcery wasn't that hard, it turned out. All it required was a sorcerer of power to trigger it through a push of energy feeding the first magic directly. Once fed, the person's sorcery was awake and aware. The hard part was teaching my coven how to control the hunger. But I had absolute faith in Demetrius and in my family.

The insatiable need of sorcery to devour wasn't for the faint of heart. But if we were going to survive another attack—and even if we were never attacked again—having the ability to use our dark power was a necessity at this point.

"I can't imagine Eva is very happy Demetrius and Ethpeal are helping out." Sassafras's ears swiveled as though he heard something, but his attention never wavered.

"Gram and Demetrius can take care of themselves," I said. "Besides, Eva's probably too busy shoving her head up her ass to even notice the world is turning around her."

Sass swatted my hand. "Sydlynn Thaddea Hayle. Language."

We laughed together. Because, language or not, it was damned funny.

"Gram doesn't seem concerned." The one time I brought it up to her she snorted and patted my cheek like I was adorable or something. "So I'm not." Okay, not much. Just enough to make things interesting.

"You'll be happy to know the entire coven is awake now," Sass said. "And making excellent progress. Even the little ones." I'd almost held off on the twelve and unders, but, to my surprise, their parents insisted and I was happy they made that choice. Everyone needed to be able to mount a basic defense, just in case. "Just let the Brotherhood try to come after us again."

I grinned at him, mind turning. "You remember what the Stronghold told me. About the difference between the Brotherhood and the Steam Union?"

Sass nodded. "That the Brotherhood are parasites," he said. "Thieves without magic of their own. But the Steam Union have earned and built their personal power."

"There has to be a way to use that weakness against them." Demetrius was, naturally, teaching the family the Steam Union way of utilizing their sorcery, Gram at Harvard doing the same for Mom's Enforcers. They learned to funnel wasted energy from decaying flora, sunlight, and their own magic into their sorcery to build the base. A Brotherhood sorcerer simply would drain whatever was around him or her to feed their need.

"I don't see how," Sass said. "There is magic in everything, Syd. How do you cut them off from everything?"

I shook my head, shrugged at last. "I have no idea.

But there has to be a way. And I'm going to find it. Time to turn the tables on Belaisle if I can."

"I have no doubt the answer will come to you." Sass's front paw rested on my knee. "Just, be careful, Syd. You know where the need for revenge can lead."

I hugged him against me, his soft fur up my nose, against my cheeks. "I'm sure you'll be keeping a close eye on me," I said. "So I don't have to worry."

When I let him go, he blinked away moisture, sniffing, turning his head away. "You'd be so lucky," he said.

I laughed, stroked his fur as our quiet moment was broken by the touch of a vast and powerful mind just before the veil before us opened and the massive form of Max, the drach leader, stepped through.

SIX

Sassafras turned and bowed his head to Max as the tear in the veil closed behind him. In turn, my big friend nodded, the light from the swaying bulb overhead catching the faint scales on his bald pate. Glittering diamond eyes swiveled to me, a faint smile on his face.

"I'm interrupting." His deep voice always sounded like there was a song behind it, the musical language of his people bleeding through.

"Not at all." Sassafras turned tail and headed for the stairs. "Will you be home for supper?"

I had no idea. "I'll try to let you know."

Sass stopped half way up, met my eyes. "You do that." And then, he was gone.

When I turned back, Max smiled wider. "He is an old soul with a young man's arrogance," he said, describing Sassafras perfectly. "I hope he knows I like him very much."

"Pretty sure the feeling is mutual." I grinned, gently punched his arm, though I could have hit him as hard as I wanted and Max wouldn't have felt a thing. "Ready to go hunting?"

"Of course," he said. "After our morning visit."

I almost rolled my eyes, but fair enough. "You know there'll be no change in them, right?" Max tore open the veil, the edges shimmering with rainbow magic. I reached for his hand, felt him pulling on me even as he dove through and into the darkness. He tossed me with practiced ease and I soared over him as his body transformed in mid-leap. No longer a giant man shape draped in a gray robe, his true form burst into life, the solid power of his wide shoulders my seat as I landed on his dragon's back and settled on the base of his neck.

Of that I am certain, he sent as his massive wings propelled us forward into the gloom. It always took me a few minutes to adjust to the darkness. When I did, the vast, web-like network of the veil came into sharp focus, the barriers between planes as clear as lines in the sand. He banked to the right, giant head leading as he spoke again. *The Fates are trapped in their loss, Syd.* His kindness and caring shone through. *We are their only connection to what's happening in the Universe.*

Consider myself chided, I sent. *I'm sorry, it's just…*

I understand your worry, Max sent. *I, too, fear if we wait too long to find the pieces, if our task of hunting them is too slow, our efforts to save the Universe will fail. But this is important, too.*

I bobbed a nod into the darkness. *It just makes me so sad to see them this way.* The Fates had lost their ability to see the future when the heart of Creator was taken. Powerful beyond measure, the Light and Dark Fates had fallen from all-knowing, all-seeing entities to a brother and sister as helpless as any newly blind normal. Broke my heart.

I, too, feel their pain most keenly, Max sent. I winced. Of course he did. He was in love with Light Fate and had been for, well, forever. Literally. And she loved him, too, only their positions keeping them apart. I knew what that was like and should have had more empathy.

Would have, in the future. Sure, Syd. Sure.

The veil split before us, Max's body shrinking as the pair of us hurtled through the tear and into the square outside the massive meeting hall. I tensed, ready for opposition from the maji leader, Zeon. He usually either stood at the top of the stairs and stared his hate and distrust or sent his cronies to do it. Maybe if he wasn't such a horse's rear compartment and actually did something about the problems in the Universe instead of treating me like some kind of magical patient zero who had to be eradicated, he might have earned a bit of my respect.

But, nope. The leader of the second most powerful

race in the Universe sat on his behind, preaching non-interference while everything went to crap around him. Threatening my son didn't endear him to me, either.

Surprisingly, there was no sign of Zeon today, nor of any of his people. The square was quiet and silent save for the burbling fountain, a woman's sculpture gracing the middle. The white marble perfection of Center always made me feel like I was in Vegas or somewhere equally contrived. Like they were trying too hard to impress themselves with their awesomeness.

Yeah, wasn't buying it anymore. I'd seen the ugly behind the curtain too many times to buy their smoke and mirror show.

My body grew upward as we approached the stairs of the massive building, the trick I learned long ago serving me well. By the time my foot touched the bottom step, the marble columns were a more normal size, the stairs easy to take, not a wall to surmount. I followed Max, staying back as he crossed the hall and to the end of the large meeting room, to another fountain and a pair of what looked like teenagers sitting on its edge.

A lovely woman, her flaxen braid swinging behind her, rushed toward us. There was a time the maji Iepa and I weren't friends. She was my guide for the prophecy I fulfilled, destroying Belaisle and then, Ameline. But we'd not seen eye to eye on her methods. It wasn't until after it was all over I realized she had as little choice in the matter as I had. Fate led us. And Iepa pushed the boundaries of her capabilities far past where she was supposed to just to help me.

I hugged her after she released Max. "So kind of you to come." She'd taken it on herself to care for the weakened and blinded Fates. Usually, their lack of physical sight didn't slow them down. If anything, it made them even more powerful, freeing them to see the future. But, without their foresight to guide them they were reduced to the darkness of normal blindness.

I couldn't even imagine how frustrating it had to be.

Max went directly to Light Fate, embracing her gently. They were an odd pair, he so giant and alien looking, she a frail, pale haired girl. But their love was as real as any I'd ever witnessed, stronger, even, for all the years they'd known each other. I settled on the fountain's edge and squeezed Dark Fate's soft hand and he smiled faintly at me, face settling back into quizzical concern.

"I must warn you," Iepa said, voice barely above a whisper. "Zeon is preaching war against you still, Syd." What else was new? "The maji are terrified you will reassemble Creator's physical form and try to take the power for yourself."

I shook my head, sighed. Whatever. "Any luck reaching the dark maji?" I'd had more positive response from them in the past, their open-mindedness at least making assistance a possibility.

"Not yet," Iepa said.

"I have an idea I want to try anyway," I said.

"Please," Light Fate's fear made her voice vibrate. Her white eyes stared at me, sent shivers through me as she held tight to Max. "Be careful, Sydlynn. The final vision cannot come to pass."

Her brother shifted beside me, hand tightening on mine. "We've had this conversation," he said, a hint of his old humor in his voice. "It's already in motion, my sister."

She turned away as if doing so would mean erasing her fear. "The end of everything," she whispered. "And it will be our fault."

We stayed a few more minutes, but I just couldn't stand it any longer. When I rose, releasing Dark Fate's hand, Max joined me with a pained expression. But he was kind when we parted ways with Iepa and the Fates, his head hanging low.

Thank you, he sent. *I know how troubling it is.*

If it wasn't the same conversation every time. I hooked my arm through his. *We have to do something before they break, Max.* I couldn't even imagine what a crazy Fate would mean for all of us. Bad enough the way they'd been before, all knowing and whatnot. But if one of them cracked... who knew if, even powerless, their fundamental connection to the Universe would alter reality along with such a breakdown? After all, they were literally children of creation, tied to the past, present and future for as long as there had been two Universes. I, for one, had no wish to test if their wellbeing meant holding things together. Not a pretty thought.

You said you had an idea, Max sent.

Thought of it last night. I joined him in shrinking to my normal size as we reached the bottom of the stairs. Still no sign of the maji and I wondered where they'd all gone. Not that I cared, really. Probably out picking daisies and singing kumbaya to each other or something.

Asshats.

When Max entered the veil, I reached out to him. *Human form*, I sent. *It's cramped where we're going and I wouldn't want you to slip up.*

I drew him along by the grip on his hand. *I think I know where you're taking us*, he sent. *The maji chamber?*

The very one. Thinking about bringing Gabriel to see Ameline had made me remember my initial conversation with the new her. About how she could feel and connect with all the maji. I hadn't asked her if she could talk to the dark version, though. Time to find out.

We stepped out together in the top chamber. I didn't trust myself enough to put us down in the tiny space below. Max didn't protest as we descended the spiral staircase underground, the carvings on the walls telling the history of this plane and my family's place in it. By the time we touched down at the bottom in the small chamber, I was hit with the same sense of reverence I always was. Old power lived here, deep underground. And now it had a voice.

She was waiting for us, smiling at me, at Max, waving a little. Ameline's glossy black hair was as flawless as I remembered, perfect pageboy bangs fluttering when she blinked her long, black lashes. Ice blue eyes that used to hold malice and hurt smiled at me, her bow mouth curving in delight, pale cheeks pinking as she watched us approach.

"Welcome," she said, reaching out with hesitation to touch my hand, just the barest brush of her cool fingertips over the back of my wrist.

"Ameline," I said. "You remember Max?"

She bowed to him and he bowed his head back. "Nice to see you again, Drach Lord."

"You're clean," he said with a hint of wonder. "The darkness has left you."

"I am only the soul of the woman Ameline Benoit," she said. "The echo of me is long gone, devoured by Syd's friend, Alison." I still woke up from nightmares at times, remembering that battle, how my former bestie and ghost turned vampirish something no one understood ate the furious echo of Ameline after I stopped her heart.

"I'm pleased for you," he said.

She dimpled. "So am I." Her gaze returned to me. "This isn't a social visit." No judgment, just curiosity. "I felt you coming. You were in Center."

Hopefully that meant this little experiment would work. "We need your help," I said. "Do you also have access to Core?" The dark maji's plane was the total opposite of the light, but I liked the supposed dark side of the race better. Go figure.

Ameline nodded immediately. "I have a connection to both," she said. A tiny frown puckered the smooth space between her brows. "But they have been quiet for some time."

"Can you try talking to them?" This was our only hope. Max and I attempted to enter Core at other times but were repelled. If Ameline couldn't get through to them we might as well just write them off and move on. But I didn't want to do that without trying everything.

Ameline cocked her head to one side, silky black hair sliding around her slim shoulders. Gone was the robe I found her in when we'd last met in the flesh, the aged look to her from tampering with my son's development. She was as young and fresh as when we'd first encountered each other, though I liked her now where we'd once hated one another.

"I can feel them," she said, voice distant. "But they aren't allowing me in."

"Can you send a message?" Maybe if I asked them nicely? I wasn't holding my breath.

"We can try," she said. "What do you want to say?"

"That the Universe needs them," I said. "And it's time to stop hiding."

Her lips pursed and she nodded, meeting my gaze again. "Sent," she said. "I will try to find you and alert you if I receive a response."

No instant gratification here, I guess. Still, it was worth the long shot if they would come out of hiding and lend a hand. "One more thing," I said, feeling suddenly nervous and a little awkward as I thought of Gabriel.

"Anything, Syd," she said, only making things worse. So weird, this new, bright and almost cheerful Ameline. How was I supposed to hate her now?

"My son." I stammered over those two words. "I'd like to bring Gabriel down here. To meet you. The new you. So he…" My lips felt like they'd grown ten times their size, my tongue seeming to swell as I fought for the words to say.

"So I can tell him it's not his fault." Ameline nodded. "Of course. I'd be honored." She paused. "He deserves to know the whole truth from me, Syd."

One more question to ask her as I breathed past the last. "Any sign of the vampires?" Six weeks ago, Sebastian DeWinter, king of his blood clan, and the aforementioned Alison, vanished without a trace, their entire family gone with them. Castle DeWinter in Austria was empty of their magic and even the house above, once populated with vampires of their bloodline, stood silent and bereft.

Ameline shook her head, sadness in her icy eyes. "I'm sorry," she said. "I have no idea where they've gone."

Was worth an ask. I refused to give up on Sebastian. We'd been through too much together. I'd saved his life twice, he my magic once, long ago. And I adored him. If I could find him and bring him back from wherever he'd gone, I'd risk my life to do it.

"One thing that may be connected to his disappearance," Ameline said, slender hand rising to stop me before I could thank her for trying. "I have noticed a shift in spirit magic."

Max sighed softly. "As have I," he said.

Ameline turned her gaze to him. "Everything is… off kilter. Wonky." Her nose wrinkled at the use of the word. Adorable, really.

"It has been," he said, "since the heart of Creator was stolen from the Stronghold."

"What does it mean for us?" I almost didn't want to ask.

Max shrugged, diamond eyes dull. "I don't know, Syd," he said. "Except that once the power of sorcery was divided, in order to protect us, spirit magic became the basis of Creator's power. I fear the effects to that particular magic will only increase with time."

I shivered while my vampire tucked herself carefully away inside me. We needed to find those pieces before the whole Universe fell apart.

SEVEN

I stepped out of the veil and into the dark basement at home, Max's farewell echoing in my head. Frustration made me stomp as I crossed the concrete floor to the stairs, tension across my shoulders giving me a whopper of a headache, one I'd carried with me all day after leaving the Fates with Iepa.

Once we left Ameline, we spent the rest of our time searching planes for the pieces of Creator. I'd never been part of a more intensely unsatisfying process as this whole search had become. When we'd first begun our task Max calmly divided the entire Universe into sections, assigning his people across the planes and, over the last six weeks, we'd been systematically touching down in each one to see if we could find trace of Creator's physical form.

With a small group of drach left behind at the Stronghold to protect Creator's statue at all times, it felt like our little adventure in futility was going to take forever. And I worried we didn't have that long.

Hey, I sent as the afternoon turned to night in my internal clock. *The critter attacks have slowed down, haven't they? Or is it just me?*

Max's affirmative mental signal was joined with worry. *I noticed the same,* he sent as we swooped over a fragrant purple field filled with tiny white flowers, pale green water rushing past. The sky was also faintly green, huge hippopotamus creatures lounging on the banks. One lifted its big head, bulging eyes so human I shuddered and looked away.

I take it that's a bad thing? How could it be? We'd been chasing creatures from the other Universe for years, crossed over first when Gabriel opened the gate and then when the demon Xeoniteridone destroyed the Node holding Demonicon's planes together. It seemed like the fight was never ending. But now, suddenly, we had the veil to ourselves again. *What gives?*

I don't have an answer, he sent. *Except that if they are gone, they have to have gone somewhere.*

Oh, yeah. Right.

I'd have to worry about it another day. For now, I stomped my way up the creaking stairs and to the kitchen, already aware how quiet the house was. The sun had set, the first floor dark. I blinked into the brightness as I flicked on the light, gaze settling on a note resting on the table.

My fingers smoothed the edges as I read Shenka's firm, scrolling handwriting:

Quaid is working late and the kids are sleeping over at your mother's at Harvard. Sassafras said he was visiting friends, but might be back when you get home. I had to run out. Dinner is in the fridge if you don't mind leftover casserole. See you in the morning.

Shenka

And, just like that, I was on my own for the night. Okay then.

I slouched over to the stainless steel door and jerked it open, wash of cold air from inside sending out a soft plume of mist. Shenka had carefully wrapped a serving of her delicious chicken specialty for me, but I just wasn't into it. The door thudded as I slammed it shut and retreated upstairs for a shower.

There was only so much time and hot water I could waste before even I got bored, especially when I was showering alone. Doing so just made me think of my absent husband and how much I missed him. We'd fallen into this uber comfortable pattern over the last seven years, mixed with kids and family that never failed to make me happy. Thinking that way as I rinsed soap from my hair made me wonder if I was being selfish about

Quaid's choices after all. Was I putting him first or was I, deep down, being a whiny baby because I didn't have him at my beck and call 24/7 any longer?

I refused to be that wife. Shudder to the gazillionth degree. And yet... it wasn't lost on me being by myself in the house with no one to talk to triggered my loneliness. Like I was going to fall apart because no one loved me anymore.

Sigh. Grow up, Syd.

Sprawling on my bed with a romance novel only made me think of Quaid all over again and the fact I was still a little ticked at him for last night and his total lack of willingness to talk about Gabriel. That, at least, I knew was justified. Or so I told myself in a huffy scowlfest. TV was a batch of police procedurals with plots so simplistic I knew who did it within minutes of tuning in. I finally got up and paced the house, wondering where this restlessness was coming from.

A quick check of the family turned up peace and contentment, though I'd learned that was a big, fat distraction. The last time I thought everything was peachy keen, a girl in flames crashed into our back yard and a third of the continent's witches ended up dead.

Okay, melodramatic much? But considering the past, I had the right to worry.

For a moment I thought about reaching out to Piers and Zoe. But I shut down my urge and shook my head at myself, standing on the top of the landing outside the bathroom door.

Get a grip. And take a night off.

I finally ended up in the basement yet again, tearing at the veil, reaching for the one person I knew would keep me company without making me feel like I was intruding. My sister's lovely, red-tinted face appeared behind the jagged slice, beaming a smile. Meira's position as Ruler of Demonicon had grown on her, and she'd grown into it. I was so proud of her sometimes I could just hug her and never let her go.

"Syd!" She was alone in her office, the towering windows behind her showing the moonlit skyline of her capital city, Ostrogotho. While I loved her husband, Rameranselot, and adored her daughter, Zuza, it was nice to have Meems to myself for once. "How are you?"

I grinned at her. "Social," I said before she could continue, or ask her usual question as to the nature of my call.

Meira laughed. "Good to know the world isn't in imminent danger."

I winked. "Didn't say that."

We talked for at least an hour about nothing and everything. Meira spun in her chair, platform boots on her desk, curving horns disappearing into her lush, black curls. It was nice to just chat without pressure or a goal, a problem to solve.

Of course I had to go and ruin it by smacking myself in the forehead. "Mom," I groaned.

Meira sat up abruptly, power crackling around her. "What?"

I waved her off. "Sorry," I said. "I have something to tell her and I keep forgetting." Bad daughter.

"Well, I have to go anyway." Meira waved to me. "Love you, sis."

Why did that make me choke up? "You, too, Meems."

She disappeared behind the closing veil and I sat there a long time, hugging myself. When I finally pulled myself together and reached for Mom, her power blocked me with a kind but firm, "Do not disturb."

Fine, then. I tried. I'd have to tell her about the shadow council later. Meanwhile, I had an olive branch to extend to a friend and this was a good time to do it. It was only then I realized why I was so restless and lonely. Because I was avoiding contacting Femke.

Oh, Syd.

I was just gathering myself in preparation for saying I was sorry, when power I didn't know tapped gently, but with insistence, on the edge of the family shields. I was so surprised I froze, jerking out of it when a second tap pulled me loose.

Polite, whoever it was.

I allowed the spirit magic through, felt the weight of

the mind on the other end. A mind I didn't know, but seemed familiar with me as she settled her power before me.

Sydlynn Hayle. She felt ancient, almost rigid, like a statue come to life. The volume of power at her disposal would have rivaled mine if she had access to other magicks. As it was, her spirit energy rippled with the weight of substantial strength.

You have me at a disadvantage, I sent in return.

You are summoned, she sent, flashing an image of a location in my mind. I'd never been there before, towering mountains in the distance, a spiraling castle climbing to the stars on one peak, clinging to the side like a delicate carving. *Your presence would be appreciated.*

For what purpose? Was this some kind of trap? She had to be a vampire. Too much spirit magic otherwise. My own vampire didn't comment, held very still inside me.

To bear witness on the behalf of Teresa Wilhelm, she sent. *At the event of her trial.*

My mind backpedaled as I tried to wrap myself around what this strange vampire just said to me. Teresa Wilhelm... wait, that was Sunny!

Her what?

The trial will commence in one half hour, she sent, her power retreating, slithering away like an old, dusty snake back to her lair. *With or without you.*

I sat there in my basement, staring into space as

though I'd been hit hard enough to stun me. Sunny was on trial? She was a vampire queen. Who could possibly be charging her with anything?

I'm afraid I might know. My vampire crept forward, her mental voice soft and strained. *They, like all other paranormal races, have a hierarchy. And Sunny is merely a single blood clan queen among many.*

How many? Okay, fine. So I was naïve to think the two monarchs I knew were the only ones. I'd never even considered the fact Sunny and Sebastian answered to anyone else. Probably because they never mentioned it. But I didn't ask, either, did I? *So, who was that? Some kind of older queen?*

My vampire shuddered softly. *The first queen*, she sent. *Or so I believe.* She turned from me, almost as though trying to hide inside me, shame radiating from her. *I remember her*, she whispered.

Before I could react, my demon and Shaylee both embraced the vampire essence, drew her out, while the family magic coiled around them all.

There is nothing to regret, my demon growled. *Nothing.*

You were hurt and afraid for your existence, Shaylee sent. *You didn't know you were harming normals when you inhabited them.*

My vampire seemed to uncoil a little from their support. *And yet*, she sent, still subdued, *the creation of the vampire race is on me.*

On Iepa. I corrected her sharply. *She made you in the first place.*

Thank you for trying to comfort me, my vampire sent, her presence solidifying and strengthening. *We all have our regrets, don't we?*

Preaching to the choir, sister, my demon sent.

Shaylee laughed. *We're quite the collection of screw ups, aren't we?*

She could say that again.

Okay, I sent. *Any idea what we're walking into?*

My vampire shook off the last of her sadness and focused, the sharpness of her spirit power pulling forward the image of the castle we'd been shown. *I'm assuming a gathering of blood clan monarchs*, she sent. *Only they would have the authority to hold Sunny to task.*

Any clue what she might be charged with? I stood, brushing dust from the seat of my jeans, turning for the stairs.

None, my vampire sent, sounding as baffled as I felt. *I'm afraid I'm so outside vampire law now I couldn't begin to guess.*

One way to find out, my demon snarled. *Kicking ass and taking names.*

We'll hold off on the violence until we know what's up, I sent. *If that's okay with you.*

Weenie, she shot back.

Might I suggest, Shaylee sent as I entered the kitchen, closing the basement door behind me, *going alone might not be the wisest course of action?*

We can take care of ourselves, my demon sent.

Agreed. My vampire paused a moment. *Still, Shaylee is correct. A show of force, even if only a small one, might help in this case.*

Exactly what I was thinking. I stepped out the kitchen door and into the cool September evening. *And I know the perfect pair to ask for backup.*

EIGHT

The dojo was a short walk away, my feet carrying me quickly as the need to hurry drove my pace. Wilding Springs was quiet around me, lights shining from houses in the neighborhood, mostly coven owned these days. I waved at a pair of young witches walking a baby in a stroller, but didn't have time to stop and chat.

By the time I reached the back door of the dojo almost ten minutes of my thirty allotted had passed. I barely lifted my hand to knock, catching my breath, when the entry whipped open and Charlotte emerged, wolf rising in her eyes.

"What's wrong?" My werewolf friend sniffed the air around me, a low growl rising in her throat. "You smell like worry."

"I need your help," I said.

"Anything." She stepped back, gesturing for me to

enter. The warmer air of the interior felt stifling after the brisk walk, my cheeks heated from the exertion. Charlotte's eyes returned to normal blue, blonde hair curling around her tanned face over the edge of the collar of her red leather jacket. She looked done up, makeup around her eyes, nice jeans, boots.

"I'm interrupting." I turned as Sage appeared. Her mate waved to me with a little frown, sea green eyes flickering with his own wolf a moment, black hair hanging across his forehead like the forelock of a horse. Sage had been my martial arts teacher for years and I owed him a lot for training me—and for loving Charlotte. Now a werewolf himself, the two of them chose to live here in Wilding Springs, Charlotte relinquishing the throne of the werenation to her brother, Danilo.

As guilty as it made me feel, I was so happy to have them here.

"It's nothing," Charlotte said. "Just a date."

Sage rolled his eyes at her and grinned. "Thanks, love."

Her flat, cold gaze didn't change at his teasing. "What's going on?"

I quickly filled them in on the cryptic message I received. "Either of you know anything about the other vampire monarchs?"

Head shakes from Charlotte and Sage both, him looking to her for information, too.

"Not a clue," she said, a faint hint of curiosity in her voice. "We've never been real friends with the vampire blood clans, outside of Sunny and Sebastian." By 'we' she meant the werenation, I was sure. "Though, now that you mention it, I've of course talked to other weres from different territories who have had run-ins with blood clans." She shrugged casually, though there was nothing casual about my werefriend. Focus made her eyes very blue. "I take it you're looking for the strong but silent types to have your back?"

"I realize there's no love lost between werewolves and vampires," I said. "And I wouldn't ask, but—" I trusted the werecouple to make sure I had the security to do what I had to do. While Gram and Demetrius would happily have come and Mom could have supplied Enforcers, I'd relied on Charlotte's quiet strength for so long, choosing her seemed the natural thing to do. I was already in mid-hesitation, wondering what I was thinking, that bringing them along could mean antagonizing the vampires, when Charlotte spoke.

"This is Sunny we're talking about," Charlotte said. "Old animosity or not, you know she's family. And how I feel about family." About the same way I did, so I nodded. "And maybe it's time the vampires of this plane finally got to see full-evolution werewolves aren't their enemy." The spark in her eye told me otherwise, that she was more interested in thumbing her nose at the undead race. But considering I was on my way to likely kick some vampire butt if that was what it took to save Sunny, I couldn't think of anyone I'd rather have with me to do it.

Neither of them hesitated a moment more, immediately stepping forward with their hands extended.

"Let's go," Sage said.

I loved them both so much.

The veil opened to me, my mind fixed on the location the mystery queen had shared. A moment later we emerged in darkness on a narrow walkway, the thin, iron railing barely offering a hint of protection from the sharp precipice. The breath of wind and change in altitude stole my breath as much as my vertigo. I'd suffered a long time from a fear of heights, partially in thanks to a fall I took once on Demonicon. Riding around the veil on Max's dragon back helped a lot to ease my fear, but every once in a while the old phobia of falling returned.

This was one of those times. I gulped for air, feet scrambling on the uneven rock at my feet, pushing me backward into the rough stone face of the path. Charlotte's hands caught me, steadied me as my pulse sped up to about a million beats per minute.

"One would think," she said in a dry and dusty tone, "the one immortal here would be the least afraid of falling."

"It's not the fall, I believe," Sage said with mild humor, looking down over the drop into the darkness of the mountains. "It's the anticipation of the sudden splat."

"I see." Charlotte's blue eyes twinkled as my stomach heaved.

"Just shut it." I glared at the both of them, swallowing the bile threatening to climb my throat. I turned away from them on shaking legs, the crisp wind hitting me full in the face. It helped knock me free of my fear enough I could focus on where we found ourselves.

Some kind of jagged mountain range, barren and cold. While extreme temperatures didn't bother me anymore, I could still feel the chill. The narrow path carved from the rock twisted up the side of the mountain, the castle from my vision towering over me as I craned my neck back and took it all in. They must have used magic to hide it from the normals. No way would a place like this go unexplored otherwise.

It was bigger than it seemed in the vision, more climbing stories than I could count, taking over the entire peak of the mountain. It kind of reminded me of the Seat on Demonicon in that way, though this was a marvel in spires and peaks, narrow towers almost delicate, and yet, at the same time, crude. A strange combination of old world and fantasy my mind simply accepted after a moment trying to quantify its appearance.

The dark rock barely reflected any light, though the blazing yellow illumination from inside cast enough brilliance I didn't need my demon's heightened vision to climb the last twenty or so feet to the giant stone gate serving as the entry. Two large vampires in heavy armor—a mix of scrolling leather and plate mail with giant bristling manes cascading down the back—stood guard, tall pikes capped with vicious looking yet intricately cast blades crossed before me.

This was exactly what I needed. Nothing like a good dose of righteous indignation and pissed-offedness to cut away the last of my fear.

"I was invited," I snarled, power shoving them both aside. They staggered, eyes wide, pikes jerking apart. I didn't wait to see if they were going to put up a fuss, instead slamming my power against the gates and shoving them wide open. They screamed on their hinges, the squeal of protesting metal echoing back from the next peak.

Way to make an entrance, Syd.

A tall, slender vampire with straight, shockingly red hair and crystal green eyes waited for me on the other side. Her slim, long fingered hands folded carefully in front of her, the floor length gown she wore reminding me of a medieval queen. The gold wire tiara just added to the façade. I guess she had no idea it took way more than someone like her to impress me.

Syd. Temper.

"Sydlynn Hayle." Her cold voice held contempt. "I've been instructed to guide you."

"No thanks." I pushed past her, forcing her off the narrow path leading to an arching bridge, the big, wooden front doors to the castle on the other side. "I can find my own way."

She spluttered at me but I ignored her, continuing my progress without slowing a step. The two guards, dressed the same as their gate counterparts, must have thought better of trying to stop me because they stepped aside long before I reached them, the doors swinging wide in welcome.

Warm light from dozens of glowing candles poured over me as I passed across the threshold. I was used to the stone construction of the castles I'd frequented in Austria and expected more of the same here. Instead, I realized I'd been right, that this place was carved entirely from the mountain itself. Arching ceilings trimmed with deep red embellishments curved overhead, the walls chipped almost smooth. The floor was rough around the edges, only a precise path down the center, leading into the grand foyer, shining as though made of glass. My sneakers slapped on the stone and only then did I feel self-conscious about how I was dressed.

Vampires flooded the entry, all decked out in the most elaborate and revealing clothing. Dresses with plunging necklines and frothing lace, gold lamé jackets trimmed in velvet and silk, dripping jewels, perfectly coiffed hair, sleeves that brushed the floor.

No time to do anything about my appearance, now. And, quite frankly, I seized on my rather plain t-shirt and jeans with enthusiasm. Let them see just what I thought of their little show.

Not much, thanks.

The vampire who attempted to escort us slipped past Charlotte and took the center of the room. There were easily a hundred vampires here, mostly female. Were there so many blood clan queens? Our guide's anger was clear in her voice as she spoke.

"You have been invited here as a guest," she said, chill with fury. "And yet, you treat us with disrespect." Her nose wrinkled in disgust at the sight of Charlotte and Sage, though the pair remained stone faced and silent. "How dare you simply barge in this way, bringing these unclean ones with you?"

Charlotte's power flared, Sage's beside her, as clear and bright as my own, the taint of sorcery long gone. The faint shift of rainbow light within it made the vampire queens gasp softly in surprise, eyes widening. I felt their focus twist from anger to doubt and a hint of fear. The vampires felt what I did. And I was suddenly glad I'd brought the pair of werewolves with me, so the queens could fully understand just what the weres had become. Let them screw with Charlotte and her people now.

This, Charlotte sent. *So worth it.*

She almost made me grin. But I couldn't allow for

amusement right now. Grasping my anger and indignation firmly in both hands, I added my own magic to the werepower and boosted it.

"From what I understand," I snapped, power rippling out of me, forming a soft rainbow mist at my feet, "we're on a tight timetable. So you'll forgive me if I'm not into the pleasantries while my friend and sister is being accused of something of which I'm certain she's innocent." I glared around the room, fishing for info. But not one of them flinched.

Damn. What kind of trouble was Sunny in?

"And keep your damned vampire paws off my wereguards," I said, though Charlotte grunted her disappointment in my head. "You touch them, I touch you. You won't like how that ends."

We hardly need the protection, she sent, though with laughter in her voice.

Quit it, I sent back. *I'm trying to be a bully*.

How's that working for you? Charlotte's faint giddiness wasn't lost on me.

I couldn't look at her. Bursting into laughter would ruin everything.

"We had been informed of your lack of respect for others." The redhead's flat tone whipped my head around.

"And I have been informed of the rudeness and arrogance of the vampire queens." That made them gasp.

Served them right. "Considering I only found out about Sunny—Teresa—and her trial a very short time ago, you're lucky this place is still standing." She glared at me while I looked her up and down in practiced disdain. "What did you say your name was again?"

Syd, my vampire choked on a horrified laugh. *Carefully.*

Screw that, I sent.

The vampire queen drew herself up, long hair shining in the candlelight, her spirit power rising to cast a white glow around her. "I am Sarameia," she said. "Queen of the Goreck Blood Clan, First Lesser Monarch to the Empress of all vampires."

Well, *la di da*.

"Which means," I said, beginning my forward motion again, "you're not the one who contacted me." She tried to block my progress, her power flaring. And, I had to admit, she was pretty strong. I might have had a real fight on my hands if I wasn't a maji. But, as things stood, she was so far out of her league she might as well have fought me with a feather.

"You will only pass when I allow it." Her teeth grit, face elongating, fangs appearing as her vampire form began to show. I'd only ever seen the true shape of this paranormal race a few times, once with Sunny herself when she fought the thrall of the Brotherhood, and I really wasn't into enduring it again. Instead, I shut her power down with a rough grasp of her magic and moved her firmly aside.

"Don't push me," I snapped. "I've had a rough day. Now." I scanned the crowd. "I'm looking for her boss." My thumb jerked in Sarameia's direction. "Stop yanking my chain and take me to your leader."

"You are here as a courtesy," one of the other vampire queens snarled at me, frothy pink ball gown shimmering with jewels. A ripple of unhappiness passed through the gathering, fangs showing, power pushing against me. "That courtesy can be revoked."

I laughed in her face. I think maybe that was what saved me. Because, if I was being honest with myself, if they decided to attack as a group, I was screwed. Knowing how fast vampires were, I might not be able to get the three of us out in time. And there was a lot of old power in this room. If I'd reacted with anger, I'm sure this would have devolved into a fight I wouldn't win. But my amusement seemed to take all the wind out of their sails as they shrank back from me.

Your reputation precedes you, Charlotte sent with her own good humor in her stern mental voice. *I can smell their fear.*

Indeed, the mental touch I first encountered joined the conversation, the weight of her ancient magic tinged with what felt like interest. *It has. You wish to speak to me directly, Sydlynn Hayle.*

"If it's not too much trouble." I kept the sarcasm to a minimum, though I chose to speak out loud, just so everyone was on the same page. "Your Empressness."

My demon snorted and even Shaylee giggled.

Syd, my vampire choked. *You are the worst.*

Don't piss me off, I sent to them. *Respect is earned.*

The crowd of vampire queens and their flunkies parted down the center, Sarameia clinging to her place at my side and refusing to join the others. I wished she'd just go away already.

Four more guards stepped forward, carrying a throne between them. I almost rolled my eyes at the arrogance of it all, only to stop and stare, and to finally feel a breath of respect.

The ancient woman on the throne looked more like a weathered doll than a person, draped in a thin robe of the palest pink silk. While her body appeared small and frail, her pinpoint bright, black eyes were full of intelligence and interest. Paper thin skin, as white as fine cotton, clung to her narrow bones, lips ridged from the teeth hiding behind them.

It's her, my vampire sent.

No kidding. I bowed my head to the ancient undead and she returned the gesture, her glossy black bob the only part of her that seemed alive, aside from her eyes. One claw-like hand rose, index finger tipped with a sharply pointed nail jabbing the air in my direction.

"You know who I am." Her voice was soft, clear, surprisingly youthful.

"I do," my vampire answered, taking over. "I remember you."

Her eyes lit with spirit fire. "And I," she said. "I remember you."

NINE

She didn't seem to move, to do anything, and yet the entire attitude of the gathering changed. The collective queens stepped back, bowing their heads, turning to engage in conversation as though I wasn't among them any longer. Only Sarameia remained, her anger a physical thing next to me.

"Great Empress," she said, fury barely contained. "Surely we shall not tolerate—"

And stopped talking. Her eyes bulged briefly, whole body rigid as the Empress turned her head slowly, glittering black eyes tracking to pin the younger queen in her gaze. I instantly admired—and feared—the intensity of her casualness, the way she didn't react with even a hint of emotion while Sarameia clawed at her chest, sinking to her knees beside me. The conversation in the room felt to silence, everyone staring with flat, judging eyes.

"Enough," my vampire said, ever so softly. "She is young, yet. Perhaps unworthy of her position. But we are ancient and meant to tolerate the errors of youth."

The Empress's sharp gaze returned to me while Sarameia collapsed, freed from whatever press of power her ruler held over her.

"Only from you," she said, "would I tolerate such chastisement. And even then…"

"Not chastisement," my vampire said with great sadness. "Grief. It was I who made you. And I am sorry."

The Empress shifted forward suddenly and my estimation of her frailty vanished. She might have been wasted and thin, but there was nothing slow or reduced about her.

"I," she said with a hint of joy in her dusty voice, "am not."

My vampire bowed my head. "Then I am grateful to know of your survival. And that you do not blame me for altering the course of your life."

Was that a smile curving the old Empress's lips? "You saved me from an existence of toil and hardship," she said. "From a life as a slave, doomed to rape and endless babies before dying of childbirth or some hideous ailment at a young age." The Empress sat back on her throne, tone returning to flat and composed. "I have been a part of you for so long, I barely remember the girl I was when we first met."

"Happy to oblige," I said, taking over. "And I'm sorry to interrupt this lovely family reunion." My vampire hissed at me, but the Empress simply nodded. "As much as I hate to break up the party, I was asked to come here for a reason. And I'd like to know what's going on."

The Empress gestured to Sarameia who had regained her feet. In a much more subdued tone, with her head bowed to her ruler, the red haired vampire gave me my answer.

"The defection of Piotr Wilhelm has led to a questioning of Teresa's monarchy. He has challenged her for her throne on the basis of his loyalty to the blood clan—which has never altered, unlike hers—and to prevent further damage to their spirit magic through experimentation with Sebastian DeWinter."

Well, wasn't this just peachy then? I'd told Sunny to kill the traitorous Piotr ages ago. At least boot his damned ass out of her blood clan. She'd always told me to mind my own business. I knew they were friends when she first became a vampire, that they had ties beyond their blood clan. But he'd gone over to the dark side a long time ago.

They were right about one thing, though. Sunny left the Wilhelm blood clan well before I was born, joining the DeWinter clan and Sebastian. Only with the death of her old queen, Yvette, at the hands of Batsheva Moromond did the opportunity arise for Sunny to take the throne herself. Did that mean her loyalty was in question? I didn't know enough about vampire law to answer that.

The bigger question was, why didn't she tell me? A wave of desperation passed through me as I reached for my vampire.

You know Sunny, my demon answered instead. *She tries to handle everything herself.*

As it should be, my vampire sent with mild chastisement. *She is a queen, after all.*

Doesn't mean we shouldn't have made sure Piotr had a convenient accident, my demon grumbled.

I agreed with her, but my vampire was also right. "You do realize," I said directly to the Empress who waited with patience as still as a stone, "the changes Sebastian DeWinter and his blood clan are undergoing only strengthen your race?" Mutters of anger. Didn't like that, huh? See how they took what I said next. "That, according to your creator, what he has become is, in fact, the final and intended step in your evolution?"

That pissed them off. The gathered queens snarled and spit at me, their fangs flashing, long claws appearing as they slashed the air in my direction. I ignored them, focused fully on the Empress before me. Her brow wrinkled, black eyes sparking with white fire.

"Is this true?" She spoke directly to the vampire inside me.

"It is," she said with my voice. "And that, I fear, is my greatest failing. That upon your creation I was too young, too hurt, to understand the truth of my existence. And exactly what you were meant to become."

They fear change, the Empress sent directly. *Teresa and her blood clan's ability to remain awake when the sun rises and even walk brief moments in the daylight have them terrified of her power.*

I knew exactly who she was talking about. *Doesn't mean change isn't a good thing.*

Agreed. She sighed in my head. *This is troubling. Though I've considered the possibility many times since hearing of the DeWinter issue.* Like he was a problem for her to unravel. *There may be a way to halt all of this, here and now.*

I'm open to suggestions, I sent.

Bring him to me, she sent. *So that he may speak for himself and allow the queens to examine him.*

I winced inwardly, knowing she felt it. *That could be a problem. He's missing. Along with his entire blood clan.*

She didn't seem surprised. *I had thought perhaps you knew of his location,* she sent, almost hesitant.

So this is why I'm really here. It wasn't a question.

I admit curiosity about you, she sent, the palest breath of embarrassment in her mental voice. *And about him.* She paused again, this time with real regret, as though knowing my answer before asking the question. *He is truly gone?*

I wish that wasn't the case, I sent. *I have a lot of people looking for him, powerful people with means beyond the ordinary. And I'm sure you've been searching for him yourself.*

She didn't answer that, but she didn't have to. *Then,* she sent, *I'm afraid there's nothing I can do. They will not relent without proof of this evolution you speak of. They need Sebastian DeWinter.*

You're the Empress, I sent, trying to prod her with pride. *They're scared to death of you.*

Vampire law has kept us from destroying each other for as long as I can remember. She actually sounded sad. *And even I cannot oppose it for fear of setting off a war between blood clans. Unless you would like that responsibility?* One of her eyebrows arched. *I understand you are quite capable of starting such fights and finishing them.*

That was a dig if ever I heard one. *Classy,* I sent.

She actually smiled at that, thin skin crinkling around her black eyes. *I'm sorry I didn't summon you sooner,* she sent. *I have greatly enjoyed our conversation. And forgive the subterfuge of bringing you here at this dire moment. I truly care what happens to Teresa and have always admired her. And our meeting was necessary, if orchestrated to preserve face.*

Don't talk to me about saving face, I snapped back. *I get enough of that crap from witches.*

Regardless the circumstances, she sent, *it has been enlightening. And I do hope to see you again.* I didn't know if she was talking to me, the vampire inside me, or both. *But I'm afraid we must return to the business at hand.*

The Empress gestured with her left hand and again the crowd parted. This time it was Sunny who appeared, glared at and hissed upon by the queens lining her path. My power reached out to her but the Empress's magic caged her tight.

Do not attempt to free her, the ancient vampire warned me with a hint of regret. *I will not allow it.*

Then don't do anything stupid, I shot back. *I won't allow it, either.*

For the first time anger appeared in her tone, sharp as a blade, as old as the earth. *I have been patient, Sydlynn Hayle.*

You have no idea what patience is. My vampire spoke for me, icy cold fury crackling back at her. *Sunny is our friend and innocent of wrongdoing. And I will defend her personally. You have my word on that. You might not fear Sydlynn, though you should. But fear me, Moa.* The Empress jerked slightly in shock. *Yes, I remember your primitive name. And the power I gave you, I can take away.*

The old vampire's presence retreated just slightly. *You wouldn't.* Fear. She was afraid after all.

I would, my vampire sent. *Though I love you like my very own, I will not permit you or anyone to harm this vampire queen for doing as I decree.*

The Empress's black eyes darted to Sunny and back to me, but she didn't comment again. Movement to my right turned my head and, for the first time, I caught the smirking, gloating face of Piotr watching me.

He's dead, my demon growled.

Later, Shaylee sent. *We'll make it look like an accident.*

No one will ever find the body. My vampire's anger still sizzled like white flames in my head.

Nah, I sent. *Why wait?*

Best thing I heard all day, my demon snarled. *Fire's a good way to kill.*

But before the rest of my egos could chime in, the familiar touch of Sunny's mind met mine.

Syd. Her power, subdued by the Empress, vibrated with tension. *Please, stay out of this.*

I won't let them hurt you. I'm sure my jaw was locked from clenching my teeth.

Nor will I, my vampire sent.

There's nothing you can do, she sent. *I'm begging you to leave it be.*

Not a chance. I cut her off as Sarameia stepped past me, seeming to have recovered some of her poise as she focused her vitriol on my friend.

"Teresa Wilhelm," she said in a voice that rang with indignation, carrying through the massive hall, "you have been accused of betraying your blood clan to further your own power by tainting your magic with that which has altered you forever. How do you plead?"

Sunny's clear, warm voice didn't hesitate. "Guilty," she said with pride swelling her magic so bright she glowed like a small star. "And I would do it again to ensure the safety and growth of all vampires."

They didn't like that, nope nope. I almost pushed past the red haired queen, but the Empress was on the case, her shell of protection holding the others back as they lunged for Sunny.

"I have no choice," the ancient vampire said with real regret in her young voice, "but to strip you of your blood clan and award your throne to your challenger. Piotr Wilhelm, step forward."

He did, with an eagerness that turned my stomach. I wanted to claw the satisfied smile from his face but held still as Sunny's blue eyes locked on mine and forced me to hold still with her gaze alone.

Power rose from her in a spinning column of white, ghosting up from her feet to the top of her head, forming a pulsing cloud just beyond her reach. She sighed and slumped ever so slightly as the magic of her blood clan hovered, the sound of soft weeping falling from it like crystal tinkling. She raised her chin, shoulders back and nodded to the Empress who slowly nodded in return before gesturing.

The magic of the Wilhelm family slammed with solid force into Piotr, sending him back two steps, gasping though he needed no air to breathe. From the discomfort on his face, the power Sunny relinquished wasn't giving him an easy time of integration, though after a moment he shuddered and relaxed.

"My first decree as king of the Wilhelms," he said, "is the immediate draining and beheading of Teresa, fallen daughter of our blood clan, to ensure her taint never damages our family again."

TEN

No one had a chance to react because I was already in motion. My power hit the Empress's hard, dividing her shields in half, wrapping around Sunny with a fist of rainbow light. She stared at me in horror, shaking her head, but it was too late.

"She's under my protection," I snarled.

Piotr flashed his fangs at me, actually nervy enough to take a step toward me, the pathetic, whining creepsalot. "Release her," he said. "This is none of your concern."

"Like hell," I shot back. I spun on the Empress who glared at me with renewed anger. Maybe she would have released Sunny after all, but no way was I taking that chance. "You want a war?" I pushed hard against her. "You want to see just what I can bring to a fight? I'll give you a battle you'll never win."

"You've made enemies here tonight, Sydlynn Hayle,"

the Empress said, cold rage clear in her voice and her power, all touch of friendliness long gone.

Boo freaking hoo. With friends like her, who needed enemies? "So have they." I jabbed a finger at the collected queens who hissed at me like the pack of rattlesnakes they were.

Oh, no they *didn't*.

It wasn't often I was in a position where I could—or would—let my power out to play. Sure, dribs and drabs of it, enough to get the job done. And less often lately, my old acts seeming to give me the advanced warning I needed to keep those opposing me in line. Tonight, though? Tonight I was feeling the urge to let it all hang out for once. Maybe it was the blatant resentment of the queens, the way they seemed to look down at Sunny, their judgment of Charlotte and Sage. Their lack of respect for everything I'd done to save their wretched hides from death and destruction over the years.

Yeah, maybe. More likely I just couldn't stand being threatened by yet another sect of know-it-all paranormals who hadn't a freaking clue what was really happening out there in the wide Universe.

The vast well of magic I held inside me often remained unseen, unfelt, because I really wasn't much for showing off.

Time they experienced just who they were dealing with.

Syd, Sunny sent in a choked mental voice as I tapped my power. *What are you doing?*

What she needs to, Charlotte cut off the former queen. *To save your ass. Be still.*

I'd never heard my werefriend use that tone with Sunny before. But it gained the silence she'd demanded. And left me to my own devices. For good or ill.

As the rainbow light of my maji power emerged, I pushed at my physical form, growing in size and height, the magic within me flaring outward, filling the entire giant foyer with the song of its combined energies. Green, blue, white, red, amber and black, all swirling in waves of pulsing light, pushing through the vampire queens, through the Empress, not harming them but allowing them to feel the immensity of what I controlled.

Heady stuff, out in the open like this. I was so used to keeping it all bottled, contained, tied neatly in a bow. I forgot just how amazing this power I controlled really felt. Grinning grimly, I straddled the center of the room, staring down at them with two balls of vibrating light in my hands, so bright the whole mountain must have glowed from it.

"Hear me," I said, voice booming, shaking the entire peak. The queen's squeals of fear brought me no satisfaction despite how good it felt to let my full power out to play. Nor did the fear of the Empress, though she hid hers far better than they did. "Your day of change is coming whether you like it or not. The very Universe is shifting, and if you choose not to change with it, your kind will perish." I glared down at them, filling my magic with stern dominance. A few fresh meeps erupted in response. "Do you understand?"

Are you threatening me? The Empress's question held no malice, to her credit, her fear more awe-filled, but with a tremor of doubt running under her mind. Doubt? About what?

No, I sent. *I'm being honest. You already know of the evolution of the werewolves.* She sent the affirmative. *And the deaths of the witches by the hand of the Brotherhood.* Again she sent she did. *All the paranormal races must come together, must be willing to work as one, including improving and evolving themselves, to guarantee our safety in the future.*

There is more going on here than you have said, she sent. Again with the doubt, aimed inward. Was she second guessing her decision about Sunny? But no, it felt far more important than that, as though her very existence depended on it. But when I pushed for answers, she deftly blocked me, side stepping my probing mind. I wasn't about to coerce her—the very idea made me want to throw up—but there was much more to her reaction than she was letting on.

I wasn't the only one holding back.

There is, I sent. *The very Universe is in danger. And I fear Sebastian's disappearance has something to do with that.*

Understood, she sent. *You can come down now.* Her fear faded, awe still in place, though a touch of amusement ratcheted up my opinion of her almost immediately.

Maybe we could be friends after all.

I slowly shrank, accepting the soft apology in her mental touch, returning to my normal size and pulling my magic back in. I felt oddly cleansed from the experience and wondered if I should let the kids out and about more often.

"Where are Frank Hayle and Chambrelle Strait?" I wasn't leaving without them. My uncle and Sunny's human servant would be in grave danger if Piotr managed to get his hands on them.

"At Wilhelm Castle," the Empress said.

"They are also under my protection," I said. No one argued with me. Smart of them. Though, from the belligerent look on Piotr's face, he wanted to fight me.

Just try it, I sent directly into his mind.

He backed off. Smart boy.

"Take Teresa," the Empress said. "But know that she is not welcome in any blood clan from this moment forth." *Forgive me*, she sent as she spoke, mental voice overriding her spoken words. *I will work on them, but it will take time. I believe, one day, the one you call Sunny will again rise to be the best of us.*

Unfair, cowardly and the epitome of frustrating. But it would have to do.

I turned to Charlotte and Sage. "Go get Uncle Frank and Chambrelle," I said. The werewolves nodded before tearing open the veil and leaving. The vampire queens watched with whispers of shock and I fought to keep my temper.

"You resist evolution," I said, "and give up so much in the denial of it." I pointed to where the werewolves had gone. "They have embraced their destiny. You call them unclean." I let them see just what I thought of that estimation in my face, in the whole set of my body judging them right back. "But they, at least, are willing to grasp change by the throat and make it do their bidding instead of hiding like poisonous spiders in dark recesses, spitefully complaining about matters that are of zero consequence to the rest of us."

No reaction aside from spiteful rage. Still. Hoped that hurt.

Sunny was shaking as I joined her, fury on her face. I knew how she felt.

Be well, Sydlynn Hayle, the Empress sent. *I hope to speak to you again.*

I didn't respond. I let my slicing open of the veil speak for me, pulling Sunny along with me.

We hit the back yard a moment later, the motion sensitive light flashing on as we landed on the soft grass. I turned to Sunny to hug her, relieved at least she was alive and well, only to stagger back when her personal power hit me full in the chest. If I'd been expecting the blow I probably wouldn't have felt it, but I was so surprised by the attack she managed to shove me away two steps before I caught myself again.

"Damn it, Syd!" Her hissing fury carried barbs of disgust. "I told you to stay out of it!"

"They were going to kill you, Sunny." It was hard not to react with anger of my own. She'd been through a lot. I really needed to stay empathetic.

"I had it under control!" More power flared, the veil opening to disgorge Charlotte and Sage, Chambrelle and Frank bursting out into the yard and the middle of our fight.

"Sunny!" My handsome, blond uncle tried to embrace her but she was too wound up. He gaped at her as she stabbed the air with her index finger, pointing it right at me.

"This is your fault!" She vibrated with fury. "You're meddling where you're not welcome. You've handed my blood clan over to the Brotherhood, Syd. And there's nothing I can do to save them now." She stepped away from me, shaking, head down, panting. "Nothing."

She so did not just blame me for this. But she didn't allow me time for a rebuttal. In a shiver of shadow, Sunny fled. Uncle Frank shot me a tragic look.

"She didn't mean that," he said.

Whatever. I let him go, shaking from the residue of

my anger as Chambrelle sighed and shook her head.

"Thank you," she said, pale green eyes full of sorrow. "My queen is simply at wit's end and has been for some time. I assure you, we know none of this is your doing."

I waved off the Amazonian normal who served Sunny and Frank. "Just take care of her," I said. Sage offered his hand, Chambrelle taking it as the pair went after the two vampires. Leaving me to stare into Charlotte's empty blue eyes and wonder if I really was to blame.

"You did the right thing," she said, before stomping through the yard and to the driveway, leaving me alone.

I went to bed, heart hurting, stressed and worried, to find Quaid still wasn't home. I really could have used his strong arms around me. Instead, I curled up in our cold bed and stared into the night for a long time before finally falling asleep.

And yes, there were a few tears involved.

ELEVEN

I woke to bright sunlight and a grumpy disposition. From the cool freshness of my husband's pillow, Quaid hadn't been home at all through the night. Way to add to my bad mood as I spun scenarios in my head going from bad to worse—as simple as him falling asleep in his office chair to dying a horrible, flaming death at the hands of some enemy. Of course, the touch of his power as steady as ever disproved my worrywart ways, which only added to the irritation I felt he wasn't there for me to question about his absence.

Rather than contact him mentally and overreact so badly I ended up screaming at him across the plane, I stuffed down my annoyance and began my own day. A shower helped somewhat, the hot water washing away some of my old anger and frustration. But it was the touch of my mother's mind that made me jump and drop the soap with a squeak of shock.

Sydlynn. I could tell from her faint amusement she'd caught a flash of where I was.

Mom. I threw a mental snowball at her. *Don't do that.*

Sorry, sweetheart, she sent. *But I thought you'd like to know we've been invited to a World Paranormal Council meeting this morning in Hong Kong. I figured you'd want to be there.*

I grumbled under my breath, ducking for the slippery bar before answering. *I'll be ten minutes.*

Meet you there, she sent and was gone. I set the bar down on the ledge and rinsed my hair before kicking myself. I should have taken the opportunity to talk to her about the shadow council. Oh well, it could wait. Not like there was a lot of forward movement on the issue right now anyway.

Faint curiosity drove me to towel off quickly and dress in something more than my usual t-shirt and jeans. Still, I refused to be typecast in a velvet skirt and silk blouse. Instead, I opted for the one suit I owned, dark blue with a pale cream shell underneath. High heels and I weren't exactly friends, but I'd managed to find a pair that didn't try to kill me every time I wore them. Their flashy red soles made me grin for some reason, so I was happy enough to slip my bare feet into them and add a couple of inches to my height.

Who would have guessed I'd look so good in a power suit? I skipped breakfast all together, not even bothering to go downstairs for coffee. I could hear and feel Shenka moving around on the first floor and reached out to her as I tore open the veil from my bedroom.

Meeting, I sent. *Be back later.*

She didn't respond, still cold with me, but I knew she got the message so I left it alone. I probably should have gone down to talk to her directly, but Sassafras's little chat yesterday reminded me she probably had her own things to work out. She'd come around and we'd find a way past this. If I'd learned anything from my fight with Sunny last night, it was to back the hell off when I wasn't wanted.

Heart still hurting from that stinging accusation from one of the people I loved most in the world, I stepped through the veil and crossed the continent and an ocean, exiting the other side of the world in Hong Kong.

The view of the huge city and harbor beyond the giant glass windows of the top floor stopped me in my tracks as it always did. I adored this place, with its cultural diversity. Once a British colony, recently returned to the control of China, Hong Kong retained its multilayered feel, still welcoming business from around the world to its towering skyscrapers and banks. A source of the normal's global economy, the entire city thrived on the unique flavor of Chinese heritage mixed with the norms and conventions of Western mega cities.

I strode down the hall, the bank of windows on my

left, mingling with the last few arriving dignitaries to the meeting. A small grin pulled at my lips as I softly grasped the large man in front of me by his very muscular arm and pulled him around. Danilo Moreau, king of the werenation, grinned down at me with a mutter of happiness, sweeping me into his broad chest for a lusty hug. I groaned at the squeeze, all the breath leaving me, while watching his beautiful wife smile indulgently. One of her slim hands rested over her round belly, the protruding presence of the next baby in their growing brood safe under her gentle touch.

"Sydlynn." Yana Moreau kissed my cheek gently, leaning over her very pregnant middle to do so. "Dani, you could have broken something." But she was still smiling, glowing as women in her condition did.

His big hand clasped me on the shoulder, loving eyes on his gravid wife. "She never complains," he said.

True enough. "Any idea what this is about?" I waited in line with them, the two Enforcers at the door carefully checking magic signatures. I understood the caution but found it irritating nonetheless.

"Not a clue," Yana said with mild curiosity. "Though, it's been gratifying to see such rapid forward motion."

I nodded as they took their turn at the door. I'd say this for Femke, she knew how to get things moving. Every meeting like this one carried us closer to forming a true whole, from signing actual treaties between territories, to enlisting paranormals in all areas of the plane to join hands with the witch councils.

Yana hugged me quickly as they passed within. "Come visit soon," she said, looking down with love at her belly. "The kids miss you and yours. Once this little one arrives in a month, I'll be swamped."

With murmured promises to bring Ethie and Gabriel to see her, I waved them off to their seats before dutifully sharing my magic signature with the two Enforcers. They knew who I was, clearly, but I sighed and complied just to keep the peace.

When I entered, I realized I was late. The Council room was full of witches, other werewolves besides the king and queen, even a few overly dressed humans I could only assume were vampire representatives. Probably best I wasn't forced to come face-to-face with their queens just yet, considering what I'd done last night. I scanned the room, the low table at the far end inconspicuous despite the gravity of the Council sitting behind it. No grand station here, no posturing. Just a line of paranormals headed by Femke Svennson.

They'd already taken their seats and the small, square man with round glasses who stood at the end was talking some mumbo jumbo about territorial disputes. I slipped down the aisle and into the open seat on the end next to Mom who slid her arm through mine and pulled me against her side.

You're tardy, she sent with a twinkle in her eye.

Long night, I sent, not meaning to be so grim.

Mom stiffened, stared. *What happened?*

And though maybe we should have been paying attention to what was going on in front of us, I told her everything about the vampire situation.

Mom's fingers dug into my arm as she bit her lower lip in frustration. *Damn her*, she sent. *Why didn't Sunny ask for help before it went this far?*

Who knows, I sent, grateful Mom was on my side. The sting of Sunny's personal attack didn't seem so sharp with my mother's power hugging me.

You did the right thing, she sent. *From the sound of the situation Sunny would have ended up dead and Frank a prisoner of Piotr. Syd, we have to deal with it.*

I'll talk to Femke when this is over, I sent. *She might be able to do something. But at least the old Empress is willing to work on the rest of the queens.*

We'll see, Mom sent. *Anything else I should know about?*

I didn't get a chance to go on. Not when a black tunnel of power burst into view just a few feet from me, flooding the aisle beside me with darkness. I surged to my feet, my own sorcery blooming outward in response, ready to take down whoever came through that gap. Only to freeze in shock at the sight of Eva Southway stomping her way out of the black. She came to a halt facing Femke and the Council, face pinched and angry as the tunnel collapsed behind her.

"Leader Southway." Femke stood, nodded to Eva with way more composure than I would have had in her place, gestured to a seat in the front row. "I was hoping you would finally join us. Your input is invaluable to this Council."

Eva didn't seem to be in the mood for gracious hospitality. Her sorcery slapped Femke's offer away with a crack of power against power while everyone gasped at her arrogance. Except me, of course. I was already on the move down the aisle, heading for her, when Femke's magic hit me hard and stopped me in my tracks.

Let me handle this, she sent before cutting off.

I was getting really tired of hearing people say that and not following through.

"I have no interest in your little game or your pathetic Council," Eva said, voice carrying sharply around the room, fed by power. "I've come to inform you the Steam Union is off limits and the next spy you send to us will be summarily executed." She gestured, a second tunnel opening, a young witch falling through with a groan. He collapsed on his side, shivering, wide eyed. I understood his reaction. Traveling through sorcery tunnels was a particularly soul devouring experience the first time around. And, from the look of things, he'd been mishandled before he was put in the tunnel in the first place.

The Council stirred, anger on their faces, Femke's hardening, blue eyes and pale skin framed by light blonde hair giving her the regal appearance I always compared to an ice queen.

"There was no need to harm him," she said, holding her ground. "None. He was a peaceful envoy, Eva."

The Steam Union leader stepped away from him, disgust on her profile as I circled slowly, my power feeding him, warming him up. He scuttled out of the way at last, heading for Femke as Eva spoke.

"You heard me," she said, a wave of sorcery washing over the room, smothering everyone. She wasn't taking power, just pushing hers over ours. To her, a clear demonstration of her superiority I could only imagine. "Stay away from us from now on. We want nothing to do with you or your troubles."

Femke nodded sharply. "Very well," she said. "You may go."

I might have been still pissed with her, fed by her attempt to keep me from smearing Eva on the carpet under my high heels, but I had to admit my friend was brilliant. The Steam Union leader's face darkened to scarlet, lips a slash of fury across her face. She twitched in rage, tunnel opening almost on top of a small cluster of witches who were forced to leap out of the way, scattering their chairs and colliding with others in their row.

"I'm done being treated like a slave," Eva snarled, gaze traveling over the crowd while I wondered what the hell she was talking about. "And being looked on like the enemy." Okay, she'd clearly cracked her nut. Except I remembered the reaction of the witches of the shadow council and finally, grudgingly, understood. She had to be facing opposition and, in some cases, blame from those who suffered at the hands of the Brotherhood. Still, it was her own fault for not acting, not taking the initiative to help us in our time of need.

"We aren't the Brotherhood," Eva's voice swelled, warbled as she glared like she'd just been mortally insulted or personally attacked. "But if you're looking for an enemy, I'll give you one!" Before anyone could react, even me, Eva stepped backward into the tunnel of darkness and vanished with a soft pop of dissipating power.

The outcry began immediately. I helped the displaced witches right their chairs before returning to my aisle seat beside Mom. By then, Femke was tapping her glowing blue gavel on the table, the ringing sound bringing order.

"We can't allow the Steam Union to run free with that woman leading them." The big king of the werenation surged to his feet two rows and the room's width away from me.

"We will handle the Steam Union and Eva Southway," Femke said. "I assure you of that, King

Danilo."

"Like you've handled the Brotherhood?" I didn't know the witch who spoke up, but her accent identified her as from somewhere in India. So Yamini Dhavan was sending her people here to cause dissent, was she? The Indian Council Leader probably wasn't working alone.

But no. The moment the witch fell silent, another stood up and focused her power on the complainer. I could tell from the force of her magic, the tone and touch of it, she came directly from Yamini. "We have had six short weeks," she said, dark skin and hair a match for the other witch's coloring, as was her accent. "Our own Council Leader is behind the WPC one hundred percent. And we've made great progress in a very short period of time." She sat down in a huff, looking up at Femke who smiled faintly, nodding.

"We realize there is a great deal to be done," Femke said, her voice soothing, a soft wave of power embracing all of us and, in doing so, proved to me yet again why she was the best choice for this job, like it or not. "And we are taking aggressive steps to ensure the safety of all paranormals. To that end, we would like to announce the creation of our very own Enforcer order." Murmurs of surprise ran through the room, including mine. It was a great idea, absolutely. "We will be drawing from the other Council Enforcer ranks in the beginning, starting with only a few to ensure we don't deplete the best and brightest." Made total sense to me and I wasn't the only one to think so from all the head bobbing. "Moreover, we would like to ask any werewolf, Sidhe, sorcerers or vampires who would like training in the Enforcer order to submit themselves for testing. It is our goal to make this a truly inclusive group, dedicated to the protection of all paranormals."

Okay, she was absolutely brilliant. Even I hadn't thought of that.

"All will be trained in every discipline possible for their race," Femke said, "and formed into teams of diversity to ensure the greatest chance of success." I could just picture the logistical frustrations and grinned. Glad I didn't have to deal with it. "All will be fully trained in sorcery, so they will never be at risk from that dark power at the hands of the Brotherhood."

Mom was nodding in time with me. I was ready to go hug Femke. This was exactly what we needed.

"That being said," she went on, "our new force needs a powerful leader, one who has experience in dealing with all manner of magicks." That was a tough one. My mind sifted over the few Enforcers I knew well and discarded them all. Had to be a European or something.

Or something.

"Please," Femke said, gesturing toward the back of the room. We all turned in our seats as once while she went on. "Welcome World Paranormal Council Enforcer

Leader Quaid Hayle."

Oh.

My.

Dead man.

TWELVE

I gaped in shock, heart thudding painfully in my chest as Mom hissed in my ear, not composed enough to connect mentally.

"Did you know about this?"

I shook my head, mute, as Quaid walked past me dressed in an Enforcer robe, cuffs banded, not with blue, but with all the colors of magic. He came to a halt next to Femke who stepped out around the table to join him. Together they faced the crowd of whispering paranormals.

"Enforcer Leader Hayle has a unique perspective. As the husband of Coven Leader Sydlynn Hayle, his exposure and experience with a multitude of magicks makes him the perfect selection for our new Enforcer order."

I choked on her smooth explanation, eyes boring

holes through my grim faced and serious husband. Did he feel how angry I was? He had to be burning up from it. Had to be.

What the hell was he thinking?

"Thank you, Council Leader Svennson," he said in his deep voice, warming up as he nodded to the crowd. "I am honored to accept this important position and will do everything in my power to uphold the laws of our Council."

If he survived me kicking his damned ass across the plane.

Mom and I sat together, fuming side by side, the occasional muttered curse escaping her. I barely had time for her anger, though I understood it. She'd been grooming him to take over for Varity Rhodes. I wondered if the old Enforcer leader knew about Quaid's defection.

How could Femke do this? Just steal Quaid out from under me? And he didn't say a word, didn't talk it over with me, nothing. Nada. Just took the damned job and that was that.

You do realize, my vampire sent softly, *Quaid is his own person and doesn't require your permission.*

That burned my socks. *We're married*, I snapped at her. *The least he could have done was warn a girl.* Damn it, how long had he known?

Still, she sent. *Perhaps a gentler approach than anger might yield better results.*

Whatever.

The meeting broke up a few minutes later, though I held my place until the room was almost empty. The cowardly bastard didn't look my way once, though I was sure he knew I was there. When he finally lifted his chocolate gaze to mine, his face was set and blank.

Don't give me that look, I snapped in his head. *Don't you dare, Quaid.*

He moved toward me, sighing in my mind. *I don't suppose you'd understand why I needed to do this.* My husband came to a halt beside me while Mom glared up at him. She stood, her power pushing against his chest, not a blow, but a steady pressure like a fist.

"I need to go," she said, voice cold, brushing her lips over my cheek. "It would appear I have a new Enforcer leader to train." Quaid's brow furrowed, one hand reaching for her, but she was already pushing past him without a word, fury in every line of her body. Blue power flared and Mom was gone, leaving him to my tender mercies.

If meat hooks were tender.

"I'm keeping the job," he said, anger in his tone though he kept his voice low, arms crossing over his chest. "No matter what you say."

He did *not* just try to bully me.

"I don't give a hot damn about the job, Quaid." With

every word I poked him hard with power. "Not one hot damn. What I do care about is the fact you didn't tell me." He flinched, guilt smothered by returning temper. So, he knew he was wrong and was trying to justify it to himself, huh? Now all his long days and absences made sense. He'd been splitting time working with Mom and with Femke, playing both sides.

"I was going to," he said. "But I knew what you'd say."

"What's that, then? Hmm?" I pulled away from him, shaking my head. "Since you can read my mind and everything."

"Can we not do this here?" His face darkened as he glanced right and left at the few paranormals still chatting nearby.

"You do not get to dictate anything to me," I snapped. "Now, answer the question, Quaid."

"You would have told me it was too much and that you needed me home with the kids." He turned his face away. "For the good of the coven."

Was he freaking kidding me? "You've gone so far off your rocker you've landed on your ass," I said. "What the hell made you think I'd say anything like that?"

He didn't answer, face stony.

Okay, Syd. Deep breaths. This was my husband, the man I'd loved since I was sixteen years old, had fought and clawed and bled to have at my side. Was he right?

Quaid finally turned back, a hint of sadness in his eyes. "I'm sorry," he said, though his voice was dull.

I wasn't ready to accept an apology. "We're not just married," I said, lowering my voice. "We're best friends, Quaid. You just broke my trust with this little stunt. I only want what's best for you and if you believe otherwise, you don't know me as well as you think." Damn it, the waterworks were showing up and I didn't know if I could hold them off. "Who do you think asked Mom to change the damned law to let you be an Enforcer again in the first place?"

He flinched from that. "Syd—"

I couldn't help it. I batted his hand away. I didn't want him touching me right now.

"We'll talk about this later," I said, turning away from him. "Once we've cooled off. I just can't have this conversation right now."

Quaid let me go as I walked away. But I didn't make it far. My breaking heart solidified into jagged splinters without my consent, aimed right at the tall, blonde woman who walked toward me with one hand half raised in a wave of welcome. She must have seen something that shocked her because Femke came to a halt with her blue eyes wide and lips parted in surprise as I stomped to her side and got in her face.

"You had to have my husband." I didn't mean it that way. Quaid would never cheat on me, I knew that. But the fury I felt at him came out at her.

Her surprise turned to shuttered anger in a flash. "I have no idea what you're talking about."

"Did it cross your mind maybe Mom wouldn't appreciate you poaching her next Enforcer leader?" My fisted hands trembled at my sides. "What the hell is wrong with you?"

Femke's coldness sent a chill down my spine as her power pushed me firmly but gently out of her space. I let it.

"I am, as all of you have requested of me, doing the very best I can to make this Council strong and viable." That was a dig at me, yup, sure was. She was still pissed I suggested she take the leadership. She could suck that up right now and choke on it. "Quaid is the best possible choice, as I said." A hint of doubt crossed through her eyes. "He didn't tell you."

"No, he didn't," I said, disgust so powerful I had to back away from her. "And neither did you."

Her anger was still there, but flavored now with self-recrimination. Didn't do much to ease my temper, but the self-righteous crankass in me was happy to see it.

"I'm sorry for the misunderstanding," she said.

Misunder… Snap.

"Besides," she leaned in, temper flaring, whispering the next words to me. "This isn't about poaching, is it? It's about Quaid, controlling him. Like you try to control everyone around you." She might as well have punched me in the face. "You should be happy for him, not beating him up for taking such a dangerous job."

I could barely breathe, lips working as I tried to speak past my fury.

"Oh, and Syd?" Femke's tone turned sweet, though her anger still flared in her eyes. "Stay away from the Steam Union and Eva Southway. I don't need your particular brand of help. I'd rather the whole plane didn't implode because you thought your way was the right way. Is that understood?"

She turned her back, Quaid brushing past me, the scent of spices and his warm musk just driving my anger higher. With a snarl, I tore open the veil and leaped through, screaming my fury into the darkness until I could only sob in frustration.

THIRTEEN

When I finally stepped through the veil and into the basement, I was under control enough to wipe the tears from my face and not go looking for a cardboard box to kick with my sharp toed high heels. Barely.

Sassafras perched on the bottom step, staring up at me with huge amber eyes. The moment I saw him the tears started again, though I didn't know why I was crying. I sank to the step and hugged him, not caring if I got silver fur on my nice navy suit. His purring soothed me enough I made it to hiccup stage and was able to tell him what happened without hitching a breath.

"The idiot!" Sassafras's snapping tone told me he was behind me all the way and that make me feel so much better. Mostly because I knew I had a temper and was worried maybe I jumped the gun, overreacted. But the way my silver Persian's body quivered in anger I knew I was right, had the right to be angry and upset. "What was Quaid thinking?"

"He thought I'd oppose it," I whispered, wiping at my nose with the cuff of my jacket. "Am I that mean, Sass?"

He shook his head, butting me solidly with it. "Of course not," he said. "But a little family consultation would have been nice. And Femke." Sass sighed. "I know she's under a lot of pressure, but if she was trying to alienate Miriam—and the other Council Leaders for that matter—she did a wonderful job." I stared at him, blank. "Syd," he said with gentleness that made it through to me, "she stole him, plain and simple. Do you think the other Council Leaders won't be nervous she'll do the same to them? They won't trust her from now on. And that's trouble."

I hadn't thought of that. They were a suspicious lot to begin with. Damn her! If only she'd mentioned it to Mom, to me…

Water under the crumbling bridge.

No time to continue my pity fest. Not when Karyn Barrett's mind reached for me. The young coven leader may have sensed something was wrong, but the mix of sadness and excitement in her mind helped distract me.

Syd, she sent. *You're going to want to come visit. I have someone here who'd like to see you.* And, with that, she let me see who she was talking about.

I lurched to my feet, Sass still in my arms, reaching for the veil. *I'll be right there.*

A heartbeat later I stepped out into her living room and crouched down next to the filthy, lopsided form of Pender Tremere.

Sassafras leaped down from my grasp and into the former Enforcer Leader's lap, purring loudly as he head butted the limp man. Pender sat, long legs folded under him, leaning softly to one side, face covered in a dirty, scraggly beard, hazel eyes slightly out of focus. His hair had grown longish, receding hairline seeming more pronounced. His skin had a pale, yellowish pallor even under all the dirt, long, lean body draped in a grime encrusted old coat, pants torn and stained. He'd never carried much extra weight and the last six weeks hadn't been kind in that department.

Pender's tongue ran over his cracked lips, eyes finally registering me. A faint smile lifted the corner of his mouth, though the light was so far gone from him I almost starting crying again. Pender had spent the majority of his time as leader of the North American Enforcers doing things that broke his heart. And now, I feared, whatever the Brotherhood had done to him finished the job.

Mom. I reached for her with desperate need. Her crackling anger hadn't eased much, but she felt my distress and focused immediately. *Pender.*

She froze. *I'm coming.* And her power left mine.

"Hello." Pender's hand lifted, the scent of decay and body odor so strong I almost flinched away, but couldn't. I let him run his dirty fingers over my cheek. "Pretty lady."

"Hi, Pender." I took his hand in mine, squeezed it. He looked away again, mouth slack as he stared into the distance, though he other hand slowly stroked Sass's fur as if by automation.

I looked up when Karyn sat delicately on the edge of the couch with a sad expression on her face. "Where did you find him?"

"On the street," she said. "It was pure luck, Syd. One of the girls recognized him by accident. He was homeless, eating out of dumpsters, living in a shelter. His power is still there, but it's like he's forgotten who he is." She wiped at one cheek, a single tear escaping. "Can you help him?"

Blue fire flared and Mom appeared, face crumpling at the sight of Pender. She crouched next to me and I moved out of the way as her hands cupped his face.

"Dear Pender," she breathed before looking up at Karyn. "Thank you for finding him. We'll take it from here."

Karyn nodded to Mom, glanced sharply at me, but I shook my head. Damn it, the stupid shadow council. And Karyn was worried I'd told Mom. If only I'd found the right time and place.

I stood as Mom tried to help Pender stand. My eyes drifted around the small living room, the run down appearance of the furniture, how crowded it seemed to be with a least a dozen people peeking out from various doorways.

"How many are living here?" Concern bloomed.

"Sixteen," Karyn said, blushing, rushing on as though she needed to explain. "Our family money disappeared when the coven was attacked. We've been doing our best to recover, but it's hard." She smiled at the two little girls who tucked in between the legs of an older woman from what looked like a small kitchen. "Besides, no one wants to live alone right now."

So, the Brotherhood had pulled the same trick on her he did on my family, using his hacker ways to siphon off the family fortune. Well, I had a possible solution to that if my old friend and recent new ally, Simon, was up for the challenge.

"Let me look into the family money," I said as Pender tottered to his feet, leaning on Mom. "I might be able to help you recover what you lost."

Relief flooded over Karyn's face. "Thank you," she said. "That's exactly why we—" Her gaze went to Mom, faint panic flaring. "Thank you."

Sigh.

A few minutes later, after a brief farewell, Mom and I

settled Pender onto a soft bed in the back of a coven house in Wilding Springs. Lula and Phon Kennecott both bent over the man, their power flaring as they examined him. I stood back, Sassafras's eyes glowing where he hovered on Pender's pillow, adding his power to the healer twins.

When they pulled back, their matching faces were grim.

"He's been broken," Phon said, one hand running through his dirty blond hair, freckles crinkling as he wrinkled his nose. "By the Brotherhood. His mind is shattered."

"I'm so sorry." Lula patted the fallen Enforcer's hand. "We can make him comfortable, but his recovery is unlikely."

Mom turned away, cheeks bright with color, eyes moist. "Do the best you can," she said.

"Miriam?" Pender's voice cracked, spun her around, drew me closer. He smiled up at her, childlike, sweet despite the ground in filth, the beard. He looked so young suddenly, sparkling.

"Pender, my dear." Mom sank to the edge of the bed, held his hand. "How are you feeling?"

"So lovely for you to come visit," he said. "I've missed our talks." Pender picked suddenly at the beard on his face. "Someone left me a donut."

Okay then.

"You're safe now," Mom said. "Lula and Phon are here."

"Syd." His head snapped up, eyes blinking.

"Me, too," I said, bending over Mom's shoulder.

Pender's face crumpled. "They're gone." His voice wailed out so sharp I flinched from him at last. "Gone just like that." His fingers snapped, the sound of cracking bone though it was just his index and thumb rubbing together. "Sebastian tried, so hard. He almost saved me." Pender's lower lip trembled. "Alison, so sweet, her ghost is a demon, did you know?" I had no idea what he was talking about, but this was the first I'd heard of my vampire friends in ages and I had to get as much from the damaged Enforcer as I could.

"Where did they go, Pender?" I prodded him softly with magic while Mom hissed at me. I ignored her. "Show me where."

His eyes glazed over a moment. "All gone," he whispered.

"Did the Brotherhood hurt them?" If it was Belaisle I was going after him right now and not stopping until I turned over the rock he was hiding under.

But Pender's mind was already spinning, his power reaching for mine in a herky-jerky twitch of magic. I let him make contact, saw images spin through his head, broken pieces I could barely make sense of.

Only one sliver of a vision made any sense and scared

the crap out of me. I pulled away, examining the moment with growing fear while Mom patted Pender's hand.

Not the Brotherhood. No, not even close. If Pender's damaged memory was to be believed, Sebastian and Alison—and their entire blood clan by association of blood ties—were sucked through a glowing white hole in the veil and vanished.

I spun back to ask more questions, only to find Pender in Mom's arms, choking huge sobs while she rubbed his back and murmured comfort.

FOURTEEN

I went home. There wasn't much else I could do. Mom joined me a few minutes later, sitting at the table with me over a cup of coffee. For a brief moment I wondered where Shenka was, knew I should fill her in on everything, but I was too heartsick and tired to do much more than talk with my mother.

"What are we going to do about Quaid?" I really didn't want to have this discussion but it was important.

Mom shrugged, a bit of her residual anger showing. "There's not much we can do." She sighed it out, toying with her spoon. It made musical clinking sounds against the side of her mug. "He's made his choice. I just wish he'd let me know so I could have found a replacement." Her eyes met mine. "He didn't tell you? Not even a hint?"

I snorted. "Claimed he thought I'd tell him to be a good baby daddy and stay home." Whatever.

129

"Considering I was excited for him to take the job with you? His argument is invalid."

"Is that what you call it?" Sassafras sniffed from over his bowl of fresh milk, clearly offended.

Mom stroked his fur in absent irritation. "We'll just have to make do," she said, stopping her petting of my silver Persian to rub one temple, a sure sign she'd developed a headache. "Varity didn't take it well, but she's going over the list of candidates now."

That was good at least.

"I have to go, sweetheart." Mom swept to her feet, hugging me before pulling away. "I'll see you for dinner. I think a nice family meal is in order tonight, don't you?"

I smiled and waved to her, turning away as she flared in blue fire and vanished. Only to turn back with a curse on my lips.

What the hell was wrong with me I kept forgetting to talk to her about the shadow council?

Perhaps you don't want to tell her, my vampire sent.

Sounds legit, my demon piped in.

You always were one for standing against authority, Shaylee sent.

Thanks for that, I shot at them. *I'll tell her tonight before dinner.* For now, I had a job to do for said shadow council that had less to do with acting behind Mom's back and more with helping the smaller covens regain their dignity.

I had no idea how many of them lost their family

money, but I could guess the Brotherhood would make a sweeping effort and had to assume it was all of them. I was already crossing the back yard with Sassafras at my feet, the pair of us entering the park on the other side by the time I reached for Apollo Zornov.

He came trotting toward me a few minutes later from the far side of the green space, his younger brother, Owen, in tow. I waved at them from the swing I rocked back and forth on, heels scraping the sand beneath me, waiting for them to join me before speaking.

"Nice suit." Apollo had this flirty, arrogant way about him that showed up less lately than it used to. And while I knew I should have been offended at times, I couldn't help but grin at him when he winked at me in brazen flattery.

"I need the help of our mutual friend again," I said. "Care to take a trip to visit BitsandBytes?" Simon was brilliant, though I didn't think much of his screen name. Still, my former close friend from high school who Ameline and the vampires ruined was now a hard core hacker. He'd freed up the Hayle family fortune, returning it to me less a hefty fee I figured was well worth it just to thumb my nose at Belaisle.

Owen extended one hand, impossibly blue eyes glowing with amusement.

"We'd be delighted, Coven Leader Hayle."

I left the cranky and offended Sassafras behind,

letting Apollo take the lead, showing me again where to go. The warehouse on the quiet street overlooking the small city I'd yet to identify looked far different in daylight. But the moment we stepped inside I realized it wasn't just the lighting that had changed. The whole place felt super charged with leftover magic. Heart pounding, I led the way this time, Apollo and Owen trailing after me, to the office door with the smoked glass now shattered and scattered over the concrete floor. I pushed past it, high heels grinding over shards as I stared in shock and fear at the shattered monitors, smashed banks of CPU's. Simon's precious computer system was destroyed and there wasn't a trace of him.

"The Brotherhood." Owen's brows pulled together, his sorcery slipping out in thin ropes, ends twitching as if sniffing the air.

Apollo nodded, grim and angry. "They found him. Took him. In retaliation."

For helping me.

Oh, *hell* no.

"We're going to find him," I snarled through clenched teeth. "And rescue his scrawny ass."

Apollo was already on the move, slipping a smart phone from his pocket, fingers racing over the screen. "Leave it to me," he said.

As much as I wanted to do otherwise, I knew he would get the job done. And then I would deal with whoever hurt Simon. They would regret the day they were even a glimmer in their momma's eyes, you betcha.

There was nowhere else to go but home. I had Max to contact, planes to search. I was surprised the big drach hadn't reached for me already. I knew if anything happened he'd let me know right away. But I had to tell him about what Pender saw, share the vision with him. Max worried, as Ameline did, the spirit magic of our Universe was in trouble. Was the disappearance of the DeWinter blood clan part of that?

If so, what did that mean for Sebastian and Alison?

I slipped off my heels at the border to the yard, wanting the cool grass under my feet. I could have landed in the basement, but I needed another dose of the outdoors to chill me the hell out. Of course, coming face-to-face with my angry husband halfway to the back door wasn't conducive to releasing my stress.

"Tell me you wouldn't have fought my decision?" Quaid vibrated with anger, his t-shirt taut across his chest, thighs jumping in his jeans. I'd never seen him so upset.

"I wouldn't." There was no other way to say it. Plain and simple and honest. I let him feel what I was feeling so he would know the truth.

It just seemed to make him angrier.

Quaid spun away from me, hands tossing in the air. "I needed to do this for me, Syd. For me. Not the family, not you and the kids. I know that's selfish, but damn it."

He stopped, head down. "And for all of us." His gaze lifted to meet mine. "I was powerless when the Brotherhood came to hurt this family. I won't let that happen again."

My words choked off in my throat as he stomped away, slamming the door behind him. The sudden flare of his departing magic told me he'd left again and I let him go. More stuff for those around me to work through on their own.

Goody.

And though I wasn't in the mood to deal with more, I forced myself to walk into the kitchen and confront my second. Shenka's face was pulled tight with anxiety, though when she noticed me watching her standing at the counter, staring at nothing as if the weight of the whole plane sat on her shoulders, her expression stiffened to forced casualness and a polite smile that didn't reach her dark brown eyes.

"Shenka," I said. "We have to talk."

"About what?" She turned her back on me, pouring a sloppy cup of coffee as her hand shook. She slammed it down again, frustration radiating from her. "There's nothing to talk about."

I couldn't let this go. "Please, tell me what's wrong. I want to help."

She barked a laugh, so bitter it hurt. "Like you helped Sunny?" How did she hear about that? And, besides, I had helped Sunny. "Like you helped Quaid just now?" She was eavesdropping?

"That's none of your business," I snapped before I could stop myself.

Shenka froze, half turned to face me, expression hard and sad. "I guess you're right," she whispered. "Thanks. You did help."

Before I could ask her what she was talking about, Shenka pushed past me and left the kitchen, the sound of her feet stomping up the stairs ending with the slamming of her bedroom door.

I forced a deep breath in and out of my lungs before my shoulders would unwind, my jaw unclench. It felt like I was suddenly living with a pack of irresponsible teenagers or something. The world had fallen apart and what? That gave everyone permission to become assholes?

Not on my watch. I spun, ready to go beat down Shenka's door and demand an explanation for her behavior when darkness flooded the back yard. I spun and ran for the door, heart thudding, though the feel of the sorcery was familiar, if not entirely right. I realized as I skidded to a barefoot halt, my heels still clutched in one hand, that the power I was feeling was Southway all right, but not Eva or Piers.

Clover, my friend's younger sister, stood shivering outside her tunnel, long, black braid swinging behind her, dark eyes full of worry.

"Syd," she said. "I'm sorry to drag you into this. I really, really am."

Another disaster? Yeah, I could handle it. "Where's Piers?"

"That's why I'm here," she said, voice shaking. "You have to help him, all of us. Mom's lost her mind."

FIFTEEN

A furry white bundle bounded across the yard toward me, Sass leaping up into my arms as I slipped my feet back into my high heels. He settled against me, breathing hard as Clover tentatively stroked his fur.

"Nice to see you again," he said. "Now, take us to your mother, there's a good girl."

Considering Clover was probably in her early twenties, his gentle but condescending tone should have pissed her off. I guess it was a testament to the treatment she was used to receiving from her domineering mother that Clover simply bobbed a nod and turned into the tunnel she'd left open for us.

I thought you were going to help the Kennecotts with Pender, I sent to the silver Persian as I followed Clover into her sorcery. A thin shield was all I needed to protect us from the hunger of her power. Not that she would have fed from us, only that this particular mode of travel left me unsettled, like being inside the belly of a starving whale in icy darkness.

You *left* me *behind on your little excursion with the Zornov brothers,* he sniped. *That tiff of yours with Quaid caught my attention, so I headed home. But when I felt Clover arrive I thought you could use my help.* We exited the other end of the tunnel into the back hall of a quiet house. At least, I guessed it was a house. The walls were dark paneled wood, old school, and reminded me of Harvard. Giant bookshelves climbed their stately way to the ceiling, a sliding ladder on wheels tucked in one corner. I could only guess there wasn't a genre novel among the collection as Clover turned to me, voice soft and nervous.

"This is the Steam Union house in Nottingham," she said in her soft English accent.

"Nicer than the sewers," I said, recalling the last time I'd seen her. When the Brotherhood imploded the Steam Union, they'd fled to a safe house under the city. While fragrant, it managed to keep them protected.

Clover wrinkled her nose but didn't comment past a flash of a smile. "I managed to escape Mum's notice long enough to come for you, but that won't last long." She froze, looked toward the large door at the other end of the room. Faint light filtered in through the heavy curtains, dust motes doing their dance of joy in their brief respite from the dimness. The scent of oppression was everywhere, age and mildew paired with unbending pride, like the house itself was stuck up. "Mum was controlling before now, Syd. She ran a tight ship." Like that was a good thing, at least from Clover's explanatory tone. But the tension in her face, the hurt in her eyes, told me things had changed to the point even loyal members like her own daughter were afraid. "Now, she's paranoid. As though everyone is out to get her." Clover shivered, hugging herself inside her pale blue button up sweater. "Especially Piers."

"He's been working on her." I knew that much.

Clover bit her lower lip. "Actually." She paused. "He's been under house arrest since he returned."

So the messages he was okay... "Your mother's been faking his contact with me." The bitch.

Clover looked away, embarrassed. "No," she whispered. "I have."

"Why?" I thought she loved her brother, was on his side. Was I wrong?

When Clover looked back at me, I saw the conflict in her and felt, for the first time, compassion for Piers's sister. She loved her mother and her brother. And was doing her best to hold her family together. But something had changed, enough she brought me here, to center of her mother's power.

That made me far more afraid than it probably should have.

The door slammed open with a thundering boom as Clover and I, Sassafras tense in my arms, turned toward the now gaping entry. Eva Southway stormed through, a handful of her people at her side.

"What is the meaning of this?" She glared back and forth between me and Clover before her face twisted with cruel glee. "Well done, child. You've caught an intruder." Eva stalked closer, eyes shining with her own particular brand of madness. And while I usually felt badly for those I'd known who'd lost their minds, Eva's insanity stank of self-preservation. Which meant I wasn't about to cut her any slack.

Unless she'd find a way to hang herself with it.

"I'm here to see Piers." No way was I showing an ounce of respect or ground giving. I pushed past Clover and matched Eva's stance, the silver Persian in my arms holding still, amber eyes glowing in the gloom.

"You are an unwelcome intruder," Eva snapped. "And you will leave immediately or I will make you leave."

I almost laughed in her face. "Piers, Eva," I said. "Now."

Before she could respond, Clover slipped up to my side. "Please, Mum," she said, voice shaking. "If you would just let him go—"

Eva's entire attitude changed, rage flaring over her face, power bubbling up beneath her like a mutant vine bursting from the ground. "Traitor," she hissed at her daughter. "You brought her here! I should have known not to trust my own blood."

Clover shrank from her mother while my temper heated up a notch.

"Listen up," I said. "I won't ask again. Bring Piers here now or get the hell out of my way."

"You have no right to be here," Eva snarled at me while her people watched and waited. Some seemed eager to back her, but the rest were as nervous as Clover. I wondered if push came to shove how many would stand at their leader's side against me.

"I have every right," I said, "considering my friend—who is no longer one of you, by the way—is being held against his will."

"So you say," Eva said, eyes narrowing. "Where is your proof?" I could feel her power testing me, but no way was she brave enough to call me out. I'd crush her and we both knew it.

"Let me see him," I said, "and I won't need any."

"We'll see about that." Eva's magic guttered as she reached out, past the walls of the house. What was she doing? "I demand you come and remove this witch at once!"

Before I could figure out who she was talking to, blue fire flared and two figures appeared a few feet away. Femke's jaw clenched when she laid eyes on me, my husband's dark gaze taking in everything, but avoiding mine. Eva wasted no time pointing at me as though I'd eaten her unborn child with strawberry jam and a nice bit of biscuit. "Time to take out your trash, Femke."

I quivered with fury, but Sass's mind touched mine.

Patience, he sent. *Don't stoop. She's lost it, Syd. We need to be in control.*

I knew that.

Damn it.

"Are you here uninvited, Coven Leader Hayle?" Femke's tone was flat, cool. She'd warned me to stay away from Eva, after all.

"No," I said. "I was asked to come, brought here personally by Steam Union member Clover Southway." I glanced at the girl, gratified to see her bob a frightened nod at the Council Leader.

Lucky, Syd, Femke sent in a private burst. "If that's the case," Femke said, turning her chill on Eva, "why am I here exactly?"

"She's yours," Eva said. "And even if my disloyal daughter brought her here, I want her out. Now."

"Considering you rejected the entire Council in the first place," Sassafras spoke up, as dry and cold as Femke, though far more cutting as was his way, "I'm surprised you think Leader Svennson or the World Paranormal Council would in any way assist you when you asked for such." He bowed his head to Femke. "It was most courteous of you to come here, under the circumstances."

Too clever by far, she sent to both of us. *But thank you for that, Sassafras.*

"Which means," I said directly to Eva, "you can't just call on them whenever you want to. Just so you know."

"Since we're here," Femke said, "may I ask why I was taken from a very important meeting to deal with this?"

"She's holding Piers against his will," I said. Clover nodded again, her misery clear as she ducked behind me. Her mother's piercing gaze of rage was all the reason I needed to step between Clover and Eva. She might be grown up, but Piers's sister had never been allowed to mature past a bullied girl. By her own mother, no less.

"Again, you have no proof past the lies of that creature." Eva practically spit in my direction. She'd disowned her own daughter with those two words. The mother in me wanted to punch her in the face and hug Clover tight while we watched her bleed on the floor.

"Perhaps not," Femke said in a thoughtful tone, as though there wasn't enough tension in the room to cut all of us to the quick if we made the wrong move. "But I, too, would like to see Piers." She smiled faintly at Eva. "Kindly have him brought here, if you don't mind."

Eva twitched under Femke's gaze. *Take that, you crazy cow.*

"He is under arrest," Eva finally blurted. "For crimes against his people that have nothing to do with you."

Femke shrugged delicately, stepping back from us. "Then, by your own admission, my presence here is a waste of time. You can't have it both ways, Eva. Either I speak to Piers right now or I leave and you deal with your intruder alone."

At least she hadn't hung me out to dry.

"Eva." Her husband, Felix, separated himself from the gathered Steam Union members watching. One hand settled on her shoulder which she shrugged off. He had the same soft features as Clover, even under the dark beard. His eyes were far too kind, too gentle and I knew where his daughter got her meekness. "Perhaps it would be best to just let Piers go."

She spun on him, hand flying across his face with a slap so hard he staggered back, the sound of contact echoing in the sudden quiet.

"I WILL NEVER LET HIM GO!" Spittle flew from her lips, sprayed him with soft dots of moisture as he straightened with a terrible, broken grief on his face. Was that what this was about? Piers leaving her? He was clearly far more like his strong willed mother than his weak father and sister. Did Piers's defection begin Eva's downturn? "Do you hear me? NEVER." She spun back on Femke and Quaid. "Get out of my house."

Syd. Femke's mind touched mine, a hint of desperate anxiety in it. *Be careful.*

Don't worry about me, I sent back as I gently set

144

Sassafras on the back of the chair next to me, prepping for a fight just in case. *Get out of here. Wait about ten minutes. Then send body bags.*

Her mind twitched, pushing against me even as a fresh tunnel of darkness opened and Gram and Demetrius stepped through. Eva drew a breath to scream at them, too, I was guessing, only to be beaten to the punch.

"Eva Southway," Gram said in a booming voice, "as a duly accepted member of the Steam Union, I declare you unfit to lead our order and demand you step down in favor of fresh blood."

SIXTEEN

Go, Gram.

And while I hadn't been expecting this turn of events, I took advantage immediately, linking my power to my grandmother's.

"Witnessed," I said. "As an impartial third party."

Sure was.

I thought Eva's little temper tantrum over releasing Piers showed the massive fault line in her psyche. Gram's nuclear bomb drop set off a visible chain reaction in the over stressed Steam Union leader. I watched her thought process—such as it was—crawl across her face, her whole body, from shock to horror to fear and, finally, inevitably, into absolute crackerjack rage.

Before she could blow Mount Southway, Gram spun and addressed the Steam Union members who watched with pinched expressions and true fear on their faces.

"We all know our order is suffering under her leadership." Gram wasn't pulling any punches, Eva twitching with every word that left her mouth. "The downfall of the Steam Union will only continue if Eva Southway is allowed to continue pulling us into the dark ages with her." A few hesitant nods, looks about from the others. Clover shivered next to me, Felix staring down at the floor, though his clenched fists told me there was more strength in him than I'd given him credit for. "It's time for a new direction, a fresh outlook."

"Are you volunteering, Ethpeal?" Eva had somehow regained control of herself, though the venom in her glare as she stared at my grandmother through slitted eyes would have done serious harm if backed by magic.

"Of course not," Gram snorted, rolling her eyes at the Steam Union leader with casual grace. "Couldn't pay me enough to shake up this lot." The watchers didn't seem to mind she'd offered a mild insult. Were they that crushed by Eva they couldn't even muster emotions of their own past sadness and anxiety?

"Then who?" Felix raised his head, tears on his cheeks, dripping into his beard. Eva spun on him but he took a step toward Gram, ignoring his furious wife. From the calm and expectant look on his face, I figured Felix already knew what she was going to say.

"I nominate Piers Southway," Gram said, power pushing her words outward. I could only guess she used her magic to make sure every Steam Union member heard her.

Good choice, I sent to my grandmother as a sigh tinted with relief rolled around the room.

No other, Gram sent.

Eva's eyes crackled with power. "He's no longer a member of this order," she snapped.

"So?" Gram's flat anger cut through the Steam Union leader's protest like a splash of icy water on a simmering fire. "That can be easily rectified."

"I can see," Femke interrupted before Eva could respond, "things are well in hand." Like hell they were. "Knowing now this is an internal matter, I will take my leave."

Thanks for the backup, I snapped at her.

I suggest you do the same, Syd. Femke's mental tone was soft, careful. *Please, don't make this worse. There's nothing I'd rather see than Piers leading the Steam Union. Give him the chance to depose his mother and make this right.*

I guess you'll find out what happened after it's all over. Irritation at her chastisement, as gentle as it was, just fired me up further. Seeing my silent husband standing next to her reopened the fresh hurt I'd as yet to deal with to my satisfaction. *Run along, now, World Leader. I'll clean up the mess witches leave behind. As usual.*

Her mind shut down, a wave of fury hitting me. Okay, maybe I'd gone too far. But damn her, this was important. And I knew if—when—Piers took over, he'd join the new WPC. Femke needed to be here.

Gram's eyes narrowed as she looked back and forth between Femke and me. "Thank you, World Council Leader," she said. "We can handle it from here."

Femke nodded once, sharp and angry, she and Quaid vanishing in a flare of blue fire.

Poorly done, girl, Gram grumbled in my head. *She deserves better from you.*

I didn't bother responding. I'd figure out a way to fix it later. Right now, Eva Southway was recoiling inward. Which told me she was planning something I wasn't going to like.

Gram returned her attention to her leader. "I demand to see Piers," she said. A few muttering agreements joined hers, Demetrius nodding at her side. "Immediately."

I watched Eva look around at the majority of nodding Steam Union members, took personal note of those who seemed to be as sullen and dangerous as she—a small minority, thankfully. And though I could tell she wanted to protest, there was really nothing Eva could do.

"Bring him," she snarled, waving in the general direction of the door.

He'll need your support, Gram sent as we waited in silence for the two young Steam Union members who went scrambling at Eva's order to return. *This is going to get ugly.*

She doesn't have many on her team, at least, I sent. *From what I can tell.*

Agreed, Demetrius sent, his soft touch tinted with sadness. *But there are enough of them if Piers doesn't seize power immediately, they could sway others to oppose him.*

Politics. My favorite.

Movement at the door drew my focus, though Eva didn't turn with the rest of us. She stood in the center of the room, scowling at the floor, arms crossed over her chest. Felix took two steps toward me, one arm extended to Clover who went to him, both of them staring toward the doorway. At the tall, handsome blond who entered.

Piers was always lean, aristocratic features sharp, pale hair a silken fall almost to his knees. But the man I watched come toward me wasn't the lanky, proud and self-assured Piers I knew so well. His shoulders hunched forward, cheeks hollow, dark circles under his translucent gray eyes. The lustrous hair he was so proud of hung in a stringy mass, button up shirt torn and dirty, a large hole in the knee of his dress pants. His shoes were long gone, bare feet crusted in soil. When he lifted one hand to brush away a lock of hair from his drawn face, I couldn't help but notice the wide, black bruise ringing his wrist.

A few soft gasps met his appearance, horrified looks passed from Steam Union member to Steam Union member. Clover covered her mouth with both hands, turning her face away, but I forced myself to stare, to take in his roughened condition and to burn the fury I felt at his mother deeper into my soul.

"Your own son," I said.

"We had no idea." A young woman with pale red hair took a step back as I locked onto her with my furious gaze. "None."

"You told us he was here willingly." An older gentleman in a three piece suit spoke up, bitterness in his tone, small, white mustache curling up at the edges as his lips tightened. "Eva, how could you?"

"Where is Zoe Helios?" I slapped them with the question, backed by power. And though they were sorcerers, they flinched from my magic.

"Here." I turned to find her hurrying forward, stopping with tears on her face, staring at Piers as though she'd never seen him before. "Oh, my love," she whispered.

He didn't turn his head. Didn't react at all. I reached for him but he blocked me out, refused to allow me inside with iron will so powerful I retained hope this might end in our favor after all. Piers wasn't broken. Just hurt to the core of his heart.

Zoe hurried to my side, tucked in next to Gram and me. "They held me prisoner here," she said in her clear voice. "Against my will, refused to allow me to see Piers or even leave my room. Threatened me with harm if I tried to escape." She met my eyes, tears trickling down her cheeks. "I couldn't leave," she choked on her words this time. "The fire wouldn't take me. I couldn't help him." Frustration warred with sorrow in her voice. "Damn you!" She threw the curse at Eva. "He loves you and you betrayed him."

The Steam Union leader just smirked at her. "Outsiders don't get to speak further." Her power crowded me, heading for Zoe. Rainbow fire sizzled along the edge of her magic and shoved it back in her face. Eva retreated with a cry, the watching Steam Union calling out in fear, but I didn't attack. As much as I wanted to.

"You try that again," I said as mildly as I could manage, "and the leadership will be wide open for takers."

She backed off, though only to turn and address her people. "Will we allow this to happen to our order?" Self-righteousness wasn't pretty on her, either. "Will we fall to our fears or stand for what we believe in?"

They swayed, but more with fear than belief.

"Oh, give it a rest, will you, Eva." Gram's testy tone actually inspired a few titters of nervous laughter. Eva spun on her, but my grandmother wasn't looking at her. Her focus was on Piers. "We've demanded a change of leadership," she said, speaking to his crumpled form as though they were the only two in the room. "And we want you to take your mother's place."

For the first time since he was led inside, Piers

reacted. Slowly, so slowly, painfully, he raised his head. I could almost hear his bones creaking, the tendons moaning from the weariness in his movements. But it wasn't from physical exhaustion, I knew that much. Just from the look on his face. He was emotionally damaged, hurt so deeply he could barely function. His tongue slipped over his dry lips.

"No," he said in the sudden quiet, barely a whisper, but it carried.

Eva smiled, triumphant, crossing her arms over her chest. "There," she said. "You see? Even my son believes I am the best leader of our people."

He laughed, soft and broken, full of gravel, stopping her amusement in its tracks.

"Mum," he said, gray eyes darkened to charcoal. Their gazes locked, the steel inside my friend showing at last. "Please. Don't embarrass yourself."

She snarled at him, power gathered, but one glance at me and she held back. So, I'd made her think twice, had I? Good, then. Though, part of me—okay, my furious demon part—wanted her to try it. Any excuse.

But Femke was right. This was Piers's fight. I couldn't win it for him.

"Piers Southway," Eva said, "I declare you an enemy of the Steam Union. For your attempt to take over my leadership, I order you stripped of power and put to death."

"Um, hang on a second," I said, halting the wave of resistance that washed through the crowd. "He did no such thing."

"Wasn't his idea," Gram said, thrusting her magic at Eva like a challenge. "It was mine. Feel like coming at me, Eva?"

"I was afraid of this," Zoe whispered in my ear while the rest of the room stared in rapt and fearful attention at Gram and Eva where they faced off over Piers. "He told me long ago he won't fight his mother, Syd. His heart is broken."

We'd see about that. *Piers, you dumbass*, I sent sharply at the wall of black he had erected. *The Steam Union needs you and your mother is making a huge mess here. Fix it or I will.*

Stay out of this, Syd, he sent, mental voice cold.

Like hell I will, I sent. *Either you take care of this or I start breaking people.* I sighed in frustration. *You are the only one who can save them. Look around you, damn it. They are falling apart, Piers. And your mother is letting it happen.* No answer. *Fine*, I sent. *Maybe I was wrong. Your people deserve better than the Southways, obviously.*

That got a reaction. He glared at me with a flash of fury behind his darkened eyes. But he held still while his mother, oblivious to our conversation, finally stood down from Gram.

"At the very least," she said, "he will have his power taken, his sorcery silenced. That is the way of our order."

Wasn't going to happen. "And he will be imprisoned for the remainder of his life." Would no one else speak for him?

Really, people?

To my utter shock, Clover darted forward, arms going around her brother. While I knew she adored him, I also understood how deeply her fear of her mother ran. It amazed me she had the fortitude and courage to stand against the woman who trod on her for her entire life. But Clover did.

With anger ringing in her voice, Piers's younger sister took her stand.

"You won't touch him," she said. "I won't allow it."

Casually, as though swinging at a troublesome insect, Eva lashed out at her child and struck her hard. I wanted to stop her, needed to do something, anything, but the pressure of Gram's mind on mine held me back.

Watch, she sent.

I didn't have long to wait. The moment Eva's power struck Clover, Piers's head snapped up, a burst of black erupting between his mother and his sister. Eva staggered back, Clover weeping as she fell to her knees beside her suddenly furious brother.

"Enough!" His bark of fury echoed through the room. "You swore to me you wouldn't hurt her, Mother. You promised me you'd leave Clover and Father out of this if I stood down."

Eva retreated from his anger, sullenness crawling across her eyes, but she was too late.

"Very well," he said, voice cold. "You asked for it. Challenge accepted!"

SEVENTEEN

From the sudden terror in Eva's eyes, she knew she'd finally pushed him too far. Piers's power roared to life, filling the room with the rumbling growl of a starving animal. Eva back pedaled, tried to combat him, but his magic was stronger, his storehouse of reserves rising from far within him. The Steam Union watchers swayed as Piers strode toward his mother, literally battering her to the floor with one pummeling blow after another. The entire house shook from the titanic effort, books falling from the shelves, dust clogging the air.

Eva finally sagged beneath the onslaught of his rage, arms over her head, weeping in fury and frustration and, for a moment, I feared he would go too far as the old wood flooring cracked beneath her with a sharp, explosive sound like the strike of lightning. As much as Eva needed to be taken care of, I knew my friend would never survive killing his own mother.

Piers. I gently, so gently, pulled him back.

His mind panted in mine, animal rage swallowing him. He'd been through so much, I could only guess, and when he snapped... he snapped.

But he responded as I continued to coax him, retreating from the crumpled ball of sobbing anger who pounded the damaged floor at her feet with both fists, a child having a tantrum. Piers's shoulders straightened, body vibrating with power as the majority of the Steam Union looked up to him, their hope shining in their faces.

Eva spit on the floor boards, meeting her son's eyes with so much hate I readied myself to take her out personally so he wouldn't have to. "This isn't over," she snarled in a voice like grinding steel. "Not by a long shot. I declare myself the leader of a new order, the Sorcerer Guild." Okay, that came too easily. Had she been planning this all along, a safety net in her back pocket?

No time to find out. Eva leaped to her feet, shaking, gestured around her. Before anyone could stop her she attacked her own people, siphoning off a portion of their power while the small group I'd taken note of filed in beside her, smooth and precise. Just as if they'd had this in mind and made prior plans to ensure escape. Piers roared in fury, lunged for his mother, but she was already disappearing into a tunnel of black, faithful followers joining her.

It snapped shut as he came to a halt before the spot, teeth bared, hands clenched, shaking all over. No one said a word, too shocked to react. When Piers finally turned his face was closed and dark, jaw tight, dust settling around him.

"Eva Southway is a fugitive from our justice," he said. "By stealing our power—forbidden to our order—she has declared herself no better than the Brotherhood we oppose." Murmurs of angry agreement met his words. "She and her Sorcerer Guild will be hunted and destroyed like the animals they've become." Louder now, their support. A people reborn, though I knew it would take much more than just an impassioned speech from a furious man to change things. "I have been asked to lead you. Would you have me?"

Their cry of acceptance brought tears to my eyes because it wasn't just the people in the room offering their support. Waves of sorcery hit all of us, coming from the Steam Union members who watched and listened from elsewhere. They'd seen everything and Piers was their only choice.

"Then," he said, bowing his head, "I accept. And I will do my very best to lead you."

Clover, back on her feet, rushed to his side and hugged him. His father joined her while Zoe quivered at my side. I gently urged her toward him, holding back as she took a few tentative steps in his direction. The grief ridden look on his face when he saw her forced me to clamp both hands over my mouth to stifle the sob trying to escape. Gram's arm went around my shoulders as Piers engulfed Zoe in his arms like it was just the two of them in the room.

Now, Gram sent, *to help him heal. She's done a lot of damage to that boy.*

You'll keep me posted on the pursuit of Eva? I knew she would.

Don't worry, Gram sent, grim but oddly gleeful. *If I'm the one who catches her*, and her mental tone told me she intended just that, *I'll invite you to the show.*

I hugged her back, leaned in to kiss Demetrius's soft cheek. When I straightened, it was to Piers staring at me, one arm draped around Zoe, the other his sister.

"The Steam Union thanks Coven Leader Hayle for her assistance," he said.

"Coven Leader Hayle is happy to see Steam Union Leader Southway take over," I said. "Anything I can do, please, don't hesitate."

When I tried to touch his mind past the formalities, he fended me off again.

I just need some time, he sent. "Thank you," he said out loud. "But we can take things from here."

I knew a dismissal when I heard one. Tried to convince myself it didn't hurt.

Liar.

I backed away, leaving the Steam Union members to close in on Piers. At least I knew they were in good hands at last. Before I could leave, someone grabbed me, turned me around. Zoe hugged me tight, lips against my ear.

"I'll take care of him," she said before leaning away, smiling and blinking back tears. "He'll see you soon. We both will."

I raised my gaze, met Gram's. She smiled, too, lopsided. And I felt a whole lot better.

The veil welcomed me as I skimmed for home, heart sore for my sorcerer friend. It couldn't have been easy for him to challenge his own mother. I should know. Though my mother raised me to stand on my own two feet while Eva, it seemed, did her best to smother Piers and Clover. I was happy to know maybe the two of them finally had a fighting chance.

My high heels tapped on the stairs as I emerged from the basement, just wanting to take a hot shower and maybe make a bowl of popcorn, gorge on some chocolate, watch a TV show and veg the hell out. But the moment I stepped through the door at the top and into the kitchen, I fell into a maelstrom of fury so powerful I almost fell back down into the dark.

"Sydlynn. Thaddea. Hayle." Mom stood in the middle of the space, fire crackling around her, vibrating with fury as she threw out each one of my names with such violence the dishes in the cupboard rattled in tune.

Um. What? "Mom." I gasped a breath, pushed back against her power enough I could enter the kitchen. "What the hell?"

"My question exactly." Her magic retreated, the young power of the Council heated with her rage, as angry as she was. "When exactly were you going to tell me you were chosen to undermine my authority?" Undermine... oh. Damn. Oops. "And that you accepted the job?"

Craptastic on a crap stick. "Mom," I said, shaking my head, hands up to ward her off. "I'm sorry, I tried to tell you, I swear." The stupid, wretched, dumbass shadow council. Why didn't I make time to fill her in? "But there was so much going on and I didn't get a chance—"

"A rather important piece of information, Syd," Mom snapped, though her power finally retreated the rest of the way. I caught a glimpse of a nervous Shenka in the corner and wondered who told Mom in the first place. Surely not my second. She'd been opposed to such a thing. "Considering everything that's happened, we need unity, not division!"

"I know!" I didn't mean to shout back at Mom, but I'd been in too many fights over the last few days, my temper on a hair trigger and my mother knew just what buttons to push. "I'm not an idiot!"

"You could have fooled me," Mom said, drawing herself up, black robe swirling around her as blue fire crackled. "You're lucky I don't have you arrested, do you know that? I still might."

"Just try it." I was done fighting, sagging against the table. "Go back to Harvard, Mom. We'll talk later when you're reasonable."

Oh, dear.

Mom left, sure did. And the house shook with her passing.

I glared at Shenka who shook her head. "I swear," she said. "I didn't say a word. And I have no idea who did."

Not like it mattered now. I turned away from my second and retreated upstairs. From the quiet, the kids were still with Dad in Boston. Probably a good thing. I stepped into the shower, shedding my suit, and spent a good ten minutes or so crying into my hands as the hot water poured over me.

The release of emotion made me feel better, though it left me worn out. I really had to find time to go clean up some of my messes. As I sat on the edge of the bed and looked out into the street outside my house, at the happy, playing kids, the parents with strollers living their quiet lives, I realized how much of an ass I'd been with the people I loved.

Okay, so they'd been asses back, and sometimes first. But, still. I knew better. I'd grown past my temper, or thought I had. I guess the pressure of all of it happening so fast just got to me, blow after blow building until I just couldn't take it anymore. Which didn't mean I couldn't do the right thing and be the bigger person.

Yeah. Attitude again. I'd do better.

The sigh of a sorcery tunnel opening turned me around. Gram exited, coming to sit next to me, Sassafras in her arms. He glared at me, amber eyes snapping, tail thrashing.

"Forget someone?"

I reached out and hugged him to me, more tears spilling over onto his fur. "I'm sorry," I choked out the whisper.

Sass's irritation fled in a rush. "Me, too," he said.

Gram's hand settled on my shoulder and I looked up, Sass and I both turning to watch her as she smiled at me.

"Sucks, doesn't it? The leadership gig?" I shrugged at her questions. Gram's grin was heartfelt, but there was old hurt in her eyes. I knew she'd had her own struggles, though we'd never talked them completely through. "Feels like no one understands, sometimes. That their problems are more important than the big picture. And the older you get, Syd, the harder it is. The more you want to just say screw it and walk away. To just be selfish and not care what happens to anyone else."

My whole body clenched against her words, though I had to admit there were times I'd thought that way. "I can't," I said.

She laughed. "Of course you can't, you ninny. You're

a Hayle witch. And we never quit, no matter the obstacles." Gram sighed, fingers sliding over Sass's fur. "Right, cat?"

Something passed between them, a feeling of irony I didn't understand.

"You didn't quit, Ethpeal," he said, indignant. "She kicked you out."

What was this?

Gram shook her head, winking at him, fixing her blue eyes on me. "A long story about the woman who gave birth to me," she said. Funny how she worded it that way, instead of just saying her mother. "Ask me again sometime." She stood, then, waved at the air before her, tunnel forming. "Emotions run high in times of crisis. You know that. You have to be the strong one, as unfair as that is. They don't have the experience with the massive stuff like you do." Gram waved, fingers wiggling. "Now, stop being a baby and go mend hearts, girl." With a grin to take the sting from her words, she stepped into the tunnel and vanished.

EIGHTEEN

I followed through with my plan to hide from the world for the rest of the day, despite Gram's suggestion. I just needed time away from everyone, to gather my thoughts, get some emotional rest. The last thing I wanted was to encounter something that would set me off again. I knew better than to jump into trying to apologize or talk to anyone right now.

Bad to worse in 3, 2, 1... good thing I knew myself well enough to lay low.

Sassafras waddled downstairs with me, staying close at my side as I peeked into the kitchen. Shenka was gone, a relief, to be honest. I wasn't prepared to deal with her yet, either. Sass hopped up on the counter and watched with cat fascination as the microwave did its thing to the bag of popcorn while I poured him a dish of milk and myself a tall glass of ginger ale. The smell of buttery goodness instantly softened my mood, mouthwatering. I rarely got to eat popcorn in peace, usually cornered and surrounded by demanding children and Galleytrot's begging eyes, so it was a treat to empty the hot puffed kernels into a big bowl in anticipation of keeping it all to myself.

I almost made it to the living room when Apollo's voice in my head brought me to an abrupt halt. With a twinge of irritation at the interruption followed by a kick of guilt for being mad about it, I greeted him back.

Syd, he sent, excitement and worry all bubbling in his mind. *I found Simon.*

Okay, had my complete attention. I set the bowl on the end table by the sofa and turned for the kitchen again. Sassafras cocked his head to me as I mouthed Simon's name.

Where? I caught the flash of a location, a row house on a city street. *On my way.*

I took time to shed my fuzzy socks and slip into a pair of sneakers, deeming my pajama pants and t-shirt would have to do. I didn't want to waste a second more. I lifted the impatient silver Persian into my arms as he pawed my leg and stepped through the veil to the street Apollo showed me. He looked up from where he loitered on the corner, eyes bright, Owen pacing behind a car in impatience.

"That one," Apollo said, pointing surreptitiously at a pale gray place with a bright blue door. "Basement."

"You're sure?" I set Sass on his feet, knowing he could take care of himself. He shook out his fur, sniffing the afternoon air.

"Positive," Owen said, joining us, shivering with the need to act from the intense look in his eyes. "They slipped in their shielding. I felt him."

Good to know. "Let me lead," I said. "But watch my back."

Both nodded with immediate grins on their faces.

"What?" I looked back and forth between them.

"Just looking forward to a little Syd ass kicking action," Apollo said. The brothers high fived each other with enthusiasm.

Boys. But I couldn't help grinning in return.

Fun, my demon sent as I strode down the street like a freight train without brakes. *That's what we needed.*

Indeed, my vampire sent, clearly amused. *Try not to do any permanent damage, Sydlynn.*

Want me to shake things up a little? Shaylee flexed her Sidhe muscles inside me, the threat of an earthquake at the ready.

Not yet, I sent. *Let me see if I can convince them to be reasonable and stand down first.*

My alter egos all laughed.

I loved them so much.

Just before my foot touched the first step to the door, I felt sorcery surge and paused. The sight of the tall, handsome Piers Southway emerging from the narrow alley between houses made me stop and stare. Clover was with him, a pair of men I vaguely recognized as Steam Union friends of his I'd met before. They both looked rather contrite, but eager, so I held my ground as Piers approached.

He looked much better, considering it had only been a few hours since he'd taken over leadership. A shower and shave, fresh clothing and his freedom had done wonders, but there was still a great deal of darkness around his eyes and his small smile was grim.

"Syd." He shifted his shoulders inside his coat.

"Piers." I nodded to him, looking at the pair grinning at me over his shoulder. More boys and their enthusiasm. They fit right in with Apollo and Owen.

"You remember Ellis Lowsley?" Red hair, freckles, bright green eyes. I wiggled my fingers in his direction and he offered a jaunty wave back.

"And Laird Meath?" Dark skin like Shenka's, glossy black hair, crooked teeth in a bright smile. Both looked like they were ready to pounce at a moment's notice.

Where were they when you needed them? I hoped I didn't come across as harsh, but they were his friends, I recalled. Had been there when Piers and I attacked the Black Souls the night we freed Charlotte's people.

Gone, Piers sent, carefully quiet. *They tried to rescue me and Mum had them banished.* He sounded sad, achingly so, but shook it off, power nudging me as he spoke out loud. "I understand you have a Brotherhood problem," he said.

I glanced at the Zornov brothers who both shrugged and shook their heads.

"I have my sources," Piers said, hands deep in the pockets of his gray longcoat. "I thought, as a gesture of thanks for your assistance, you'd allow the Steam Union to help you take care of things."

An alliance. Brilliant, really, and so soon after his takeover. I wished I'd thought of it, though never would have considered he'd be ready for something like this just yet.

"How thoughtful," I said. "Happy for the help."

Piers's smile widened, lost some of its hard edge. "Shall we?" He strode up the stairs at my side, Sassafras sneaking between our legs, the Steam Union and Zornov brothers watching our backs.

"Should we knock?" Maybe Piers needed a little fun himself, from the sudden flare of playfulness in his eyes. I was happy to see him recovering so quickly and shrugged, nice and casual.

"Fair play and all that," I said.

Piers laughed, relaxed suddenly. "Syd," he whispered. "Thank you." And raised his right hand.

His knock broke the door from its hinges, crumpling its center and sending it spinning inward, the shards impacting the wall at the end of the hallway like arrows. I strolled inside to the sound of panicked shouting, my demon cat sashaying in front of me. A Brotherhood sorcerer appeared, face pale with shock under his short, dark hair, staring at us as though he had no idea what to do. Sassafras's demon fire burst in his bulging eyes, sending him falling backward with a frightened cry.

Piers crushed him easily, the push of his sorcery sweeping the house. "Down," he said at the same moment I felt Simon's soul through the weakening field of the Brotherhood's dampening energy.

Owen had been right. I let the Zornovs and the Steam Union deal with the handful of sorcerers upstairs, Sassafras and Piers joining me as we crossed to the kitchen and to the basement door. The stairs were dimly lit, not that it mattered. A flare of witchlight hovered over our heads as I tossed the glowing blue ball ahead of us to light the way.

A ring of young Brotherhood sorcerers, six or so, surrounded a steel cage in the center of the basement. From the terror on their faces they knew what was coming. I grinned and waved at them, relaxing into the joy of taking action.

"Hiya," I said. "Heard you had a friend of mine. Thought I'd talk to you about playing nice."

One of the sorcerers whimpered. But the one in the lead scowled at me, power gathering, bolstering the others.

"We're not afraid of you," he said, first hint of a goatee marking him as a Liander Belaisle wannabe.

Piers laughed. Doubled over, gasping for breath, one hand on my shoulder as his amusement filled the suddenly quiet basement. He took the time then to artfully wipe the tears from the corners of his eyes while I met Simon's nervous gaze. He looked okay, undamaged, and when I wiggled my fingers at him, he waved back, a bit dazed.

"Be with you in a sec, Si," I said. "Just need to take out the trash."

The fight turned out to be little in the way of entertaining. Whether Belaisle himself instigated the kidnapping, or if it was the brainchild of their sad and sorry little leader, they hadn't left nearly enough protection. Piers's power roared through the space, mine in counterpoint. While he bowled them over with a powerful push of sorcery, my maji magic sliced through their shielding and cut their bonds to their stolen power. It rose from them with a musical sigh, escaping their clutches. I sealed them off from stealing more while Piers caged them in a smoky bubble of semi-opaque darkness.

It might have been cruel, but they were the enemy. With some help from the blossom of sorcery beneath me, I made the seal severing their sorcery access as permanent as I could. Sure, Belaisle might have been able to reverse it eventually, but it would take a great deal of power to do so and I doubted he cared about this small group of foot soldiers enough to make the effort.

Piers let them go when he realized what I'd done, nodding his satisfaction. While I turned toward the cage, he addressed them, his friends and the Zornovs herding the rest of the defeated Brotherhood down to join them.

"My name is Piers Southway," he said. "I am the leader of the Steam Union. As Brotherhood, you are the enemy, parasites devouring power for your own gain." My fingers traced over the lock as I listened, a soft surge of power opening it, the door to the tall, steel cell swinging open. "You've chosen the wrong side, but, I would offer you an alternative."

I turned as Simon exited, shaking but physically fine. *Tell me*, I sent to Piers, *you're not going to make your mother's mistake.*

He didn't answer me. "I know what Liander Belaisle told you," he said. "But there is a better way. And if you're willing to explore that, I'm willing to show you how."

The leader spit on the floor at Piers's feet. "Forget it," he said. "Master Belaisle is our leader. We don't need another way." He was shivering, probably an after effect of being cut off from his power. "He'll come for us, and when he does, he'll kill you and restore our magic."

Piers shook his head, blond hair rippling like a silk waterfall. "You're mistaken," he said. "Belaisle isn't coming and you know it." No protests, not this time, just unease, shifting of feet as the young men stared at Piers with growing worry. "He doesn't care about you," he said. "And he never will. The Brotherhood is about power. Without your own, you're dead to him."

"Don't listen!" The young leader whipped his head back and forth, trying to meet the eyes of his friends, but they were muttering among themselves, uncertain. "He's lying to make us betray the master."

"The only master you need," Piers said, "is yourself. Think about that." He turned his back on them, gesturing for his people to stand guard while he crossed to me. Sassafras pawed Piers's leg and my friend bent and lifted him into his arms, stroking his fur as he met my eyes.

"I'll handle things from here," he said. "I won't do what my mother did. They are Brotherhood and always will be, thanks to how their power was woken." I'd never heard that before and would have to ask him more later. Interesting. "Still, with some proper guidance, they are young and fresh enough they might at least learn to get along with others."

Sorry, I sent. *I shouldn't have said that. About your mother.*

He just smiled, handed me Sass, softly kissing my cheek. This close to him I could see the weariness clinging to the lines in his face, deep in his gaze. But he seemed happy enough as he moved away, fixing his gray eyes on Simon next.

"I understand you're very important to Syd," he said. "Which makes you a friend of mine." He held out his hand, and, to my relief, Simon shook it without hesitation. His recent attitude shone on his face, but it wasn't aimed at Piers.

"Likewise," he said. "Thanks for the rescue." Simon glared, fearless, at the Brotherhood sorcerers. "Don't go easy on them," he growled.

Piers's grin was so much himself I wanted to hug him. "Trust me," he said. "If they decide to accept my offer, their lives will be hell for a very, very long time." He winked at me. "And now, if you'll excuse us, the Steam Union has work to do. But we are happy to have instigated this alliance and hope such agreements can be furthered in the future."

I saluted him with one hand, Sassafras tucked under the other, balancing his front feet on my palm.

"Steam Union Leader Southway," my demon cat said solemnly. "Well done."

Piers turned away as Sass's mind met mine.

And that, he sent, *is what a real leader looks like. Taking notes?*

I snorted at him. *Smartass cat.* But, he was right. Any remaining residual worry about Piers's state of mind washed away as I waved at Apollo and Owen. The pair joined us, Apollo and Simon sharing a distinctly guyish hug, slapping each other on the shoulder before parting with grins on their faces.

"I guess I don't have to warn you about telling anyone what you've seen today," I said to Simon.

He shrugged. "You're just going to mind wipe me or something anyway," he said, sullenness returning.

"Actually," I said, mind shuffling over, "I was hoping that wouldn't be necessary." Sassafras's head turned, amber eyes meeting mine.

"What did you have in mind?" Simon let out a little chirp of shock, staring at the demon cat. Sass just blinked at him. "In for a penny," he said in his sarcastic cat tone.

"The Brotherhood has proven they will use mundane methods to come after the covens," I said. "You do know I'm a witch?"

Simon nodded, swallowed. "When these guys took me, it all came back," he said. That was how he knew about the mind wipe. Being subjected to sorcery must have triggered his memories. I'd have to check into that. "The Star Club, you and Darin…" he trailed off, guilt passing over his face. "Rupe."

"But, you knew about the Brotherhood before this happened." I'd assumed he was aware of other things, too.

"I thought they were some shadowy underground mafia," Simon said. "I had no clue until the wipe broke who they really were. And even then, I've just been piecing things together." His tight jaw told me he had lots of questions and I was more than willing to answer. But, not right now.

"Turns out Belaisle targeted the other families, too. I need help returning their money to them." Simon's face pinched, suddenly shrewd. "Think you could handle it?"

I worried maybe he'd say no. After all, he'd been kidnapped, his computers destroyed, all because he helped me. But the flare of anger in his eyes, the defiance, gave me my answer before he could speak out loud.

"Any chance to stick it to these buttmunchers," he said. "What did you have in mind?"

"Feel like moving back to Wilding Springs?" His eyebrows shot up. "Coven house, your own, under our protection. All the equipment you want or need. And the freedom to pursue your own projects, as long as you don't bring any trouble to us."

Simon didn't even think about it, sticking his hand out. "I'll take it," he said.

You do realize, Sass sent as I opened the veil, Simon's shock flashing over his face at the sight, *you've just hired a criminal to live with the family.*

I'm sure we'll be a good influence, I sent as we stepped through for home.

Sass's soft answering laughter cracked me up.

NINETEEN

I left Apollo and Owen with Simon in the small house at the end of the street the pair had claimed as their own. The three bachelors would be great roommates, I figured, at least until one of the determined ladies pursuing the Zornov brothers actually managed to pin one of them down.

Staying out of it.

Leaving them with a credit card and license to replace Simon's equipment, I winced at the thought of how much he would spend. I'd been more than generous with his fee when he liberated the Hayle fortune for me, but I felt responsible for his kidnapping and, after all, it was only money.

The best part of the whole affair happened as I turned to leave the boys to their shopping. Simon stopped me, chasing after me, pulling me to a halt in the driveway while Sassafras paused at the edge of the street to observe in his quiet cat way.

"Um, Syd, I..." Simon shuffled his feet, nervous fingers adjusting his glasses. He reminded me more of the boy I used to know than the man he'd become in that moment. "I just wanted to say I was sorry." His eyes met mine through the lenses of his glasses. They'd become bent somewhere along the way, leaning slightly to the right, his dark hair falling over his forehead in need of a good haircut. So young, yet, really. "I didn't remember... and I blamed you for everything." He hugged himself though the afternoon was one of those warm September days that reminded me of summer not long past. "You were the only part of the whole mess that stood out in my head. That, and this horrible feeling I couldn't shake, that something was wrong. I associated that with you." He shrugged, dropping his arms. "Now I know you saved me. And I never thanked you for that."

"Twice," I said. Simon's head shot up, eyes wide and I grinned. "I saved your ass twice, Clement. And don't you forget it."

He grinned at me, punched my arm gently. "Don't get all high and mighty about it, Hayle," he shot back. "Just saying."

I hugged him and he embraced me back. I'd been through a roller coaster of emotions lately, and this moment was no exception. "Missed you," I whispered.

Simon nodded against my shoulder then let me go. Flashed me a wicked smile. "Now, if you'll excuse me," he said, "I'm off to spend your money."

Groan.

Sassafras and I strolled down the street toward home. I was in no hurry as the sun slowly set over the tree line to the west, lighting the tall windows of the Hilltop Hotel overlooking town. That place still gave me the creeps, even after all these years. Too many memories of the Dumont family and their evil intentions, though my recollections of Ameline had altered enough, I was surprised to discover, thinking of her in that setting didn't raise the old hate like it used to.

Sass stopped at the end of our driveway and looked up at me. "You're not coming inside," he said in no uncertain terms. "You have work to do."

I sighed, nodded, hands stuffed into my pajama pant pockets. "Think Mom will care I'm not dressed for the part?"

He turned his back on me and waddled toward the kitchen door. "Just go apologize to your mother, Sydlynn. There's a good girl."

A waft of his magic opened the screen door for him and he disappeared inside with a flick of his tail. I grinned despite myself. No matter how old I grew, I knew Sass would always treat me like the irritating teenager I'd been.

But, he was right about mending fences. My

resolution with Simon put me in the mood to make amends. Slipping up the side of the driveway past the low-slung red convertible I had been unable to resist buying and around the bumper of the more practical gray minivan I drove more often than not, I reached for the veil out of the sight of the street and went to Harvard.

I could have showed up right in Mom's office, but I wanted a show of contrition so she'd know I was serious. Instead, I let my power announce me as I exited in the dark paneled and formal sitting room outside her door, refusing to look at the glum, grumpy portraits of all the Council Leaders who stared down at me like I'd offended them somehow.

A moment later, the door to her office opened and Philip's smiling face peeked out.

"One second, Coven Leader," he said, nose wrinkling his numerous freckles before his red head disappeared again, the door sighing shut behind him.

I paced a moment, hands clasped behind my back, trying to decide what I was going to say. Every conversation I staged in my head went from bad to worse in a matter of seconds, forcing me to rewind and try again. By the time the door opened again, I was so wound up and ready for the worst I was surprised to see Mom kindly waving off her secretary. Philip grinned at me on the way by, his mood high, at least. And when I met Mom's eyes, all the fighting I'd been doing in my twisting brain shut off.

"Mom," I said.

"Syd," she said, at exactly the same time.

"I'm sorry." Again, in unison.

Mom came toward me, and I to her, our arms around each other before we could fully come to a stop.

"I know you would never do anything to jeopardize the Council," she said.

"I swear I was going to tell you and tried to stop them from even forming a shadow council," I blurted over her.

We laughed together, soft and full of understanding. Mom led me into her office, closed the door. I sat in one of the big chairs in front of her massive desk while she took the one beside me, crossing her legs as she leaned toward me.

"Tell me," she said.

I shared everything I could remember, including my suggestion to train all witches in sorcery.

"Agreed," she said. "I understand there has been a shift in power in the Steam Union." Her eyes glittered with delight she'd caught me by surprise. "Yes, I heard about Piers. I'm proud of him."

"He'll be a great leader," I said, sinking back into the cushions, finally relaxing as weariness washed over me. "I'm also going to see what I can do about restoring the stolen funds from the covens."

She nodded. "Simon," she said.

Did she know everything? Probably a good thing, honestly.

"I have no real objection to the shadow council," Mom said. "As long as you keep me posted—and they don't attempt something detrimental to the safety of our people. If feeling like they are in control gives them courage and comfort, I'm fine with it." She hesitated with a little smile. "Besides, if I trust anyone to have the best interests of the covens at heart, it's you."

Nice of her to say so. "They're afraid, Mom," I said. "I'm hoping Piers will be willing to allow his people to train ours so they won't have to fear the Brotherhood anymore."

"Let me see what I can do in my official capacity," she said. "I planned to reach out to him and congratulate him tomorrow. To encourage him to join the WPC." I had a feeling there'd be no fight there. "And to ask him to help us. Even if he can't at this point, I know he'll give it a fair hearing."

Unlike his mother. "Any news on Eva?"

Mom shook her head. "My sources aren't that good, sweetheart," she said. "But if Piers wants help tracking her, we're more than happy to do what we can."

Working together. What a concept.

Sydlynn. Max's massive mind touched mine, making me jump. *Forgive the intrusion.*

Where have you been all day? I sat up straighter, Mom's

little frown registering the distraction. Mind you, I'd been busy, but we usually patrolled together and I felt guilty for forgetting about him.

All is well, he sent, amusement clear. *But we have an appointment I don't think either of us should miss. Council Leader Hayle, your permission to enter your territory.*

Mom's eyebrows shot up. *Granted, always, Max,* she sent. *How polite,* she sent to me in a tight touch of power.

Touchy times, I sent back as the veil opened and Max stepped through. I stood to join him, Mom coming to my side. He bowed to her before offering his hand to me.

"Forgive me," he said. "Syd and I must go."

"Of course." She hugged me before I could take his fingers in mine. *Funny,* she sent with a catch in her mind, *I forget sometimes just how small the problems are the rest of us have to deal with compared to the ones you carry with you every day.* I tried to protest, but she let me go with a smile. *Leave this to me,* she sent. *Just keep the Universe turning, please.*

I kissed her cheek and grasped Max's hand, leaving my mother behind as he pulled me into the veil. *Where are we off to?*

Ameline contacted me a short time ago, he sent. *She has an answer for us.*

The dark maji. My heart sped up as the mess I left behind was shunted sideways in favor of bigger problems. *Any idea what they said?*

We're about to find out. The veil opened and Max and I

were in the maji chamber. I guess he was more confident in his ability to pinpoint our landing than I was. Ameline stood by the altar, smiling at us, though there was strain on her face.

"Thank you for coming so quickly," she said, stepping aside to show us she wasn't alone. "I didn't think our guest was willing to wait much longer."

The tall, dark skinned maji was as familiar to me as Ameline. "Trinol," I said, greeting her old guide with a smile. "It's good to see you."

He nodded to me, though nervously, black eyes flickering to Max and back to me again. "Sydlynn Hayle," he said. Sang Max's drach name. "I don't have much time."

"What's going on?" I took a step toward him but he backed away from me, holding his hands up to ward me off.

"I shouldn't be here," he said, deep voice shaking, dark skin taking on a gray tint. The hem of his long, black robe trembled over the floor, though he held himself as rigid as stone. "But I owed you answers, after everything that happened."

He'd been Ameline's guide way back when we were still struggling to fulfill the prophecy. Told her far more than Iepa ever told me. And yet, I'd always felt a closer affinity to his people than to the ones meant for my side of the fight. Which made me wonder whose side the light maji were really on. Not so cut and dried, the second race.

"We need your help," I said. "You know about the sorcerer Belaisle and his connection to Dark Brother?" I still couldn't believe the idiot sold his soul to Creator's sibling in the other Universe. Then again, this was Liander Belaisle. And any offer of Universal power would make him salivate.

Trinol's sharp nod was no surprise. "We are well informed," he said. "Part of the reason my people have closed off from the rest of the Universe." He hesitated. "They are afraid, Sydlynn. As am I."

"You're the only ones who can help us," I said. "Max and the drach are stretched thin. We have to find the pieces of Creator before Dark Brother does."

Trinol's distress was clear on his face. He'd always come across as so composed to me, almost as emotionless as the Sidhe. I'd never seen him so torn, so upset. "We can't," he said at last, turning sideways, away from me. "Our focus has been defense. We seek tools, weapons we can use against Dark Brother when the time comes. And the time is coming, make no mistake." He turned his head to meet my eyes. "An army is coming for us, the likes of which we've never seen."

That sounded promising. And like a ton of fun. Yikes.

"We have no promise of that," Max said in a gentle voice. "The Fates can see nothing."

"Perhaps," Trinol said. "But the final foreseeing has

been triggered and you know it, Lord of the Drach." He shuddered. "Whether through an attack of Dark Brother's army or in the final battle between my people and the light maji, we are doomed." His voice dropped, softened, and he repeated the words I'd heard from Light Fate a few times now. "The end of everything."

"Not if we can find Creator's pieces first," I said. Totally grasping at straws.

"For all we know," Trinol said with great sadness, "it is the assembly of Creator's physical form that brings about our final downfall."

Hadn't thought of that, honestly.

"We want to help, Sydlynn, we truly do." Trinol's shoulders sagged forward, large hands spread out before him, eyes flaring with rainbow light and frustration. "But we fear triggering the retaliation of our brothers and sisters of the Light. We just can't risk doing so, especially with Dark Brother in the mix."

It wasn't his fault, but that didn't help my temper any. "Thanks for nothing."

Trinol finally turned back completely, nodding, sad. "I know you think us cowardly," he said. "We have spent our existence controlling the fate of others through subtlety and manipulation. You are an anomaly to us, as Ameline was." He smiled at her soul and she smiled back. "Children of pure action, of passion and immense power. How terrifying in your freshness." He paused, drew a deep breath and let it out again. "If anyone can prevent Dark Brother from reassembling Creator's form, it will be you. Not us. We are too far past our days of direct intervention."

"Do you know what will happen if he succeeds?" I still didn't have a satisfactory answer.

Trinol shrugged. "It's unclear," he said. "Though the final vision is of the maji at war. So I can only assume that control of Creator's form means Dark Brother will rule both Universes."

More guessing and supposing. Great.

Trinol's head snapped up, eyes going distant before he shuddered, rainbow light surrounding him.

"I can tell you one thing," he said, hurried, words tumbling over each other as the power pulled at him. Clearly, someone wasn't happy he was here. "You already have the means to track the pieces in your possession. Something the other seekers do not. And make no mistake," he shifted, wrestled with the magic tugging at him, "there are more players seeking Creator than just you and the sorcerers."

"Trinol!" I reached out to him with power, but his magic held me off.

"You just have to know where to look," he said, eyes glowing. And vanished in a flash of fire.

TWENTY

I pulled myself up to sit on the edge of the altar, Ameline leaping gracefully beside me. Max joined us, feet firmly on the floor, but at least we were now at eye level.

"Any guesses what that cryptic little remark was about?" I swung my feet, hands palm down on the stone behind me, leaning back and squinting at the writing on the wall across from me, secretly hoping some mystery message might appear and solve all my problems.

Ameline shook her head, turning sideways, tucking one foot under her thigh. "It's obvious the dark maji are now as reluctant as the light to do anything besides save their own skins." Her old irritation was showing, though it felt more like my own so I wasn't freaked out by it.

"While it's comforting to know we have something in our midst that will help us," Max said, "until we can pinpoint that advantage, I'm afraid we're no further along that we were before."

Ameline's distress pulled at the corners of her bow lips. "I'll keep working on Trinol," she said. "He's never been so reticent before."

Max leaned forward and gently patted her knee, giant hand almost engulfing her leg. "You've done well," he said and, to my shock, she flushed and ducked her head with real pleasure.

She really had shed all her bad parts.

"The spirit magic glitches are growing worse," Ameline said when she'd recovered. "I'm feeling blips, as though there are gaps in the power that seal themselves when the parts go missing."

"How frequently?" I sat up straighter, thinking of Pender and the image his shattered mind shared.

"Not very, just yet," she said, "but far too often for my liking. And there are small gaps, at times, bigger ones in others. As though the spirit power is thinning. Does that make sense?"

I showed them both what Pender showed me and Max hissed in a breath of air.

"As I feared," he said. "I have no idea where Sebastian and his vampires have gone. But if that image is correct, what you've been feeling, Ameline, is other blood clans disappearing as the DeWinter one did."

So, not good. "Then we have a visit to make," I said, hopping down from the stone altar. She might not want to admit it, but the Empress of vampires had a serious problem on her hands. And while I didn't really feel a keen sense of loyalty to the other blood clans, my vampire essence urged me through worry alone to go check in and see what was up.

Max and I left, Ameline promising to share what else she learned, the veil engulfing the drach leader and me as I did my best to puzzle out what Trinol was talking about.

Where are we going? Max let me take the lead even as I focused on the ledge.

To talk to a stubborn old vampire, I sent. Cold air struck us as we emerged, Max looking around with glittering eyes at the dark mountain peak.

"Nepal, I believe," he said. "Your plane."

So that was where the castle resided. I hadn't managed to figure that out.

The two guards at the gate stepped aside the instant they saw me, keeping their distance, and this time there was no greeting party on the path to the bridge. I crossed it in a hurry, mind reaching forward with a discreet tap, much like the one the Empress offered me when she first contacted me.

See? I could be polite.

Welcome, Sydlynn Hayle, her ancient mind met mine.

That was easy. I strode through the open door into the giant, arching foyer, now empty of the gathering of queens. A slim young woman in a skintight, black leather cat suit, hair cut to a perfect bob, bowed to me. Her dark eyes slanted slightly upward, belying her Asian heritage, and she moved like a graceful animal when she gestured for me to follow her.

Not a vampire, from the feel of her. Some sorcery at her disposal and a hint of witch magic, but subtle, like she'd never developed it. Her core of power was based in spirit magic, though I'd never experienced that in a mortal before. How interesting.

She led us through a curving corridor, one side carved out with windows looking over the mountain range. A thick, deep, red carpet muffled my footfalls and, not for the first time since I left home in my pajamas, did I regret not stopping for a change of clothes.

Our guide stopped at a small door carved with the face of a dragon. The briefest smile passed her ruby painted lips, lifting her pale yellow skin, rounding her cheeks. She bowed to me, fluid, almost inhuman, and gestured for me to precede her.

"*Lóng*," Max said with respect in his voice. "I had thought your kind extinct."

I looked back and forth between them, hating being in the dark.

"My people are few," the young woman answered in a crisp British accent. "Faithful to the one who saved us." She bowed to him. "I am Jiao."

Max sang his name to her and she stood there, rapt,

until he was finished.

"I am honored," she said, lowering her head with genuine humility. Her dark eyes then lifted, met mine. "My mistress awaits, Light One."

So, she knew about my extra circulars. Also very interesting. I stepped past the girl, Jiao, surprised by the minty, yet dusty, scent of her, catching the faintest hint of scales on her collarbone. That startled me. Was she like Max? But, no. Not drach. And her power refused to let me examine her further.

Determined to grill Max on who she was later, I let it go. For now, I had some questions to put to the Empress and I needed my full focus.

The room on the other side was dark, walls painted the same lush crimson as the carpet in the hall. A heavy fall of fabric hung from the ceiling, draping around the giant bed in the center of the room. Three young women, all beautiful, all human, arranged themselves in various positions of languidity, only rising when a hand rose from the velvet coverlet and waved them away. They swept from the room in a scented breeze, the mix of flowers and spices making me feel slightly nauseated.

"Come forward." The Empress's magic slipped back the fabric, two young men in black jackets tightened to their waists with white cummerbunds attaching the weight of the drape to large gold rings embedded in the wall. The resulting effect resembled the spread of drach wings. I strode to the base of the bed, trying not to be too impressed, Max joining me. The Empress leaned forward, beads of black eyes lighting up at the sight of him, a real smile on her face.

"Lord Drach," she said, muttering something else in a language I didn't know. It sounded as old as she was.

He answered in the multi-layered song of his people, to which she swayed as if entranced, then went on in the same language she'd used.

Way to leave me out of the conversation. But it was over quickly, the Empress sinking back into her cushions as the young, dangerous Jiao, came to stand beside the bed, eyes locked on me.

"It has been too long since we met," the Empress said, a hint of regret in her voice. "It is good to see you well."

"And you, Moa," he answered with a happy rumble.

Max obviously knew her. Part of me was peeved he hadn't told me so. Then again, I really hadn't been forthcoming when I informed him who we were visiting. But knowing the trouble the Universe's spirit magic was in, I would have thought he'd have brought her up by now.

As for the Empress, she preened, though the twist of her lips told me she knew she was being ridiculous. "Not so pretty as when I saw you last, great lord."

"You are as lovely as ever," he said with absolute

sincerity. "It is the courage of the heart and the beauty of the soul's song that appeals to the drach."

She laughed, a soft and happy sound, childlike. I still struggled to reconcile her ancient appearance with the young voice that emerged when she spoke. "Flattery," she said. "It's been too long."

"Empress," I said, "I don't mean to break up the party, but we're worried about your people."

Her sharp eyes went to me, back to Max. "You are aware of the disappearances of other blood clans." Not a question.

"We are," Max said. "And we want to help, if we can."

The Empress sighed, shook her head, almost angry as she cut through the air with one hand. "We both know that isn't possible," she said. "Greater things have been set in motion, Fated." She fixed her glittering eyes on me. "Correct?"

There wasn't much I could say to that. "We're doing everything we can," I said. "The maji are staying out of it. That leaves the drach to carry the work." As usual.

She nodded brusquely. "I've never had time for the maji," she said. "Too reticent, too afraid of their own magic. But you," she jabbed one of her sharp fingers toward me. "You are different. One of them, and yet." She licked one finger, as though tasting the very air on it. "Perhaps there is hope, then."

I didn't know why her saying so made me feel better. I guess because, for once, one of the leaders of my plane wasn't a douchenozzle from the get go. I actually kind of liked her, no matter Sunny's present predicament.

Something to be tackled for later, it turned out. About a heartbeat before the black tunnel opened beside me, Jiao, perched at the Empress's bedside, tensed and crouched, hissing. The slim, black clad woman leaped forward, an impossible jump high in the air, landing at the foot of the bed directly in the path of the tunnel. I barely had time to erect a shield in front of the portal before she was slashing the air with silver claws so sharp they sang, embedding in my wards with the force of her blow.

She glared at me, eyes shimmering with chrome, as Piers Southway emerged. I almost gave him hell for being a jackass, barging in here like this, until I caught sight of his face—and the fact he wasn't alone. Charlotte leaped out beside him, vibrating with tension, her wolf in her eyes, muzzle forming and retreating. Her blue gaze met mine, fury so intense in her face I shivered and let the whole intrusion thing drop.

"You have great courage," the Empress said in a flat and angry voice, "and for that reason only I will let you live long enough to tell me why you've intruded on my private quarters, master of sorcery."

Piers bowed gracefully as Jiao retreated, though not far, her gaze flickering from Piers to Charlotte and back again, endlessly.

"Forgive the intrusion," he said, voice rough with anger. "But the matter is absolutely urgent. And though my companion was inclined to deal with the issue directly, in the spirit of working together instilled by the new World Paranormal Council, I begged her to come to you first."

Charlotte could barely contain herself and my heart sped up at what could possibly have pissed her off this badly.

What's going on? I shot the question directly at her but she didn't respond, just growled low in the back of her throat. The Empress's bodygirl hissed back.

"Tell me," the Empress commanded.

"The queen of the werenation has been kidnapped," Piers said. "And Piotr Wilhelm took her."

TWENTY-ONE

He what? I gaped at Charlotte, understood her absolute fury and, in the instant it took me to go from shock to rage of my own, the Empress reacted. Her tiny body joined Jiao's, springing forward to the end of the bed, fury on her face. But this anger was aimed at Piers.

"What reason has the Steam Union to come here, to make such accusations?" I could feel her defensiveness, wondered if she already knew by the way her voice vibrated with anger. It was the reaction of someone carrying guilt around.

"The evolving werenation is young and still growing," Piers shot right back at her. "Unlike other magic races, the Steam Union are here to support and protect in whatever capacity is required. Including standing beside them as allies and spokespeople." He glanced at Charlotte. "For as long as they will have us."

My werefriend's sharp nod sealed the deal.

The Empress's attitude didn't change, though I could tell she wasn't happy her avenue of argument had been cut off. "You have proof." Again, not a question.

"Not direct proof, no," he said, standing his ground.

"And yet, you come here, accuse one of my monarchs of kidnapping a werewolf." She said the word like it was an insult.

Okay, so didn't like her so much anymore. "The werenation is a duly accepted and recognized paranormal species," I snarled. "And you'll do well to speak of them with respect in my company."

That got her attention. Her head whipped around, her bodygirl hyper focused on me. Let them try it. Just let them try it.

"Explain," Max said, breaking the taut temper holding the room in shaking thrall.

"Yana's convoy was attacked," Piers said, one hand settling on Charlotte's shoulder to hold her still. I wanted to go to her, but held my ground with Max who, at least, had the Empress's respect. "She was returning from Kiev, a shopping trip for the new baby." My mind recalled the swell of Yana's belly at the meeting, the glow in her face. How happy Danilo was of late. They bred like rabbits, those two, their third already since Danilo took the throne. "Her wereguards were slaughtered and she was taken."

"If they were killed," the Empress said, "you have no way of knowing it was vampires." Sullen, bitter. Angry. Was that guilt? Did she believe him and refused to admit it?

"One of the guards survived long enough," Piers said, firmly, with sadness. "The queen is eight months pregnant, Empress. King Danilo is beside himself."

"Why do you bring this to me if you have all your answers?" She turned her back on him, Jiao draping her bony form in a thick, red robe. I felt Max shift beside me, looked up to see anger in his shining diamond eyes.

"You know why," he said in his rumbling voice. "You granted that throne to a vampire you were aware held a personal vendetta against the werenation." Charlotte's head snapped around, muzzle appearing and staying put. The Empress's shoulders twitched and she half turned.

"Perhaps," she said. "But the monarchs of my race are autonomous, outside of core vampire law. It has nothing to do with me."

"Like Sunny's removal from her throne had nothing to do with you." The Empress flinched from my sarcasm. What was really going on here? Was I right? Did she already know about the attack on the werewolves?

"Then you will stay out of it," Max said, "when Sydlynn and her companions kill him for this affront."

The Empress turned the rest of the way around, snapped something at him in her language.

"Indeed I do," he said, refusing to share in her privacy. "And I will challenge your authority until the end of days, Moa. Because as much as you've grown to consider yourself a goddess, we both know even I am not Creator. And that the years of bitterness in your heart cloud your judgment."

She turned away again. "Do as you will," she said. "But know that the vampire race will not stand for his death if he is proved innocent."

Charlotte's teeth snapped together and she finally spoke. "I'll deliver his treacherous head to you personally," she growled. "You can ask him yourself."

I crossed to my werefriend and took her shaking hand. "We'll be back, Empress," I said, gesturing to Max. He shook his head, veil opening beside him.

I will return to my people, he said, voice sad. *Go on with the search. These matters are not for one such as I to interfere.*

Could use the backup, I said, feeling selfish about the whole thing.

You don't need me, he sent as he entered the veil. *You never did.* And he was gone.

Piers didn't waste time, dragging Charlotte and me along with him back into the tunnel. *This is bad, Syd*, he sent, tight and angry. *Danilo is ready to tear Piotr apart. They're on the verge of war. And I don't need to tell you what that might mean, right?*

If Danilo went after Piotr, the whole werenation

would follow. And though it had been years since I freed the werewolves from the taint of the Black Souls who created them, there was still more than enough old prejudice between vampires and werewolves to set off a powder keg that would take a hell of a lot of trouble and time to clean up.

War between two races of the World Paranormal Council would pretty much mean the end of all alliances. I could see it now, spilling over into camps supporting one side or the other. And then, as we stepped out into a bright office and my eyes settled on Femke and Quaid, I understood what this was really about.

"Belaisle," I blurted to her as the two leaders stood to greet us. "He's at it again."

"At what?" Femke seemed truly startled, our mutual anger gone for the moment. "What's happened?"

I didn't get to answer. The door behind me, the portal to her new office, slammed open so hard the wood splintered and Danilo, king of the werenation, hurtled through. He was in half wolf form, his humanoid werewolf body looming over us, a howl so loud ripping from his chest I actually winced and covered my ears.

Femke faced him down, a tall, slim willowy blonde, giant silver Alpha were towering over her with saliva dripping from his jaws. Quaid held back, though from the feel of Femke's magic she was insisting he keep his distance. She held out one hand, pressed it fearlessly to the wereking's chest, face creased in concern for him.

"Danilo," she said. "Please, tell me what's going on."

He shrank into smaller form, though he didn't revert to human completely. "Yana," he said. "They have my wife and unborn child."

And then he collapsed, suddenly human, sobbing into his hands. She hugged his naked body, gesturing for help as two nervous Enforcers hurried forward, urged to do so by my husband who circled to finally join Femke. His two witches draped the shaking king in a black robe. Femke eased him into a chair, looking up to meet my eyes.

But it was Piers who filled her in while Quaid and I carefully avoided gazes. I just didn't have time to fight with him right now. Femke's face darkened and she nodded brusquely. "Do we have someone inside the blood clan we can talk to?"

Why didn't I think of that? I reached out immediately, felt for the one I was looking for and, without permission, jerked her firmly through the veil and deposited the trembling form of Isabelle Wilhelm in the middle of Femke's office.

Danilo shouted something incoherent at the sight of her, but the Enforcers were faster. Quaid leaped on him, held him back bodily and with power, my husband straining to keep the furious and heartsick wereking in check.

The only vampire I still trusted in her blood clan,

Isabelle burst into tears, falling into Femke's arms. I hadn't seen her in a while, but the young undead hadn't changed at all thanks to the gifts of her race. She'd been there for me in the past, friends with Charlotte, though my werefriend avoided her eyes when Isabelle reached out to try to touch her hand.

"I've been trying to escape," she wailed, "but they knew not to allow me to leave, that I would bring you down upon them." She turned toward Danilo, terrified clearly, but with hands outstretched. "Dear king, they have your queen."

"That's it, then," Piers said, rage crackling in his voice.

Femke hesitated, the diplomat in her struggling with her need to act.

"Don't even think about it," I snapped while Piers joined me, shoulder to shoulder.

"The Steam Union will not tolerate such blatant attacks against our allies," he said.

"Nor will the North American Witches Council," I said, speaking for Mom and hoping she'd forgive me. "And we're not assembling a damned committee to look into it, Femke. We're going to get Yana now. End of story."

Danilo lurched toward me, but I held him off better than the Enforcers had.

"You," I said, pushing him into the chair again, "are

staying put. No arguments. You," I pointed at Femke, "stay here and out of it, just in case this goes wrong so you can claim no culpability." The World Paranormal Council was still so young to be faced with such a giant mess this soon. I worried her involvement before we had all the t's crossed and i's dotted might create more problems than it solved. Better to investigate and claim later Femke was behind taking Piotr down if things went well. I'd take the heat personally if they didn't. I'd worked too hard to make sure everyone was playing nice to let Piotr Wilhelm screw this up. "Piers and I will make sure that vampire asshat knows he's crossed the line."

Femke's accepting nod was all the answer I needed.

"Except," she said, blue eyes sparkling, the Femke I loved shining through, "screw culpability." She must have known where my head was and didn't care. Which proved to me once again she was exactly the leader we needed. And that I had to stop trying to protect her from doing her job. "I'm coming with you."

TWENTY-TWO

Femke took a few minutes to whisper some hasty instructions to a harried older witch while Charlotte paced back and forth behind her brother. Before I could stop myself by thinking about it too much, I opened my power and called out to the one person I needed in on this the most.

I just hoped she wasn't still pissed at me.

Sunny. Her mind latched onto mine in an instant.

Syd, she sent, softly desperate. *I just heard about Yana. Where are you?*

Femke's, I sent, relief flooding me. *Hong Kong. Can you come?*

The beautiful vampire queen—and she would always be queen to me—hesitated.

I have no standing any longer, she sent. *I might only hinder you.*

Bull pucky, I sent. *We need you.*

Then, you shall have me, she sent. I barely had time to turn and open my mouth to tell Piers, when the air shimmered behind Danilo's chair and Sunny appeared. Gone was her elaborate gown, replaced by a sober gray suit, but she was as stunning as ever, supermodel features twisted in grief as she circled to face the wereking. He looked up into her eyes, lunging to his feet, but I needn't have gasped a fearful breath. He didn't harm her, except maybe to crush her a little in a gargantuan hug.

"Danilo," she said, voice clear in the silence that followed his embrace. "We'll bring her back to you."

He let Sunny go, nodding, body trembling. "I want to go with you." But his dull tone told me he knew that wasn't going to happen.

"Please," Femke said, finally joining me, Sunny coming to my side with a sorrowful smile on her face. "Trust us. You know we have your best interest at heart. Charlotte will stand in your stead. And we will see justice done."

My werefriend bowed her head to her brother. "I'll bring her back safe," she said, "or I'll kill him for harming her."

Danilo turned away, didn't watch as I reached out to everyone. "Mind if I handle transportation?"

No one objected. "Might I suggest," Sunny said, "the throne room? He'll likely be gloating there, thinking he's won some victory."

"It's not Piotr I'm worried about," I said, tearing at the veil toward the suggested location. I latched onto their minds collectively as I led them through. *This smacks of Brotherhood interference, an attempt to spark a war between the vampires and werewolves.*

And shatter the new alliance, Femke sent while the others muttered angrily. *Makes sense, Syd.*

I almost wished she'd argued. *For now, we deal with Piotr and bring Yana and the baby home safe. Then we kick that damned vampire's ass off the throne and make him tell us where Belaisle is.*

Dibs, Piers sent.

Wait your turn, Charlotte snarled.

We'll talk it out later, I sent. *Now, are we ready?*

Affirmatives all around. I drew a breath and tore open the veil on the other side, shields at the fore, dropping us in the middle of the Wilhelm throne room. The first thing I saw was Piotr, smiling at me with his sharp teeth exposed.

The second hit me like a blow, though I supposed I should have guessed she'd show up after the assault on her privacy. The Empress sat in her throne chair, held aloft by four of her guards.

Max told you to stay out of this, I sent directly to her.

The drach lord has no sway over me, she answered, though I could sense the tremor in the back of her mind, knew she was lying.

But the third member of their little party was the most shocking of all. Blonde hair spiked, gray eyes snapping with vengeful hate, Eva Southway flanked the vampire Empress on her left. She was alone, but felt far more powerful than the last time I'd seen her, after stealing magic from her own people. Clearly she'd made a habit of thievery. I didn't bother glancing at Piers. I had a feeling I'd know what I'd see on his face.

"What are you doing here, Mother?" His crisp tone didn't hide his anger very well.

"Supporting my allies," she snapped back. "Nothing to do with you, child."

Nice attempt at an insult. Not particularly effective, but an effort, at least.

Let him deal with his mother. I had other, more important details to handle. My power pushed against Piotr, though the Empress attempted to stop me. For a moment, I let my magic linger against hers, weighing her strength against my own, letting her feel just how outclassed she was. To her credit she didn't retreat, and I was forced to firmly push her aside to get to him.

The moment my power touched him, he hissed at me, turning to glare at her.

"You swore to protect me!" Nice way to talk to his Empress. Then again, from the power of the Brotherhood thrall he was obviously under, it was likely he was too far gone to know what he was saying.

"Silence." She didn't raise her voice, didn't have to. I let her power cut mine off, gave her that small victory, more out of resignation than any need to protect her obviously thin-skinned ego.

"You knew," I said, though it really wasn't a surprise now. Just a disappointment. "What was going on with him. That they owned him. And you let him take the Wilhelm throne."

She didn't answer me, but she didn't have to.

"I don't know what your game is," I said, advancing on her, stopping short of climbing onto her throne chair and shaking her, "but you could have had a place in the future of our plane. Instead, you've made an enemy of me today. And of the Lord of the Drach." I had no doubt Max would agree, though I really was into taking liberties with other people's decisions today.

The Empress settled back in her seat, regret in her little black eyes, but lips a slash of determination.

"You have no idea what is in play," she said. "Perhaps, when you've lived as long as I have, maneuvered the pieces needed to see the whole picture, you and I will speak again."

Pieces.

Oh. My. Swearword.

Was I reading too much into this? But no. Trinol warned me there were others seeking the fragments of

Creator. And there was no way she used that terminology by accident. But she was a vampire, unable to travel to other worlds.

Who was she working with? And why? Max's comment about her not being a goddess made me shudder.

"Is that what you're after, Mao?" I didn't speak much above a pitying whisper. "Why you summoned me in the first place? Not to defend Sunny, or even to meet me, but to assess what I could be worth to you? What the essence could do for you?" My vampire hissed softly inside me. "And to follow me, to find the pieces yourself. To become Creator after all?"

She looked away, shivered. "Take what you've come for," she said. "This particular move of the game is over."

She disappeared in a shudder of shadow, leaving Piotr to stare after her in fury and horror. When he turned and met my eyes, his fear won.

"Where is she?" I had no qualms about shaking him until his bones fell out of his miserable skin. Eva lunged between us, just saving him from an eternity of agony, but not for long. I'd take them both on, no problem. "Get out of the way," I said, right in her face. "You really don't want to make me angrier than I already am."

Piotr backed up, almost ran into the steps leading to his throne. "They were planning to attack me," he said, faint hysteria in his voice. "Plotting to kill me. With her."

He stabbed an index finger at Sunny.

"My dear, dear Piotr," Sunny said in her mildest, sweetest voice, "you matter so little to me I can't imagine caring what happened to you one way or another."

Piotr twitched, turned to look for support from his family of vampires, but none of them would meet his eyes. I wondered as horror dawned on his face if he was just realizing how deeply the control of the Brotherhood ran and could only imagine that was the case. I felt the power controlling him flee, leaving him barren and alone, facing all of us without even the push of the Brotherhood to keep him afloat.

"It's not my fault!" He screamed the words at me. Charlotte bounded past me in wolf form, hit him full in the chest, drove him back onto the steps with a thud. She stood over him, lupine body shaking as she howled in his face.

He tried to fight her, sparks of spirit magic singing her fur but she held him down, her own rainbow light, so much like mine, smothering his energy with hers. She half shifted into werewolf shape and snarled.

"Where is Yana?"

Piotr wailed softly. "Bring her!"

A handful of vampires scrambled from the room, running, I hoped, to fetch the werewolf queen. Charlotte didn't move while we waited, her jaws drooling strings of steaming saliva onto his pale skin.

I spun at the sound of footsteps, turned with my stomach clenching tight at the sight of Yana being led toward us.

Correction. Carried, her head slumped forward, body emaciated even after a short stint in the care of the vampires. Such a dramatic change from just earlier this morning when I'd seen her with Danilo. Charlotte howled and spun, racing for her sister-in-law as the vampires holding her let her go and dove back out of my werefriend's reach. But it didn't matter. She wasn't interested in them, not when Yana began to fall. Charlotte shifted to human, tatters of what remained of her clothing whispering around her as she gently eased her queen to the floor.

I fell to my knees beside her, reaching out with power to support the fallen werequeen. Her eyes flickered open, caught mine a moment, a whisper escaping her.

"The baby," Yana said. "Save the baby."

I pushed magic into her, but there was nothing to anchor it to—except the unborn child. Yana was lost, I knew that already. From the faint puncture wounds on her skin, still unhealed, she'd been drained over and over again, on purpose, weakened to the point of death. But her mother's heart refused to quit, focusing everything she had left on the child still living in her wasted and dying body.

Syd. Femke's power latched onto me. *We need to go.*

213

Now.

And let him get away with this? I spun to glare up at her.

No, she sent, tears in her eyes. *Because if we don't get Yana to Danilo immediately, she'll die before she gets to say goodbye. And he'll never forgive us for that.*

Damn. It. All. To hell and back again.

I swept to my feet, continually feeding magic into the fading wolf in Yana's soul as I spun on Eva, Piotr and the rest of the Wilhelm clan.

"This isn't over," I said. "And when I come back, you'd better be ready to hurt."

The veil swallowed us before I could change my mind and personally wipe the smirk from Eva Southway's face.

TWENTY-THREE

I don't know what I was thinking, what carried me, not to Femke's office, but the throne room at the werepalace. Charlotte vanished the moment we emerged, and I could only guess she went for her brother.

My power eased Yana to the floor, her body shriveling almost before my eyes. Wereguards crowded close, their fury and fear a weight on me I finally had to push back with almost violent force. They retreated, more so when the air split and Danilo came roaring through, Charlotte on his heels.

Femke stepped back, allowed him past, but closed the gap again to keep the others away. Danilo fell to his knees, arms slipping tenderly around his wife as she looked up into his eyes, body straining. A wet, tearing sound twisted my stomach in a knot, a flood of blood and amniotic fluid rushing out from under her dress.

Sympathy pains fed by experience made my entire body clench while Charlotte dove forward, hands scrambling to retrieve the tiny baby, her own power pulsing into the child as her extended claw cut the cord. She bent over her sister-in-law, laid the softly squalling infant on her chest, gore spreading from between Yana's legs to puddle at my feet.

"Saved her," she said with a faint smile of triumph. And died, sighing out Danilo's name with her last breath.

I stood there in a pool of blood, tears streaming down my cheeks, as the werewolves raised their heads to match their king and howled their grief.

I sat on the bottom step of the broad, sweeping staircase to the upper levels, the carpet soft under me. My sneakers were clean again, the blood magicked away because I simply couldn't stand to have Yana's death on me. I wiped at my raw nose, my sore cheeks, too much crying leaving me chapped inside and out. Soft footsteps descended behind me, the owner of them pausing to sit next to me and take my hand.

"I'm sorry," Femke said. And that was all she needed to say.

We sat there a long time, in silence, just holding hands, my power hugging her and hers me. All the anger and frustration, the blame and shame, was gone. I missed her, I realized, more than I wanted to admit.

"I'm worried about him." Femke cleared her throat, a soft, apologetic sound.

Danilo. "So am I." There was no way now he wasn't going after the vampires. This was so many kinds of bad I could barely stand it. "We could appeal to the Empress," I said. "Or just go in there and excise Piotr's ass. Give him to Danilo. That might take care of the honor thing."

Femke shook her head, biting her lower lip. "You know we can't do that," she said. "I won't start a war between nations by delivering a vampire king to the leader of the werewolves. No matter what he's done. But." She sighed in irritation, releasing my hand. Damn, were we fighting again? But she ran both through her hair, fingers shaking. So, no. She just needed the outlet. "Arresting his ass? You better believe it." I gaped at her a moment. She what? "Already done." Well, what did I know? She met my eyes as I processed that and wondered what the Empress thought of Femke's move. "You saddled me with this job," she said, accusation in the words, but not her tone. "And I have to follow the rules, Syd. We can put him on trial for murdering Yana and the other werewolves. But answering one death with another without following protocol is inviting a bigger mess than either of us is prepared to deal with." Pain in her blue eyes pushed my empathy to the surface.

"I know," I said. "I'm sorry. I wish there was another way." And I'd settle for his arrest. For now.

217

She shook her head with a soft laugh. "We both know there wasn't," she said with great dignity. "And thank you for trusting me."

"Just don't get my husband killed," I said with a weary smile of my own. "And it's all good."

She opened her mouth, grief on her face, but I knew what she was going to say and waved her off before she could say it.

"He's a big boy," I said. "And, like you, perfect for the job."

Heavy footfalls interrupted us, Piers thudding his way down the steps with Charlotte padding along silently beside him. The pair came to a halt at the bottom, swinging around to face us. From the expressions they shared, they had been talking and were in complete concord. I just hoped they'd thought through what they were about to say.

"This assault can't be ignored," Charlotte said, all cold and collected, which meant she was dying inside at failing her brother.

"As we see it," Piers said while Sunny drifted past me to observe, quiet and withdrawn, "this is partially my issue to deal with. My mother has clearly aligned with our enemies and, for all I know, was part of the plot against the werenation."

A terrible worry gnawed on my innards. "Piers," I said, voice flat and angry. "Tell me you didn't know Eva would be there."

Wouldn't you know? He refused to meet my eyes. The only thing that saved him from a solid punch in the chest was my werefriend.

"And," Charlotte said, interrupting my need to throttle Piers for keeping damned secrets when he knew better, "it is *my* issue, and that of my people, to avenge the unlawful death of the queen of our nation."

Femke sighed softly, tilted her head toward Sunny. "Any other takers in the blame department?"

"Indeed," my beautiful, undead aunt said. "If I hadn't lost my throne to Piotr, if I'd been stronger and braver about eliminating him instead of allowing him to undermine me out of an old sense of loyalty, Queen Yana would still be alive and this would not be an issue." She shrugged her graceful shoulders.

While I was an equal opportunity guilter, the three of them really needed to get a grip.

"Listen up," I said. "This is the Brotherhood, and you all know it." Three blank stares. "Their attempt to get us to fight amongst ourselves." Totally not getting through to them. "And if you start a war over this, you'll be handing us all over to them."

Crickets.

Lovely.

"Does that mean you won't help us?" Charlotte's rigid fury spoke volumes. I'd never said no to her before.

PATTI LARSEN

But, like Femke, I was seeing the bigger picture here.

Way to be a grown up, Syd.

"Piotr and Eva will be dealt with," Femke said. "The king of the Wilhelm Blood Clan is in custody as we speak and will face justice."

"Let me guess," Piers said, bitterness almost tangible. "My mother escaped."

"For now," Femke said with such confidence behind those two words even I felt better. "I promise you she will be found and arrested and will stand trial if she's had a part in this." Femke stared the three down a moment, letting her assurances sink in. "But we must do this the right way. Through the Council. Or we lose everything we've built."

"You know we'll act with or without your permission," Piers said, flat and cold.

Femke nodded. "And if you interfere with due process or try to have my prisoner killed while in custody, I'll have you arrested."

Okay, that was going a little too far. "Deep breaths," I said. "Let's do it Femke's way." Charlotte's denial was swift and violent, a shake of her head, flare of power in her eyes. *I'll make sure she lets you execute him when he's found guilty*, I sent directly into her mind.

Somehow, Femke caught it. She stared at me in shock tinged with horror. *Syd.*

You really want to deny her family that? Femke turned at

last and nodded heavily to Charlotte who seemed to latch onto that promise like a drowning woman to a life buoy.

I rose to my feet, sighed, when Charlotte's wolf flared in agreement. "You two," I said, pointing at Piers and Sunny. "I'm counting on both of you to keep the mess to a minimum." I knew if Piers caught his mother first, there would be no trial, no Femke. Though I worried harming Eva might do him irreparable harm. They both nodded, Piers surly, Sunny thoughtful and quiet. I turned my back on them to ascend the stairs. If it weren't for the wellbeing of my friends, I could care less if accidents happened to Piotr Wilhelm and Eva Southway.

They'd have to wait. Right now I had the heavy task of talking to the mourning wereking before I could go home. And I really wasn't looking forward to our conversation.

TWENTY-FOUR

I stopped at the top of the stairs, hesitating to break through the crowd of waiting werewolves who hovered, heads down, emitting rage and fear as they waited outside their king's quarters. Gritting my teeth against opposition, I slipped into the press of bodies and was surprised when they parted for me easily, sliding out of the way with slow nods of acceptance at my presence.

By the time I traveled down the hall and to Danilo's door, I was shaken by the eerie silence, the only sound the occasional chops licking from the half turned wereguards standing watch. They parted to allow me to enter, closing the door softly behind me.

A pair of familiar faces looked up at my entry, heads rising from their whispered conversation. The former Council healer twins, Lula and Phon Kennecott, smiled faintly at me, as identical as fraternal siblings could be.

Matching hazel eyes watched me cross the elaborately decorated room, passing Victorian furniture and approaching the vast, marble clad fireplace where they waited.

Lula ducked her head to me as I joined them, hand squeezing mine. I'd called them immediately after the death of the queen, wishing I'd done so earlier, though knowing even these two with their immense talent couldn't have saved her any more than I could. She'd simply given up too much to save her daughter.

"The baby?" My heart constricted with worry, though I'd heard her soft, mewling cries as she lay on her mother's dead breast. Still, the trauma Yana went through could have adversely affected the child in some developmental way.

"Healthy and whole," Phon said in his soft tenor voice. "She'll be fine. Her mother saved her life."

I sagged slightly in relief. Bad enough Danilo lost Yana. But if the baby had been harmed... this way, maybe we'd be able to convince him to keep his revenge to Piotr and not focus it on the entire vampire race.

"Thanks, you two," I said. They nodded.

"We didn't do much," Lula said. "But I think Danilo was happy to see us." She jerked her chin in the direction of the next door, leading from the sitting room and into the bed chamber. "He's waiting for you."

Why did that make my jaw jump? I left the pair and

crossed to the bedroom door, knocking softly with my hand while pushing out a bit of magic as warning before slipping it open and easing my way through. I closed it as softly as I could, eyes searching the room. Past the massive, canopied bed in rich purple velvet, the elaborately carved posts carrying the drape, the textured, woven carpet on the floor. My gaze flittered over the dark stained wooden walls covered in landscapes and bits of armor and swords.

I found the faces I sought tucked in the corner near the balcony doors. Even the massive bodies of the two men I approached seemed dwarfed by the enormous size of the room, the king himself diminished where he sat, hunched and silent, shoulders shaking, in a wingback chair.

His mother, Olena, sat next to him, cradling one of his big hands between her smaller ones. She looked up first, nodded to me. I always saw Charlotte in her, unlike Danilo. Here was my werefriend's blonde hair and blue eyes, nothing like her dark haired son and mountain of muscle and bone that was her father, Oleksander. The former king of the werenation rose and came to me, engulfing me in his arms. His silvery beard felt coarse against my cheek as he bent to kiss me softly, before leading me toward his grieving grandson.

"Sydlynn." Olena's accent was stronger than Charlotte's, thick but elegant. "We will always be grateful for your assistance in freeing Yana from the vampire scourge." The wolf in her flared in her eyes.

Exactly what I was hoping wouldn't be her attitude. But she and Danilo had spent a long time trapped in the bodies of wolves, Olena decades, so I suppose it was understandable she carried a grudge, though the vampires had nothing to do with her entrapment. They were just more animal—and ruthless—than even the rest of the werenation.

"I wish I could have done more," I said, choking up as I spoke. I had to clear my throat, look away from Olena before I could go on. "Yana was so courageous. She committed everything she had—she and her wolf together—to saving her daughter." I turned and met Danilo's eyes as he slowly raised his head. Winced at the smoldering fury there. "A true werequeen."

He nodded to me, free hand tightening on the arm of the chair so much the wood beneath cracked with a sharp rapport. "She will be avenged in blood and fire," he said.

About that. I had to be so careful here it wasn't even funny. One slip, one out of place word, and Danilo would refuse to listen to me. Hell, for all I knew he was already too far gone to take in a word I said. From the matching anger in his mother, I feared I'd lost already. Only Oleksander seemed more grief stricken than furious, hovering behind Danilo's chair with his deep set eyes locked on me.

"I fear there are larger concerns here, great king." Cautiously, Syd. Oh, so cautiously. Appeal to the monarch in him and not the vengeful husband. His nostrils flared in response to my words.

"What could be of more concern to me than the murder of my wife?" His voice started out soft, but grew in volume until it vibrated around the room.

I had two choices. Be nice, gentle, kind. Or smack him in the head.

Guess which one I chose?

"Pull yourself together," I snapped. His eyes widened, temper crackling, but I cut him off with a surge of power. "Your grief is understandable," I went on. "But you are a king, Danilo. You accepted the monarch's seat of the werenation. They are looking to you for guidance right now." I jabbed a finger toward the door where his people waited for him. His eyes flickered that way then back to me, the barest hint of acceptance rising. "I know it sucks," I said. "I know." I hit my chest with one fist in a deep thudding sound. "When my first husband was murdered right in front of me, I wanted nothing more than to kill the one who took him from me. To tear the whole world apart and not think of who I was hurting or what Fate needed me to do. I didn't care if everything fell to ashes. I just wanted revenge."

Danilo sat intensely still, the burning in his eyes fading to a faint, waiting boil. I was getting through to

226

him after all. Time to do my best to finish this. If I could.

"But, like it or not, Danilo, I didn't have a choice." I leaned away, lower lip quivering as I relived in my mind the day Liam died. My hate for Max for holding me back, the loss of time as I floundered to accept what happened. The worst day of my life. "I was responsible for everyone's safety. Carrying my dead husband's child. And I had a job to do." Did I get to kill Ameline in the end? You betcha. But I put my duty first. Mind you, I was forced to by fate. But it amounted to the same thing.

Danilo's hand loosened on the arm of the chair. "I had no idea," he said, voice thick. "I'm sorry for your loss, Sydlynn."

Right. He'd been a wolf when it all happened.

"And I yours," I said, leaning toward him, reaching out to squeeze his knee. "This duty of ours, it's a heavy weight, my friend. It binds us to the good of others first. Forces us to bury our hurts and losses until we've done the right thing. Only then do we have the freedom to grieve, often alone." He nodded heavily, sighing as he sank back into his chair, fresh tears trickling down his face. But his eyes were clear again, shoulders relaxed, his wolf retreating.

Holy. I'd really done it.

"You speak wisely," he said. "And, as always, I respect your opinion, Sydlynn. But this blatant attack on my people cannot go unpunished."

"We agree on that, big fella," I said, flat and with a crackle in my voice. "The woman who killed Liam isn't around to talk about it." Eagerness flooded his face. "But." I paused a long moment while he drew a slow, shaking breath and exhaled. "The choice was calculated and not fed by emotion. But by decision." Well, not entirely true, but it seemed to impact him in the way I wanted. Considering I'd been fighting for my life and Gabriel's about a second before I had the chance to stop Ameline's heart...

"But," Danilo said.

"As king, you must uncover the true motivations of the attackers." I didn't want to say vampires. No way I was lumping the whole race into this mess when it was Piotr and, to my renewed anger, Eva Southway who seemed to be responsible. The Empress I'd deal with later. "I believe this horrible crime was perpetrated by none other than Liander Belaisle and the Brotherhood."

Danilo grunted. "To what end?" His mind was still spinning clearly, making it hard for him to grasp.

"The World Paranormal Council is our first attempt to work together," I said. "That has to scare the bejeebuz out of him. If we all figure out how to be a team, he's no longer dealing with a fractured, untrusting collection of races. He's up against a powerhouse and he knows it."

"You believe my wife's murder was an attempt to begin a war." Danilo looked away from me. "To weaken our alliance."

"I truly do." I wished I had something comforting to say to him. But there was little comfort in any of this. "If you want to strike a real blow against those who killed Yana, you will target Belaisle, Danilo. Not the vampire race."

Danilo's head whipped back, mouth a grim slash under his beard. "And the Wilhelm clan," he said.

Did he know Piotr had been arrested? Likely. But I knew now the king's hate wouldn't die so easily, and could I blame him? I was fooling myself thinking I could get through to Danilo, with his life steeped in the werewolf drive for vengeance. I sighed and shrugged.

"Do what you want," I said, pushing myself to my feet. "But please, be a ruler. And weigh everything you consider with the rest of us in mind."

He looked away, refusing to meet my eyes. With time maybe he would accept. But I was fairly certain the powerful drive of honor and duty, their unreasonable *сан*, would supersede everything I just said.

I left the three weres to their grief, though Oleksander followed me to the door and engulfed me one more time.

Thank you, he sent. *For trying. I understand his pain, but perhaps I am older and more accustomed to the ache of loss. I see more clearly than he and will advise him with your request in mind.*

Relief was a rush. I hugged him tight. *Take care of him, Oleksander.*

The old werewolf bowed to me and showed me out.

I wasn't in the mood to deal with Femke and the others again, so as soon as I rejoined Lula and Phon I opened the veil and took them home. The rules against using power like that in the werewolf palace would just have to kiss my ass.

I dropped the twins off at their home with thanks before padding my way back to my own driveway. It gave me time to think, and, finally, to decide to leave a packed bag everywhere I went so I didn't have to spend stressful days like this one in my pajamas.

The soft, steady presence of spirit magic in the kitchen alerted me I had a visitor, and I wasn't surprised to find Sunny sitting there, waiting for me. She rose, came to me immediately, hugging me tight. Her skin was warm, which meant she'd fed, at least. I loved her, but the chill of her skin pre-blood meal always gave me the shivers.

"I'm sorry," she whispered, pulling away, crystal tears on her flawless face. "You saved me, saved Frank. I was just so angry, Syd." Her hands shook as she dropped them from wiping at her wet cheeks. "I thought I could handle things, that when I had the opportunity to speak directly to the other queens they would see his accusations were false. Too naïve, even now." She shook out her long, blonde hair, shimmering in the light. "By the time I realized they were already set against me it was far too late and I was on the defensive." She touched my hand, apology on her face, in her gaze and power. "With everyone." I squeezed her hand as she went on. "None of that matters now," she said. "Except my regret I allowed myself to be such a fool. But you must understand there is far more to this than you might realize. I don't know what the Empress is up to, but she's playing more than one side."

"Tell me about it." I paused, shuffled my feet. "I'm sorry, too," I said. "I shouldn't have interfered. I get so frustrated and just want to fix everything."

Sunny's soft chuckle made me smile a little. "When you have as much power and passion and heart as someone like you," she said, "it can't be easy to let the rest of us stumble around and make a mess of our lives." I shook my head but she shrugged, elegant as ever. "I needed your help," she said, "and, like a fool, resented the fact you saved my behind." Her fingertips brushed a piece of loose hair back over my ear. "But I love you for caring enough to put yourself in danger for all of us, Syd."

I sank into a chair, Sunny retaking hers. The house was quiet, and I found I missed my kids suddenly with a rush like pain. Probably triggered by Danilo's loss, talking about Liam. As soon as I was done with Sunny, I'd be taking a trip to Harvard to hug and kiss my children until they begged for mercy.

"I'm not just here to apologize," Sunny said with a rueful smile that faded immediately. "I'm worried, Syd.

I've been trying to contact some of my friends among the other blood clans, and can't seem to reach them."

"You're trying to muster support to regain your throne." Of course she was. That's my Sunny.

She leaned back in her chair, arms over her chest, foot bobbing on her crossed knee. "This was a setup," she said. "I should have won. Whatever the Empress's reasons for wanting me off the throne, I'm sure she was behind it." The conversation I'd had with the ancient vampire ran through my head. That wasn't the impression she gave me, but then again, after that many years, she'd probably learned to become an excellent liar. And, after this debacle, who knew what side she was on but her own?

I told Sunny everything I knew about the Empress and the spirit energy issues happening in our Universe. She shuddered, hands running up and down her arms, eyes wide.

"So Sebastian is gone forever?" Tears tinted her tone.

"I have no idea," I said. "But I really hope not. It's possible he and his blood clan are either on the other side, in the Dark Universe, or are trapped in some kind of limbo." Of course, I had no idea if this was true or not, so I could have been lying to her without knowing it. But it seemed to ease her tension and she sat back again.

We were interrupted by the push of sorcery and both sat up straighter as the back door slammed and Piers entered the kitchen, panting slightly from his hurry.

"You're not going to like this," he said as I groaned and slouched at his worried expression.

"Now what?"

Piers sighed while he caught his breath, real regret in his voice. "King Danilo of the werenation just declared war on the Wilhelm blood clan."

TWENTY-FIVE

"Well, I can't say I'm surprised," Sunny said.

I was disappointed, to say the least. "I thought I talked him down far enough." Damn it, Oleksander, what happened?

"I think it would have been okay," Pier said, sinking down next to Sunny, "but two werewolves were dumped on the front lawn with their throats cut and their bodies drained of blood just after you two left." He shook his head, disgust on his face. "Danilo lost his mind and everything went to hell."

"Belaisle is determined to see this devolve into chaos," I said. "Did you tell Femke?"

"She was there," Piers said. "Tried to diffuse it, but Danilo kicked her out, me too. Locked down the palace. Charlotte's still there, as far as I know, but she's wired up too, Syd."

Freaking werewolves and their stupid *сан*.

Sunny rose from her seat, face grim. "I feared this would happen," she said. "And though they are no longer my responsibility, I must attempt to save my family from this if I can."

"Where are you going?" I reached for her hand but she shook her head and backed away.

"The Empress will tell me everything she knows," Sunny said in a voice so cold mist drifted from between her lips. "Or her long existence will come to an abrupt end." She shuddered into shadow and vanished.

"Bloodthirsty," Piers said, tone light and amused.

"She's a vampire, after all." I sighed and sank lower in my chair. "Thanks for letting me know. I'll let Danilo calm down a bit then go shake some sense into his fool head."

"Syd." Piers stiffened slightly, words careful as he spoke, index finger tracing a complex pattern on the tabletop. "The werenation is under the protection of the Steam Union."

"What the hell is that supposed to mean?" I kicked him under the table and he winced as my sneaker caught his shin. "Don't tell me you're going to go to war with them out of some stupid pride thing, because I'll do more than kick you, Piers."

"I just mean," he said with a deep frown, "I won't abandon them." His gray eyes darkened slightly as he looked away, watching his finger making circles and swirls on the wooden surface. "I'm seeing things differently now, like clouds have cleared, wiped away all the rubbish." His hand stopped moving. "I've made this new gateway to the future by taking over Mum's position. Putting all the pieces back together is going to take time, but I feel like I'm finally seeing things the way they are supposed to be."

Sparks fired, gears turned and I gasped as an epiphany so powerful it took my breath away roared through me. I lunged and grabbed Piers, kissing him soundly on the mouth.

"You," I laughed, giddy with sudden understanding, "are a genius."

Wide gray eyes full of startled good humor stared back at me. "Took you that long to see it, Hayle?"

I know I shouldn't have been in the mood to laugh, but Piers's little speech fit together the puzzle of a bigger problem on my plate. Gateway. Pieces. Seeing things clearly.

What had Trinol said about us having access to a tool the others didn't? I knew what the tool was. Only it wasn't a thing.

It was my son. Our advantage was the Gateway.

"I'm so proud of you," I said, sweeping to my feet. Piers joined me, frowning around his tiny smile. "If you need anything, you let me know."

"You're not going to ride off into the sunset and save the day?" He was talking about the war between the vampires and werewolves, but I had a bigger battle to fight.

"You can handle it," I said. "Lean on Femke. Besides, if what I'm thinking is right, I might be able to get your real enemy off your back finally." Belaisle would lose his crap if he found out I knew more than he did about how to find the pieces of Creator.

Piers hugged me, the warmth of his skin on my cheek through the thin fabric of his button up shirt. We kissed again, but platonic, familiar. I knew he loved Zoe, and he knew I loved Quaid. But we'd been friends a long time and it felt wrong to just peck him on the cheek.

He released me, grinning. "Whatever you're up to," he said, "have fun. I'll try to keep everything else from falling apart while you're handling the big stuff." With a jaunty salute that was the most like him I'd seen since his mother took him captive, Piers stepped through a dark tunnel of magic and disappeared.

I almost jumped, letting out a little squeak, at the sight of Quaid standing right behind where Piers had just been. And he didn't look happy.

"What was he doing here?" Um, hello yourself, grumpy ass.

"Sorting out the werewolf mess," I said. "Why? What's it to you?" Oh, Syd. That was uncalled for.

Quaid's forehead creased in an angry frown, arms crossing over his chest. He stared at me under lowered brows like he always did when he was pissed at me. The whole physical attitude triggered my own temper.

"I didn't expect to come home after a long day and find my wife kissing another guy." He totally didn't just pull the jealousy card, did he?

"Get over yourself," I snapped. "You know Piers and I are just friends. Stop being a jerk. You want to fight? Fine. But don't drag him into it. Just admit you're in a bad mood and feeling guilty for treating me like an ass and we'll get started with the screaming and yelling already. But be honest, Quaid."

I'd never seen his jaw jump quite so vigorously. "Go to hell, Syd."

"Best you can do?" I called after him as he spun on his heel and stomped upstairs. "You really have to work on your snarking skills. You're slipping."

He muttered something incredibly rude about my mother and heritage before slamming our bedroom door. I stood there, breathing slowly to keep myself from going after him and forced myself to let it go. This fight would have to wait. And it would. We'd figure it out, forgive each other, and move on. Once he felt comfortable in what he'd done. And, I guess, I'd let him have that without a battle. Because like I told Femke, I agreed with her he really was the perfect Enforcer for the job.

As I reached for the veil to return to Harvard I had a thought. What if he was worried about not being able to fill the role? Quaid always came across as so self-assured, in control. But it was an act, as much as anyone's outward persona. I knew the man I loved had his share of weaknesses and worries, self-doubt among them. He was human, after all. And the husband of the savior of the Universe. Did he worry he had shoes too big to fill?

I almost went upstairs to talk to him, heart aching suddenly. But, I left it alone. He needed to cool off, wouldn't hear a word I said if I jumped the gun and tried too soon. So, I sighed and went to see the rest of my family, leaving him home to work out his own crap.

Sad, really, I was more comfortable dealing with giant disasters than having a heart-to-heart with my husband when we were fighting.

Still in the veil, I called out for Max. He answered immediately.

Meet me at Harvard, I sent, exiting in the familiar space of the sitting room. But this time it wasn't empty, a pair of excited kids squealing at the sight of me, bounding up from where they'd been lying on their bellies on the floor with crayons and paper. Galleytrot's big, furry head lifted, faint glow of red in his black eyes observing while Ethie reached me first, as always, wrapping her little arms around my neck and kissing me with gusto. I swung her around, tucking her tight against me while her legs wound around my waist, nose pressed to my ear.

"Missed you, Mom," she whispered so loud I'm sure they heard her across campus.

"Ethie, pumpkin pie," I said, kissing her forehead, "I missed you so much I can't stand it."

She grinned, round cheeks flushing, brilliance in her blue eyes. "Are you staying?"

"For a bit." I set her down and pulled Gabriel into my arms, snuggling him close. He clung to me, the scent of the earth and fabric softener for the first time making me smile instead of teary. Yes, he looked like Liam, felt like Liam in a lot of ways. But he was Gabriel, with my strength and curiosity. As he looked up at last into my eyes, green sparks firing in his gaze, I grinned at him.

Couldn't help it.

"Syd." Mom appeared with a strained smile of her own. "Hi, sweetheart." *I heard about Danilo*, she sent in a tight touch of magic. *Is everything all right?*

Not really, I sent. *But Piers is on it. I have something else to do, and I need Gabriel to do it.*

Mom's immediate tension only grew worse as the air of the room sighed and opened to the veil, my big drach friend stepping through.

Ethie squealed and ran for him, climbing up into his arms to grip his wide face in her tiny hands. She kissed him on the end of his nose before pressing her cheek to his. Max's smile was genuine as he began to softly hum to her. She loved the musical sound of the drach language and sighed her contentment as he finished a short song.

"Max." She hugged him around the neck. "Where have you been?"

"Busy, I fear," he said as he crossed to me, my tiny daughter held carefully in his large embrace. "But I've mourned every moment away from you, dear Ethpeal."

She sat up, wrinkled her nose at him. "Mom told you to say that."

"Indeed she did not," he said, diamond eyes glittering with amusement. "You know I adore you above all others."

Ethie turned to me and stuck out her tongue. "Keeping him," she said.

Fine by me.

"Darling," Mom said, coming forward to relieve Max of my daughter's insistent embrace, "I think your mother and Max are here to talk to Gabriel."

Instant Ethie pout face. But she went to Mom anyway and stayed with her, watching with a fascination she didn't seem able to control as Max knelt with great grace at my son's side. Gabriel still had to look up into his eyes, but seemed more at ease. Max turned his diamond gaze to me and waited.

"Trinol," I said, Max frowning at the name before turning his big head abruptly and looking at Gabriel again. "Our advantage. What if Gabriel's power can help us track the pieces?"

My son's frown wasn't worried, just curious as he looked back and forth between us. I perched on the edge of the chair beside me and held his hand.

"Sweets," I said, "when you open gateways, can you tell where you're opening them? Do you have a destination in mind?" We'd talked of this briefly a month ago, when Mom started his training, but I'd been too busy to follow up.

"Sure!" His face brightened. "I can tell you who lives there, too."

Max's soft smile added to my hope. "If I allow you to feel something," he said, "could you find more like it?"

Gabriel's frown returned, but he shrugged. "I can try," he said.

Syd, Mom sent, careful but stressed. *Is this dangerous?*

I don't know, I sent, worry surging to replace my excitement. *But Max and I are here. And we need to find those pieces.*

Galleytrot joined us, a soft growl rumbling from inside him. *I won't let harm come to him, Syd.* Whether he meant it as a reassurance or a threat, I had no idea. Chose to believe the latter.

Neither will I. I dug my fingers into his fur, scratching one ear. *But I feel better knowing you're here, too, big dog.*

He's your son, Mom sent when Galleytrot sighed agreement in a gust of hot doggy breath. *Your choice. Just, be cautious. He's enthusiastic still, and wants very much to please you. I worry he might push too hard if you ask him to.*

Right. "Gabriel," I said, pulling him to me, hugging him. "I love you. And no matter what happens, even if you can't find what we're looking for, I want you to know you are the most amazing boy with the most incredible talent. And I'm so proud of you I could just eat you up."

He smiled at me when I let him go, softly stroking my cheek. "I know, Mom," he said, joy pouring out of him. "I'll do my best, I promise."

I nodded to Max, power drawing close, ready for anything. Or, hoping I was, at least. The giant drach's magic answered mine, a net of protection forming around Gabriel, pushing out in a second layer to guard Mom and Ethie for good measure. The Council power augmented those shields.

We were as ready as we were going to get.

The idea we might be stepping through a gateway in a second to retrieve a piece of Creator made my heart skip. Max reached out to my son and touched his mind ever so gently, the vastness of the drach consciousness held back with care.

This, Max sent. I felt the touch of Creator, the same feeling as the Stronghold's personality, filled with so much life my soul stirred and danced. Gabriel's eyes flew wide, a huge smile on his face as he bobbed a nod and turned away from us, power surging, gesturing with one hand.

And nothing happened. Gabriel's face fell, frown returning, forming a scowl as he pushed and pushed. But a gate didn't open and, from the frustration in his whole body, this had never happened to him before.

"I'm sorry," he finally sagged in angry defeat. "I know how to look, I just can't seem to get to it."

"I have an idea," Max said, showing me a flashed image of the Stronghold. "Perhaps a more intimate connection would make things easier."

We left Mom and Galleytrot behind with Ethie, all three of them nervous though only the hound protested.

Don't interfere, I sent. *And protect my daughter.*

It was clear Galleytrot was going to argue, until Mom's power cut him off. He finally backed down with a deep groan of unhappiness.

"It'll be fine, Trot," Gabriel said, smiling and waving at the dog. "You'll see."

Oddly, Ethie just clung to Mom and didn't demand to come along. She was usually so insistent on being in the middle of everything. But even she, at six, must have sensed how important this was and let us go without a peep.

Gabriel held tight to my hand as we crossed over the veil and into the statue chamber of the Stronghold. He released me the moment we arrived, walking closer, staring up with awe at the giant form of Creator.

"Who hurt her?" His little voice was soft, respectful, sad.

"She did this to herself," Max answered him in his deep and musical voice. "To save us all, Creator gave of herself to assure our salvation."

"She's beautiful." Gabriel took one last step, touched the toe of her intact foot. Shivered. "This is what you want me to find. Her pieces."

Too damned clever for his own good. "You got it, sweets," I said. "Feel like trying again?"

TWENTY-SIX

My son stepped back from me, still looking up at the massive statue. He didn't answer my question, but from the gathering of his magic and the focused, almost glazed, look in his eyes, he certainly did want to give it another shot.

Be prepared, Max sent, a hint of excitement threading through his power. *I believe this might work.*

My power still coiled, ready and waiting, engulfing my son in protective energy, so my drach friend didn't have to tell me twice. But the moment Gabriel turned and gestured beside him, all of the power I had at my disposal didn't seem to be enough to keep him safe.

With a rushing burst of energy, I was pushed back, away from my son, Max staggering next to me. A giant gateway opened, my child tiny in comparison, though from the blankness of his expression he barely knew what he was doing.

Max! This was a terrible idea, and the sinking, whirling feeling in my gut told me we'd pushed Gabriel too far in a place where he never should have been allowed to open a gateway.

Stop him immediately. Max's magic battled side-by-side with mine as the two of us reached for Gabriel.

But it was far too late for that. My son slowly turned toward me while I hit my knees, force of magic expelling from the gateway he'd made like the gale force wind of an oncoming hurricane. I squinted against the dust and debris it raised, calling out his name, though my words were lost, ripped from my lips and carried away before they could make a sound.

But it was the swirling light in his eyes, white spirit light, that gave me the most fear, the way Gabriel's body went rigid as the gateway behind him began to shift. At first it was as black as the deepest night without stars or a moon, unnatural black, like the soul of one long lost to feeling. As Gabriel turned to me, images began to appear in the gateway, flashes of planes I'd never seen before, skies of blue and gray and orange and white, creatures and cities, purple oceans and giant expanses of desert the palest shade of turquoise. All beautiful, whipping past faster and faster as the power of the statue's chamber gravitated toward Gabriel and fed him.

And fed him some more.

No amount of my magic could cut through what was happening, not even my sorcery. It was as though the very Universe moved through my son, spinning out every plane in his mind, through the gateway. It might have lasted thirty or so seconds but it felt like forever. The moment it stopped, the wind died abruptly and Gabriel, his now normal eyes rolling up into his head, collapsed sideways on the ground.

I felt deaf from the sudden silence, slow and stupid, shaken to the core by what I'd just witnessed. I rushed to him, even as the image in the gateway shifted one last time. I froze with my unconscious child's body hanging limp in my arms.

Massive soldiers, dressed in some kind of medieval armor, stood in a thick formation in the center of a giant plane. Black shapes with vast wings wheeled overhead, spiked mountains stabbing the burnt red sky in the distance.

They began to march, coming right for the gateway, as the edges pushed outward, began to expand further. My heart galloped in my chest at the sound of their feet falling in precision, the clank of metal as they approached. The leader towered over them, helmet down over his glowing blue eyes, a wicked blade in his hand. Relentless, coming for us.

Max landed next to me, hitting the ground so hard it shook beneath us. Or maybe that was from the approaching footfalls of the army about to invade this space. His hands grasped my son, his energy pushing into Gabriel.

"Wake," Max said with so much desperation in his voice I couldn't breathe.

Max was afraid. Which meant I needed to be terrified, yup yup.

Gabriel's eyes flickered, a soft moan escaping. "You must close the path, Gateway," Max rumbled, still stuffing power into my son. I joined him, trying to bolster Gabriel. I sat up at the same time, wove shielding in front of the gateway, feeling the push of the army approaching and knowing there was no way, absolutely none, I would ever be able to hold them back. Thousands. Hundreds of thousands.

Oh. My. Swearword.

Twenty feet. I could hear them breathing in unison, like machines full of magic, each step absolute perfection of timing.

Fifteen feet. Gabriel groaned and twitched, trying to sit up, Max supporting him as I wove shield after shield in an attempt to buy us more time, only to have them shredded from the inside with casual precision.

Ten feet. Doom loomed over us as my son opened his eyes, looked up into the approaching army. And screamed.

The army stopped as one at the sound of his wordless

shriek. The edges of the gateway sizzled, began to collapse as Gabriel's magic rejected what he saw and triggered a closing of the way. The leader saluted, though whether to my son or all of us I had no idea. But I held Gabriel tight and rocked him while the gateway finally collapsed with a clap like thunder.

I just cuddled and swayed for a long time while he sobbed on my shoulder, Max sprawled out next to us, gray toned skin pale and translucent from shock.

"A close thing," he finally said, not a hint of music in his roughened voice. "And my fault, Sydlynn. Gabriel, I am so sorry I even suggested this. I should have known better. My pushing in the past has led us to disaster before." Max sat up, shook his head, hands linking together around his bent knees.

"Who were they?" I whispered the question over Gabriel's head. "What happened?"

"Mom." My son looked up at me, wiping at his wet face, though he'd calmed somewhat. "I didn't mean to."

I shushed him, kissed him softly. "You were amazing," I said. "You did nothing wrong."

"I tried to find the pieces," he said. "But the Universe wanted to show me everything when I did." Gabriel shuddered. "Everything, Mom. Remember sometimes I said I can see it all when I open gates?" I nodded. "I had no idea, really. I thought I was seeing. But *this*." Gabriel wiped his nose on his t-shirt collar. "It's so big, Mom."

He looked off into the distance, at the statue. "I was right there with her." Awe filled his voice, no longer shaking with fear, just a different kind of wonder. "And then he came." Terror returned in a snap. "And dragged me to the barrier between Universes."

"Dark Brother," Max said, weary and quiet.

Gabriel bobbed a nod. "I tried to fight him, but he made me cross. She fought with me, but it was too late, the way was open. Mom, if we hadn't closed the gateway…"

I swallowed hard. "Who were they, sweets?"

My son shuddered, huddled against me. "The Order," he whispered. "And they are invincible."

"The army of Dark Brother," Max said while I choked on my son's words. "Our doom."

I was so used to being the strongest kid on the block, the idea of having an unbeatable foe to face made my blood run cold. "They have to have a weakness."

"They are in the other Universe," Max said. "That is their only weakness."

I spun on him, glared. "How do you know?" Not his fault, and he didn't deserve my surge of anger in response to hating being afraid, but it had been a tough few minutes.

He let it go, obviously understanding my state of mind. "Because," he said. "I encountered them once before. When the Universes split. Just before Creator saved us all."

I hated first person evidence. "It's been a long time since then," I said. "Maybe something's changed."

Max paled even further. "Don't even suggest it," he said. "They were bad enough in the beginning let alone if they've somehow evolved."

Just freaking great.

"Gabriel," Max said, "can you tell us if any of the planes Creator showed you hold the pieces of her physical form?"

My son pulled free of me again, but didn't move far. "I don't know," he said. "It's so jumbled in my head."

Before I could stop him, Gabriel gestured and a gateway opened. But this one was soft, tentative, with little power behind it and I rapidly smothered it in shielding to protect him from the magic in this place. Whether it knew the havoc it almost wreaked or not, the chamber left my son alone. A field of pale blue grass, sky tinted softly green, appeared on the other side, a fat, rabbit-like creature with six eyes and four arms popped up and looked our way, nose twitching.

"Wait a second," I said. "I know this plane, Gabe. You showed it to me the first time you told me you knew what you could do."

His little face scrunched up in anxiety. "Sorry, Mom," he said. "It's just not working."

The lazy rabbit creature returned to munching grass,

clearly content with us as it watched from a short distance away.

Gabriel's afraid, I sent to Max. *Obviously reaching for planes that make him feel safe. Let's give him a rest.* My protective mother instincts finally kicked in and, for a moment, I wondered about myself. What kind of mom was I really to allow my seven year old to go through something like this? I had to be the worst mother ever.

Ever.

While I flogged myself for my wretched parenting skills, Max's paleness faded and his face returned to bland calm. *I wonder*, he sent. "Thank you, Gabriel," Max said. "For your bravery and for trying again though you were afraid."

My son bobbed his head, strawberry blond hair soft under my hand as I stroked it.

"I wish I could have helped more," he said. "Are we safe from the Order now?"

Max nodded. "Your mother and I will never allow them to cross to this Universe." He sounded so confident even I believed him. "But there may come a time you are forced to face them. Do you think you can do that?"

What? No. Freaking. Way. But Gabriel was nodding with that particularly stern and focused look he got that reminded me of Liam at his best.

"I'll be ready," Gabriel said.

We'd just see about that.

The boy needs to feel in control again, Max sent as the three of us climbed to our feet. *Knowing he has the courage to face what happened is the best way to ease his mind. I'm not suggesting anything, Syd.* Why did I get the impression Max wasn't telling me everything? *But I want him to have a healthy reaction to this near disaster. So he's not plagued by fears later.*

I'll handle my son, I sent, snappish. *I don't know what I was thinking. I'm a terrible mother.*

You are a wonderful parent, Max sent, gentle and kind. *With an extraordinary son who must learn to control his talent. Before it destroys us all. Imagine if that had happened when we weren't with him.* I froze in my tracks, hand tightening on Gabriel's so hard he looked up, startled. I eased my grip, tried a smile. *While unlikely without the touch of Creator, the possibility Dark Brother could reach him isn't one to be taken lightly.*

I pondered that as we returned to Harvard. Ethie was gone, Galleytrot lurching to his feet from where he lay at the threshold, guarding the door to her room. Mom emerged from her office with open arms to my son. He went to her, hugged her as my mother's mind met mine.

How did it go?

You don't want to know. I grimaced, let her feel my fear for him.

Ethie's gone to bed, she sent. *I'll put Gabriel down with her and Galleytrot.*

I wanted to go with him, to lie down next to my son

and protect him. But when Mom led him away, Galleytrot's big head leaning into my son after a judging glare aimed at me, Max's power held me back. *There is something I want to investigate*, he sent. *The boy is safe for now. Indulge me, if you would.*

Hesitation almost held me back. I put the Universe ahead of my own flesh and blood. I should be fulfilling my mothering duties right now, not running off with the leader of the drach. But I had a job to do. The words I spoke to Danilo rang with me as I turned and nodded to Max.

"Where are we going?" I took his hand and followed him into the veil, heart heavy but with a duty to complete.

I thought you guessed, Max sent. *To retrieve a piece of Creator.*

TWENTY-SEVEN

I slipped onto his back as he shifted into drach shape. *But it didn't work*, I sent, thinking of the rascally rabbit creature. *He showed us a plane that he felt safe to explore.*

Perhaps that's all it was, Max sent. *But Creator knows we seek her parts, Syd. And she showed Gabriel the entire Universe before Dark Brother interfered. Consider the gateway he chose to open when I asked him to try again was the same one you recalled from before.*

You think subconsciously he knew what he was showing us? Was it really that easy?

There is only one way to find out, Max sent. *Shall we?*

I clung to him with faint hope and wondered if he was right. Didn't matter now. Like he said, it either was the right place or it wasn't. Worth a shot, considering all the jabbing in the dark we'd done so far. I held my breath as we cleared the giant slice he made in the veil and soared out into the open sky of the plane in question.

We're flying? I could feel the thrum of intelligence in the power of this plane. Usually we landed and moved around on foot or through small slices in the veil when we visited other places. But Max's broad wings swept through the crisp, clean air as he banked softly to the left toward what looked like a small, but pre-industrial, city.

I needed to stretch my wings, he sent. *I have us shielded from view. It's rather pretty to look at, isn't it?* A wide river dumped into the vast ocean beyond the port city, vibration of magic in common use explaining to me why this culture hadn't adopted fossil fuels to grow and expand. I wished with a wistful sigh our plane had that luxury, that the Brotherhood's need for dominance hadn't crushed our willingness to share our talents with normals and saved our plane from all the ecological damage normals inflicted. One of our most sacred duties as witches was to reverse as much of that damage as possible, though we were fighting a losing battle.

How far would we have come if the Brotherhood had never been?

Max wheeled toward the edge of the city, setting us down behind a low, stone building the loveliest shade of pearl blue. I ran one hand over the rock, feeling the warmth of it as power zinged through the structure.

"An interesting species," Max said. I turned to ask

him what he meant and burst into laughter.

I hadn't laid eyes on one of the main inhabitants yet, but seeing him in his adopted form gave me all the information I needed. He was still quite tall, but had a round, jutting belly with six perfectly circular indentations, all filled with sparkling jewels. His skin was tinted softly blue, like the stone, six eyes layered on top of each other making me squirm a bit. His hands seemed normal enough, like mine when I looked down to examine them, pearlized surface of the nails glinting in the sunlight. I had a similar belly to his, though I had hair. His bald head sported four twitching antenna that seemed to have lives of their own.

"Adorable," I said. "You look so cuddly."

Max's smile was indulgent. "Better news," he said, reserved excitement telling me he was more than a little worked up, "I believe my hunch might have paid off."

My jaw dropped as he turned and circled the building, giant feet flapping on the ground like a pair of flippers, non-existent butt waddling back and forth, tucked under his giant belly. My stride felt normal, but I assumed I looked just as silly following him.

Like I cared. If there really was a piece of Creator here, I owed Gabriel a giant hug and kiss and anything else he wanted for the rest of his life.

This way, Max sent, leading me on. We cleared the edge of the building, crossing into a long, narrow road that led, in one direction, deeper into the city and, in the other, toward a towering construction of some kind. The wide, shrub dressed lane reminded me a bit of the Parade on Demonicon, the vast expanse at the base of the Seat where Ruler addressed the populace. But the tall and almost graceful building seemed different than the rest of the city, less a palace feel and more some kind of temple.

We avoided the strolling natives, though I caught myself giggling a time or two at how ridiculous they looked. How could they stand it? Then again, I guessed as I passed a pair of young women—their long, flowing hair was the only real giveaway, since they all looked the same to me otherwise—if they saw my true form they would probably think the same thing.

Antenna waved and bobbed, giant bellies bouncing over flat feet.

Yeah. Naw.

I followed Max to the front of the building, relieved to see we weren't the only ones going inside. It would be awkward if there was some kind of taboo to us entering, though it would mean we'd have to sneak in instead, something to which I wasn't at all opposed.

I can feel it. His excitement had grown past the ordinary and into buzzing delight. Max happy about something almost made me nervous. *This civilization must have located the piece,* he sent as we strode into the interior. I expected darkness, but, to my surprise, the walls themselves seemed to reflect light inward, making it just as bright indoors as it was out. *Perhaps they are using it as a focus of their worship.* This was definitely some kind of temple, with lines of benches and bars of padded material I realized were belly rests when I spotted an older resident with his giant paunch settled on it.

This could be tricky, I sent as we moved forward down long aisle toward the back of the building. It reminded me a bit of a cathedral at home, though much more open and bright, the center aisle wider, bench seats spread out in a semi-circular hub around the middle altar. The walls and floors were made of the same blue stone, the warmth of it reaching up through my feet. Almost as if it were alive. That was a creepy thought. *If we try to take their sacred relic, we could run into problems.*

We have instantaneous means of exiting this place, Max sent. *And though I have no desire to intrude on their worship, the piece is far too valuable to leave in their hands for this simple purpose.*

I totally agreed with him.

As we approached the altar, I scrunched my nose at the sight of the towering thing standing in the middle. Made of the same stone, it had seven trunks like an elephant's, eleven arms and was covered in deep purple spots. A towering tuft of what looked like grass waved over its carved head.

Um, I sent as two of the residents bowed to their faces in front of it, big bellies bouncing off the floor, *I don't think so, Max.*

How curious, he sent. And kept walking, this time around the altar to the right. I trailed after him, looking around and expecting opposition, but no one paid us any attention. Convenient.

Max passed through an archway and beyond, out of sight of the worshipers, into a long, low room behind the altar. It was a little darker in here, but not much, and I was drawn immediately to the sound of happy humming not too far away. Max slowed, waiting for me to match his pace, and the pair of us, me smiling my most diplomatic and hoping it wasn't an insult on this plane to do so, circled a giant chunk of stone and came face-to-face with the cheerful hummer.

He—I assumed it was a he—jumped with a squeal like a piglet, dropping a large chisel from one hand. It bounced on the floor with a soft ringing sound as he clutched both hands over his bouncing belly.

"Dear Creator," he said in a high pitched but masculine voice. "You frightened the jewels out of me." My eyes traveled to the stones in the indentations on his bare belly and a giggle fought for freedom.

"Our apologies," Max said. "We had merely wanted to meet the finest sculptor in all the land and were told this was the place to find him."

Our new friend's blue cheeks darkened, a blush, I assumed, and he bobbed his head, antenna waving madly.

"By the Creator's blessing," he said with false modesty. "I've been gifted with the ability to render Her essence into life." He gestured at what he'd been working on and I flinched from the odd looking duck creature with a giant fluffy tail growing out of its alligator-like behind.

Yikes. This place was off the charts.

"Stunning craftsmanship," Max said. "We are honored to be in your presence."

"Come to worship at the great Shrine, have you?" His six eyes seemed to study Max and me both at once. Creepy. Subtle hesitation rose in his voice, his manner, and I guessed we really weren't supposed to be back here. But Max was already moving, turning slowly, gaze sweeping the space. Which left me to deal with shmuckface.

Lovely.

"We are art critics," I said, wincing inwardly. Was that even a job here? But, from the instant reaction of enthusiasm from our new friend I'd hit the nail on the nose.

"Blessed be!" He lunged for me, pulled me closer. "I knew the Originator would send you one day. Please, give him my absolute best." He paused, looking his sculpture up and down with what I could only guess from his expression was self-criticism. "Don't judge my work by this mess," he said, spinning me around. "My collection is vast and varied." One of his chubby arms swept forward and I realized I missed the fact we were in some kind of warehouse space, packed with sculptures like this one. "Tell me, does he have a particular piece in mind?"

I grinned. "Now that you mention it…"

Max chuckled in my head. And turned from one of the long tables with a large, white hand in his grasp.

I froze, heart pounding suddenly. *Is that…?*

Indeed, my drach friend sent with a surge of fierce joy. A silver thread wound around his wrist. *Both safe*, he sent. *We must go.*

The sculptor's suspicion rose, immediate and so powerful I felt him switch from excitement to anger. "Release it at once," he said. "My greatest carving is not for sale, even to the Originator."

"You had nothing to do with the creation of this piece," Max said, voice soft. "And you know it."

The sculptor's belly jiggled as he lunged for my friend, but Max held him off easily. The song of the drach rose from the ribbon of silver, our carver friend coming to a halt at the sound. His six eyes widened, antenna drooping, as he backed away with sudden fear oozing from every pore.

"Guards!" He backed into his sculpture so hard it teetered slowly over, crashing to the floor. I suppose I could have used magic to save it, but it was ugly enough not to bother. Meanwhile, the sculptor simply kept back pedaling. "GUARDS!"

Time to go, Max sent, reaching for my hand.

I reached back—

—and everything. Stopped.

The Universe inhaled.

Exhaled.

And shifted.

TWENTY-EIGHT

I staggered, though more from shock than actual loss of balance. The sculptor was gone. Just gone. Poof. Vanished into thin air. And, from the sudden and utter silence, he wasn't the only one.

"What the hell?" I took a step away from Max who followed me as I crept out and into the main temple.

Empty. Not a soul left behind. I gaped at the loss of people, reaching out with my power to discover the city, once thriving and bustling, had fallen completely and utterly still.

"Where did they go?" I spun on Max who shrugged his big shoulders, pressing the hand into my grip. The silver ribbon that was the drach soul guardian of the piece slipped its coolness around my wrist, humming softly, vibrating my bones with its song.

"I don't know," he said, grim and dark, "though I can guess. The Universes, Syd. They are beginning to merge thanks to the damage done not only to spirit magic but from the gap in the protections holding the Universes apart. The loss of Creator's heart, the shifting of her power around the planes after being so long dormant…" He held very still, almost statue like, reminding me of a vampire in his total physical silence. When Max finally shuddered gently, returning to normal, I shivered in turn. "I'm guessing," he said, softly angry, though with himself, I could tell. "I have no real answers, only fears. But, one thing is certain. The people who lived here are gone."

To the other side? "Are they okay?" Impossible to know. Why was I asking him, adding to his obvious stress? Because I shared it, I guess.

"Perhaps," he said. "Total speculation. But it's possible they now exist in, if not a parallel plane, one where they might encounter their alternates. Of a darker vein."

That didn't sound good. "What can we do?"

Max's tension didn't ease as his magic swept out past me, leaving me to huddle around the hand, holding it tight to my chest. Funny how the rock didn't feel heavy, though the piece was easily the size of my upper body. It had to be the drach soul keeping it from pulling me to the ground with its weight.

"We need to go." Max retreated at last, a flash of

worry in his voice. But he was too late, and, from the grim anger on his face as he lowered his big head to meet my eyes, he already knew it.

I could do nothing but stand there as a ring of black tunnels opened around us and the Brotherhood stepped through.

Liander Belaisle hadn't changed, not much, anyway. A little smugger, more weasely looking with his ugly goatee and pale gold eyes. He was just my height, a small man in more ways than one, compensating for something. At least it made me feel better to think so.

Sorcery crushed in around us, the twenty or so Brotherhood members who joined him all young, all male, all fiercely attached to his cause from the press of their power and the eagerness on their faces. I tried to tear at the veil but my magic was instantly smothered, so I retreated on purpose, protecting myself and my energy while Max just stood there and glared with a mix of sadness and resignation on his gray face.

He'd dropped our disguises. Guess we didn't need them anymore.

"What have you done, sorcerer?" Max's voice echoed through the empty temple.

"Don't be such a sore loser, drach," Belaisle said with his own particular brand of irritating arrogance, wiping at an imaginary fleck of dust on his pinstriped lapel. "Just hand over the piece and this will all be over."

"Come and get it, Belaisle," I said, clutching the chunk of Creator tighter to me.

He rolled his eyes, sighed dramatically. "Seriously, Sydlynn," he said as though to a petulant child. "You've lost. Accept it." A nasty grin curved his lips. "I might even leave you alive and whole to track the rest of the pieces for me, if you're a good girl."

Asshat.

"What have you done with the people of this plane?" He had to have told Dark Brother or something, triggered the shift.

To my surprise, he seemed genuinely confused. "I have no idea what you're talking about," he said, "nor do I care to." Only then did I feel him drawing in power, sucking up the very lifeblood of the plane around us. I moved to cut him off but he was faster, stronger, at least in sorcery. And pouring my energy into countering him would just leave me vulnerable.

I couldn't let him take the hand.

We're in trouble here, I sent to Max. *Can you get through the veil?*

I cannot, he sent.

Belaisle is building power, I sent. *If we let him go much longer, we're toast.*

I'm open to suggestions, the drach said. *Perhaps my true form might give us a size advantage.*

Can we please just go home now? Who the hell was that?

Whoever it was talking directly to my mind sounded whiny. I didn't have time for whiny, thanks. *First you manhandle me, then you just stand around and do nothing while I'm in danger.*

Oh, *hell* no. Tell me it wasn't true.

Some rescue this is, the hand sent.

You have a personality, I sent back, thinking of the Stronghold. At least I'd liked him. He was nice. This one was already a pain in my ass.

So do you, the hand shot back. *Borderline.*

It was lucky I didn't chuck it at Belaisle and be done with it. No, him. Definitely a whiny, meeping little him.

You try spending eternity trapped in a hand, he snapped at me. *Not so much fun as you might think.*

Can you help against Belaisle? That would be too easy. While I waited for a response, I addressed the sorcerer directly. "You do realize," I said, "you're tearing the Universe apart, you dumbass. That if you succeed, Dark Brother will send his army over and there will be nothing left, Belaisle. Nothing. Not even you."

He just laughed at me while the hand sighed in my head.

You're wasting your time, he snapped. *Get on with it.*

A little help?

Sydlynn, Max sent, bemused. *Who are you talking to?*

I didn't get a chance to respond. As I prepped a biting comment about Creator's hand and his attitude, something hit me hard from behind, driving me to my knees, jerking my arms open.

And the hand fell to the stone floor with a clatter. Then disappeared as it rose for a second bounce.

I looked up, terrified, into Belaisle's furious face. But wait, that meant...

He didn't have it either.

I spun just in time, while Belaisle shouted and Max lunged, to see Trill crouching next to me, her arms wrapped around the reappeared hand, disappear in a flare of magic. Trill, my friend, maji blooded, supposed to be on my side.

Stole the hand from me.

The silver ribbon remained around my wrist, sighed sadness, sagging off my skin to fall to the floor. I barely had time to gather myself for an attack when Belaisle and his sorcerers all disappeared through tunnels of darkness, the red faced leader of the Brotherhood screaming incoherent orders at his people until they were gone.

The sudden silence gave me a headache. Max crouched beside me, one big hand lifting the ribbon from the floor, the other guiding me to my feet. I staggered a little, knees weak, in complete shock.

"What the hell just happened?"

"She appeared from nowhere," he said. "Hit you and stole the hand." He shrugged, anger in his gesture, though not aimed at me. "This deceit was planned, Syd."

Which meant… "But how?" I spun in a frustrated circle, shaking with building rage. Someone was tracking us. Max. Me. Or Gabriel. All three? Damn it. "How did they come here in the first place?" It shouldn't have been possible. The only way for other races to cross the veil into foreign planes was through things like demon effigies. With the kind of power I possessed. Or—

"Gabriel!" I almost ran right then and there, but Max grabbed me.

"He is safe," he said, cooling my jets with those three words, though he had no proof, did he? "Your family would have called for you if Gabriel was missing." Okay, heart, you can start beating again. "They had assistance. The Brotherhood has obviously been gifted the ability to cross planes by Dark Brother. And Trill is as much a maji—if human and mortal—as you are."

Damn it. What was she thinking?

"Trinol did warn us," Max said, the silver ribbon pooled in his free hand. He slowly released me, one finger stirring the silent drach soul. "That there were others seeking the pieces, not just us and the Brotherhood. Trill must be working for one of them."

Not for long she wasn't. Not when I was through with her.

"Forgive me, my brother," Max said, a single tear falling to splash on the ribbon. "I've failed our people yet again."

Compassion found a way to win over my anger and I hugged Max for mutual comfort. "I'm sorry."

"As am I." He sighed heavily, as though releasing some old hurt through the exhale. "We should go, Sydlynn. We have other pieces to find. Now we know how to do so. But next time we will be better prepared." There was enough anger in his voice I pitied the one who got in his way.

I pulled free, kicking myself as I made a connection. "The heart," I said. "That's who took the heart." Of course. And I'd given Trill free access to the Stronghold. Trusted her, if not her new friends. Not Belaisle after all—mystery solved. The Stronghold did his job, as I asked him to. Couldn't counter her when she snuck into the chamber and stole Creator's heart to prove me a fool.

"I'm going after her." I pulled Max along into the veil, leaving the quiet, abandoned plane behind. It felt good to move, to escape the deathly, fresh silence of that place once bustling with life. The veil welcomed us, drew us along. I turned to look back at the soft, sucking sound I'd never heard before. And watched as the plane behind us collapsed and disappeared, the veil tightening in around it.

This is worse than I feared, Max sent. *The very Universe is dissolving, Syd. If we don't do something soon, I worry it will be too late to stop a complete collapse into each other. One Universe, controlled by the winner of this contest. We have to succeed.*

Now he tells me.

TWENTY-NINE

Max dropped me at home, winging off on his own to consult with his people. I let him go, though it would have been nice to have him with me when I confronted Trill. Not that I expected to find her right away. But he'd come running when I tracked her down and I knew where to start looking, at least.

Loud music shook the windows of the boy's kitchen, hitting me with the deep percussion of heavy bass as I stepped through the Zornov's door uninvited. Apollo, Owen and Simon all froze in mid-chomp, a half empty pizza box sprawled open between them. They must have guessed from my expression I wasn't in the best of moods because all three set down their dinner, Owen gesturing at the stereo on the counter, silencing it.

"Where," I said through grated teeth, "can I find your sister?"

Owen swallowed audibly, the last of his bite of pizza going down hard. "What happened?"

Apollo stood up, faced me, wary but curious. "Your guess is as good as ours, remember?" He shot a look at his brother who shrugged while Simon sat back and resumed munching the thick crust. The scent finally got through to me, making my mouth water and I realized I hadn't eaten in ages. But there was no time for pizza.

"Is there any way to track her she wouldn't be able to trace back to us?" I could just run off on a tangent and make tons of magical noise, throwing my weight around looking for her. The younger me would have, and made a mess and sent Trill scrambling for cover long before I caught up with her. I knew better now. Stealth, then attack. As much as it would be more satisfying the first way, only the end result of catching her really mattered to me right now.

Apollo's curiosity turned to real concern. "Syd," he said. "What did she do?"

I shook off the need to smack him. "She stole something very important," I said, shaking a little from the strength it took to just stand there and not beat the crap out of him for not answering my question. "Two somethings, if my guess is right. She betrayed me. And I want her and what she took. Right. Now."

That got a reaction from the brothers. Owen joined Apollo with real fear on his face, brilliant blue eyes snapping anger. "It's Cable," he said.

I cut him off with a sharp gesture. "I don't give a sweet freaking damn who is responsible," I said. "Nor do I want to discuss it. I need to find Trill with minimum fuss in a way she won't know I'm hunting her. And I expect you two to help me."

Both nodded.

"Cold, Hayle," Simon muttered from behind them.

"You have no idea," I shot back. "And, until you do, mind your damned business, Simon."

He just shrugged and focused on his pizza.

"She'll be expecting one of us to try to reach her," Owen said, while his brother nodded, gnawing on the side of his thumbnail in anxiety. "But there's one person she might react to." He snapped his fingers. "Nona."

"Your grandmother." Why didn't I think of that? Probably because I was still wound up from the theft. The betrayal. Why, Trill? Why? I latched onto the two brothers with power and my hands. "Where?"

Owen showed me, a rickety old RV parked in a quiet corner of a trailer park. I pulled them along into the veil, leaving Simon behind. We emerged in the tree line, covering the last of the distance to the RV on foot. Owen beat me to the door, knocking softly. It opened almost immediately, a lined and inquisitive face peeking out, thin hands tucking her pink fluffy robe around her. The Zornov matriarch I knew best as Nona smiled at the sight of her grandson, though when she looked up and saw he wasn't alone, her face tightened.

"Sydlynn," she said. "What's Trill done now?"

"You knew," I said, entering behind Owen as his grandmother retreated. Apollo joined us, the RV rocking with our entry. Nona sat on the long couch that hid the kitchen table and sighed, head bobbing on her scrawny neck, hair as black as a teenaged girl's without a trace of silver despite her advanced age. Her dark eyes glittered with anger as she gestured for me to take a seat next to her.

"I knew she was up to something I wouldn't like," Nona said. "Though from the anger I sense in you, she's gone too far at last."

I told the Zornovs everything as we sat there in the closed space of the RV, the scents of cinnamon and over cooked onions mingling with faint traces of candle wax burning. Nona held silent and still, her old face crinkled in a scowl so deep her lips disappeared into a thin line, dark eyes mere pinpoints of sparks under her heavy brows. Owen and Apollo stared with their mouths open, as though having trouble absorbing the massiveness of what I was telling them.

Frankly, I was having a bit of a hard time myself and I was in the middle of it.

"That damned *păcăli*," Nona snapped as I finished. "What is she thinking?"

"She claimed from the beginning she's not my enemy," I said, unable to stop the disgust and chill in my voice, "but I'm having a really hard time believing her right now."

The old woman bobbed her head, thin, wrinkled hands clutching at the soft fluff of her robe.

"Nona," Owen said, tone filled with hurt, "can you find her for us? Make her talk to Syd? There has to be an explanation. Maybe Trill took the two pieces to give to you?" He focused on me in his last sentence. There was a desperate need in him to believe in his sister, and I could hardly blame him for that. It would be like Meira turning on me. I'd had it happen, briefly, but she was under the influence of the demon power boosting drink, nectar. She was purposely hooked on an enhanced version of the drug and controlled by demons out to destroy me and Dad. This was something far worse. The entire Universe was at stake.

"Trillia would never betray you or her bloodline." Nona shook her head at last, though it didn't sound as though she believed her own words completely. "There must be an explanation."

"Trill is the only one with access to the heart," I said, shoulders slumping as the truth finally hit me. Yes, I knew, intellectually. But this was heart sureness, down to the depths of my soul understanding. My friend, who I trusted, did this terrible thing. And I allowed her access, left the Stronghold vulnerable because I believed in Trill.

"We will uncover what's what," Nona said, sitting suddenly forward, spry for a woman her advanced age. "Now."

Her maji magic felt of mine, but more fundamental, fed by her blood. Creation power, long reviled by witches as evil and punishable by death was the stock and trade of the human-born maji. They understood the incredible power in blood magic, the very reason the Brotherhood used witches so long ago to create an overwhelming revulsion against its use. Blood magic was almost strong enough—pure creation power—to counter sorcery.

Trill's magic tied directly to her darker power had to have consequences. But I didn't care about that right now. Or, even, who she was working for, though I wouldn't turn down the information if it landed in my lap. All I wanted was the maji woman and the two pieces she stole from me.

The rest would wait until I beat some sense into her.

I hovered in the background as Nona reached out to her granddaughter. Trill answered her immediately, so trusting.

Nona, she sent, a faint hint of relief in her voice, backed with grief I didn't understand.

Trillia Elderia Zornov. Her grandmother's mind lashed against hers. *What have you done?*

I didn't give Trill a chance to answer. My maji power

leaped out after her, netting her with energy, holding her tight. *Don't fight me, Trill*, I sent. *I don't want to hurt you.* Not exactly the truth. A little hurt might be in order. But if she gave me what I needed, I'd consider letting her go.

Consider.

I'm sorry, Syd. Trill's mental voice slipped from sad to determined. *You don't have all the information. And I'm doing what I need to do.*

Get your ass back here, I snarled, *with the pieces. Then we'll talk. And you can fill me in on what I don't know.* Sarcasm much?

Trill's power flexed, twisted against mine, and, as though I had no hold over her at all, she slipped through my net and out of my grasp. The greasy feeling to her combined power refused to be contained, no matter how hard I tried to catch her and pull her back.

You just have to trust me, Trill sent. *Syd, I'm on your side, I swear. But I have to do this my way.*

Fine, I sent. *Do whatever the hell you want. But turn over the heart and hand.* I reached for Max, felt him coming for me, his power roaring toward me, but knew he'd be too late as Trill's mental voice grew more distant. Why did I wait so long? Still, for all I knew,he wouldn't be able to hold her either.

I'm sorry. She whispered the last. *This will all be over soon. You'll see.*

The outside of the trailer shook violently, the door

jerking open, the giant form of my drach friend's entry making the RV rock so much I had to hold on. His magic flooded the room, poured after Trill, joining with mine and, for a moment, I thought we had her.

Protect the gateway, drach lord, Trill sent, spinning free of us both. *I will see you soon.*

And, just like that, she was gone.

TRILL! I screamed after her, rage erupting from utter frustration. *I will hunt you down if it's the last thing I do!*

No answer. I stormed to my feet, power lashing out between the Zornov's searching for the touch that was Trill. And cut her off, completely.

Nona gasped, hands over her mouth, tears flooding her dark eyes, but I shook my head, relentless, refusing to back down.

"If she tries to contact any of you," I snarled, "you will tell me immediately. But until Trill is caught, she will get no support, no protection. She's on her own. Is that understood?"

They all nodded, Nona dropping her hands, trembling as Owen crossed to her, sat next to her, hugging his grandmother gently in his arms.

"We'll find her, Syd," Apollo said, voice angry and cold, but not aimed at me. "And we'll bring her in."

THIRTY

Max and I left the Zornovs with their grandmother, Apollo promising to drive her to Wilding Springs and park her RV in their backyard until the mess with Trill was sorted out. I knew how independent Nona was, but she seemed relieved by the offer and I was happy to hear she'd be safe and sound with us.

The veil welcomed my drach friend and me, he keeping his human form, crossing over to the empty plaza on Center, the burbling fountain the only activity in the place. Again we were met with silence on our visit instead of aggressive rejection, and it had me wondering what the maji leader, Zeon, was up to. He'd threatened my son, threatened me along the way. And though I honestly considered the old maji a coward at heart, I was on a knife's edge waiting to see what he would do when he finally made his move.

Max didn't seem to worry about it, entering the main temple and crossing to the private room at the back. I joined him, finding it hard to kick the depression settling around me at the realization of Trill's unfaithfulness. She could claim to be on my side all she wanted, but the proof was in the theft.

"My love!" I hadn't heard that much excitement in Light Fate's voice in a long time, the sun in her tone bringing my head up and awakening a bit of hope inside me. As blind as her brother, she stumbled toward Max, falling into his arms, but the smile on her face brought me instant relief.

"Tell me, dear one," Max said. "What has you so bright today?"

"We *saw*," she said, stressing the second word. "Both of us." Tears trickled down her cheeks as I looked past her to her twin, Dark Fate, who nodded with a delighted smile of his own from where he sat with Iepa on the edge of the pool. "Only for a moment, but we saw, my love. Our power can come back again."

Was it Max and me finding the hand that triggered it? "What did you see?"

She turned her head toward my voice. "I don't know," she said. "All we caught were flashes of planes, whipping past us as though we traveled the veil at great speed."

Gabriel. "When the gateway opened," I said, not

really meaning to speak out loud.

"So it would seem," Max said. And gently sat Light Fate down to explain to her and her brother what happened while Iepa listened with a soft frown of anxiety pulling her brows together.

"He is well, after such an ordeal?" Light Fate fumbled for my hand and I took it, squeezed it gently in gratitude for her asking.

"As far as I know," I said, my old friend guilt reminding me I hadn't seen him since we left him with Mom at Harvard. "He's a strong boy. But seeing the Order scared him."

"Scared all of us," Max said.

Light Fate shivered delicately. "As they should," she said. "We, too, saw them before our vision died, felt the malevolence of their presence. The pure need in them to devour and nothing more." And I thought the Brotherhood were bad. "They must not be permitted to cross to our Universe."

I almost said "duh", but held off because, well, she had gone from all-knowing, all-seeing to a blind girl without much hope. I was willing to cut her some slack.

"There is nothing we can do," Max said, "but hunt for the next piece of Creator. And guard well the path we take to get there."

"How did Belaisle find us?" That rankled.

"He must have had us followed," Max said. "While he

may not be aware of Gabriel's ability to track the pieces—something we must shield from everyone from this point on," he wasn't kidding, "he must know we have better odds of locating Creator's lost parts. Perhaps he simply is waiting for us to find them after all. So our fearful drive to locate them is founded in nothing."

"Except both Belaisle and Trill found us," I said, hating them with a passion so powerful I tasted bitter bile in the back of my throat for a moment. "So did he follow us and she followed him?"

"No way of knowing," Max said, gently enough it softened me so I could unclench from the need to immediately hurt the both of them in permanent and painful ways. "At least, not until we investigate further. But we now know we are traceable. And that is something we need to deal with."

"And you now know there are other players in place," Dark Fate said. "While it's likely you're correct, I would say assuming only you have the key to finding the pieces could lead you to trouble."

"Unless the other hunters are all waiting for us to lead them right where they want to go," I said, bitterness a given. That would be just peachy.

Or, my vampire sent, *gives us an advantage further than Gabriel.*

Why hadn't I thought of that? *You're brilliant,* I sent to her before speaking out loud. "What if we used that to lead them on a wild goose chase or two?"

Dark Fate's grin was nasty. "I love how you think, Sydlynn."

"You can thank my vampire," I said as she shifted inside me with a faint touch of modesty. "We just have to work out the logistics." Would be nice to stick it to Belaisle for once.

Take it a step further, even, my demon sent. *Set a trap. For all of them.*

Even if we can't hold them, my vampire agreed, *we would at least see exactly who else we have to deal with. For, surely there are other players we have, as yet, to uncover.*

I made the suggestion to the others. This time, Dark Fate laughed.

"We have spent far too long with the entirety of the Universe in our minds," he said. "Such cunning is delicious."

Optimism, I love you.

Max and I left shortly after, promising to keep the Fates and Iepa up to speed as things moved along. My brain whirled with possibilities, so much I missed the fact when Max led me out of the veil again we were nowhere near my house in Wilding Springs. Instead, we touched down in the quiet, power filled statue chamber under the Stronghold. I turned to look up at him with a curious frown.

The drach leader looked out over the empty room,

diamond eyes turning with multihued magic.

"I take it there's a reason we're here," I said. My voice barely carried, the vastness of the space swallowing my words.

"There is," he said, deep voice sad. "I have information I must divulge before we can go any further. Before you can decide, truly, to trust me in this matter." Max paused, head down, hands clasped before him over his gray robe. A terrible fear lit inside me but I smothered it, refusing to jump to conclusions.

"As long as you're not playing for another team," I said, "we're all good, Max."

He shook his head. "It's nothing like that," he said, finally meeting my eyes. Tears glistened in his. "Far worse."

Okay then.

"You have the right to know, Sydlynn Hayle, it was I who first cracked the Universe."

I knew that already... no, wait. The drach—

I gasped. "You, as in *personally*, you?"

Max nodded, heavy, ponderous in his guilt. "I was young," he said. "Impulsive. But there is no excuse for what I did." The song of the drach rose in his voice as he went on, mournful, so sad I found myself crying in sympathy. "I pushed at sorcery, felt the potential in it, but refused to trust in Creator. My family begged me to relent, but I refused in my arrogance. It was I who triggered the division of magicks and, in doing so, it was I who signaled the end of Creator as we knew her and forced Fate into two paths. So many repercussions." He looked off into the distance again. "The Dark Universe just one of them. I've catalogued so many over the centuries, Syd. Tracked the result of my actions in hurts and cracks so deep I fear I will never survive my regret."

I thought I knew guilt. I had no freaking idea.

"Max," I choked out, but he wasn't done.

"So, you see," he said, "this is all my fault. Your Liam. Gabriel. The Brotherhood. All of it, Syd. Had I done as I was told, had I believed in Creator and not my own self-important needs, the Universe would have developed as she intended, and things would have been far different." He sighed deeply, one big hand running over his face. "I was left behind, my family choosing to sacrifice themselves to guard the pieces, leaving me to lead my people, as first drach. Not as a punishment, but as a hope I would grow and learn and become the drach they knew I could be." He nodded slowly, as though to those he'd lost. "And I have striven to do so all the days of my life since." He left me, crossing to Creator's statue. One big hand opened and, as I joined him to watch, he let slip the small, silver ribbon that had been his brother to pool next to the silent thread of his mother.

"There was a time I believed in what I did," Max said. "But now, I wonder if I am the right one for this particular task, Syd. I've failed Creator before, now twice my family again when I swore to protect them." He looked up and into my eyes. "I am going to step down as leader of the drach. And I want you to choose my successor."

THIRTY-ONE

No. Way. In. Hell.

"If you're over your little pity party," I snapped, "maybe you'd like to get back to work."

Max's hurt expression wasn't helping his case any.

"Sydlynn—"

I cut him off with a firm punch to his shoulder. "I don't want to hear about it," I said. "We've come too far and been through too much together for you to quit on me now, you big lummox." Max straightened slowly, turned to face me. "I need you, no matter what you think of yourself, no matter what you've done in the past. A long freaking time ago, if I might add that little bit of fact to this ridiculous conversation." A frown creased his brow. "And, by the way, have you ever considered the fact maybe you were meant to crack magic wide open? Did Creator give you a hard time, dressing down, kick your butt when you did it?" He slowly shook his head. "No? Didn't think so. Because, I assume if you'd crossed her you'd be a smear on the floor, Max, and not leader of the first race of creation."

"If you're trying to convince me I was fated to this path," he said, "I've thought of that myself. But I can't believe."

"Why not?" I tossed my hands in the air. "Fate is tricky—both of them. You of all people know that." I had no idea if I was getting through to him, but I had to. He was not abandoning me now. "Max," I said, laying one hand on his massive arm, "what came before now, is. It's done and gone and neither of us can change it. All we can do is our best going forward. Besides, you should know trying to ditch me just makes me mad and more determined to drag you along into this disaster with me."

Max smiled. "Indeed," he said. "I should."

"Like it or not," I said, "and I've had this conversation with myself, believe me, there's no one else." Max sighed softly as I went on. "No. One. Else. We're it, flaws and lumps and warts and all."

"I stand chastised for my old angst," he said, a hint of humor in his voice. "Thank you for reminding me no matter how old I become, I am still an arrogant young drach at heart who thinks he knows what's best."

I hugged him hard, his arms slipping around me in return.

"Join the club," I said.

We parted ways, him heading up into the main level of the Stronghold, me for Wilding Springs. We both needed rest before we could begin planning our trap for Belaisle and the other seekers of the pieces. I had a few ideas, but wanted to be as clearheaded as possible just in case this idea was actually full of crap and I just couldn't see it.

The house was dark when I arrived at home, directly outside my room for once. I'd been hoping to catch Quaid unaware, to corner him and have that talk I wanted to have, but he wasn't home. And, honestly, it was probably a good thing. As tired as I was, thinking I could plan a trap for my enemies was about as good an idea as trying to patch things up with my irritable husband.

I considered it a lucky break and sat down hard on the edge of the bed, yawning so wide my jaw cracked in response.

The house felt quiet, the kids still at Harvard. Sassafras and Shenka were in the kitchen, and I considered joining them. The bed beckoned, though, temptation powerful to just crash and sleep instead.

What a day.

The rush of sorcery in the back yard made my decision for me. I slipped down the stairs and out the door, into the cool grass. Piers waited for me, blond hair swinging in the soft, September evening breeze, eyes smiling as a tiny, sad grin pulled at his wide lips. I went right to him, hugged him, inhaling his scent and allowing his power and his body to support me a moment.

Wished it was Quaid.

That drove me back a half step, pushing my hair fallen loose from my ponytail behind my ears as I grinned up at my friend with matching sadness, illumination from the back door light making his gray eyes translucent.

"Tell me you have good news," I said.

"Well, no one's died, yet," he said. Winced. "Sorry, poor taste, considering. No one but Yana." I nodded as he went on. "Danilo's war is hitting a snag. A snag named Femke." I knew she'd get in his way. "So far, so civil, though I'm sure that will change when the wereking gets his fill of her kindness and diplomacy."

"And you?" I crossed my arms over my chest, shivering a little in the wind though I wasn't really cold. More a reaction to being over tired. "How are things at home?"

"The Steam Union is a mess," he said, in his blunt British way. "I won't make any apologies for it. But I'll do my best." He didn't have to tell me he was worried. And why. I could see it all over his face. Had just heard the same thing from another dear friend of mine. Wasn't taking it from Piers, either.

"You're all they've got," I said, thinking of Max. "You're the only man for the job. Remember that." I laughed, couldn't help it. "I've been wondering, you know, why we're all so testy, so cranky. Yes, the attack, okay, got it. But, seriously. We love each other." Sunny, Mom, Quaid, Shenka, Max… Piers and his mother. "I'm finally understanding, it's not about what happened, is it?"

Piers slowly shook his head. "It's about all of us being afraid it's our fault," he said. "And that we're going to screw it up again so badly, let each other down, we can't stand it."

I loved epiphanies in my back yard with dear friends to help me work things out.

We smiled gently at each other for a long moment before I broke the silence.

"How's Zoe?" The moment the words left my mouth, his face fell.

"She's gone, Syd." His voice shook, caught.

"Let me guess," I said, grasping his hand in clear understanding, excitement, even. "She had a vision."

His eyes widened, sadness fading. "She found the fire again," he said. "How did you know?"

"Trust me," I said, "she'll be back. But if she's like another pair of friends of mine, she's trying very hard to figure out what's going on." I really needed to track her down and tell her everything.

Piers shook off his grief and shrugged. "Thanks for that," he said.

"Might I suggest," I said, "in the meantime, you keep

yourself busy with other things?" The idea had formed when I watched him with the young Brotherhood sorcerers, but it grew as I stood here next to him. "Like actively recruiting new Steam Union members?"

Piers grinned. "Way ahead of you," he said. "It was Mom's policy—Steam Union policy—we not approach newly wakened sorcerers, to only admit those of bloodlines tied to our order. But I'm a little tired of the Brotherhood culling the herd of freelancers out there."

I couldn't agree more. "So you're changing your policy?"

"Already done," he said. "Took a bit of convincing. Until I told the elders I'd much rather young sorcerers find us instead of the Brotherhood. They finally agreed."

Just like me to worry about something that was already handled. "And you thought you weren't the right one for the job."

Piers ducked his head, cheeks pinking. "Smartass," he said. Sobered a little. "How's Quaid?"

Did he know about our fight over my husband's jealousy? Or was he just concerned because of Quaid's position as WPC Enforcer leader? Either way, it didn't matter. I shut down a bit, shook my head.

Piers hugged me again. "I'll see you soon," he said.

I let him go, waved as he retreated into a dark tunnel, sighed out my stress, even more tired than before. But at least I had some deeper understanding and maybe could use that to take the edge off my reactions to the ones around me.

That would be a novelty.

Wouldn't you know, as I turned to the back door, Quaid was watching me with a blank expression on his face? I wasn't in the mood for an argument, not tonight, but tensed myself for one anyway.

"I'm sorry," he said.

I exhaled, tears springing to my eyes, expecting him to rush toward me, hug me, swing me around. I pictured it in my head, spun out the imagined moment, so clear to me I gasped in surprise when it never happened. He stayed where he was, just watching me.

"I should have told you." Quaid's body didn't shift toward me, shoulders stiff, expression guarded. So, there was more to this apology than just a few simple words to make everything all right again. "And I know better than to doubt you, Syd. With him." He gestured into the darkness behind me.

"Thanks for that." Sarcasm, really? Too late. I watched a hint of anger crawl over his face. "I'm proud of you," I said.

That helped, seemed to. What was this sudden distance between us? I hesitated to close it, to try to hug him. Why was I so afraid he'd reject my arms around him? Maybe because if he did I'd devolve into a sobbing mess. That I'd find out things were more broken than I first thought. Better not to find out.

"Thank you." He cleared his throat. "I have to go back to Hong Kong. Just home to pack a few things for the night." When Quaid met my eyes, he had to see the resistance there. "I'll be home tomorrow. Maybe we can take the kids for dinner and talk."

I nodded, shivered though I wasn't cold, rubbed my arms as he lifted the small bag I'd missed seeing lying at his feet, hoisting it over his shoulder. Quaid crossed to me swiftly, as though fearing, as I did, he wasn't welcome, and kissed my cheek. The barest brush of flesh, scratchy stubble on my skin tingling, not long enough even for me to lift my hand to touch him, hold him, keep him with me before he backed away again.

Blue fire engulfed him and he was gone.

I refused to cry. We'd figure things out. We loved each other. I just wished I could work with him for once instead of on my own. Like always. But Quaid had his own duty to fulfill and I knew I had to stay out of it.

With a heavy heart to match my weary body, I went inside.

I was two steps inside the back door when Sassafras came trotting around the corner from the kitchen and hurried toward me. I bent and scooped him from the floor, wanting comfort. But his agitation resonated with me as clearly as a struck bell when his ears collapsed to the sides, whiskers sinking downward.

"Syd," he said, voice breaking. "You have to do something."

Seriously, Universe. Now what?

"Shenka," he said. "Hurry."

I strode past the stairs and around the corner, hitting the kitchen at a near run, only skidding to a stop at the sight of my second standing at the door.

Hand on the latch.

Suitcases at her side.

Oh. My. Swearword. Was everyone leaving me?

"Syd." Shenka's voice was quiet, trembling just a little, but she held herself rigid as though expecting a battle.

"Where are you going?" She might as well have just ripped out my heart and stomped all over it. I shook as I stood there, staring at her, not knowing what to say or how to say it, to change her mind even though I could feel she was in no mood for conversation.

"Tallah's asked me to return to our family." Shenka used her sister's name like a weapon before softening a little. "And I realized I couldn't say no."

So that's what had been bothering her since she got back from California. "You're my second," I stuttered, mind blanking as I took in the luggage, her tight posture, the way her gaze dropped from me to the floor. She couldn't just leave me now.

"It's my family," she said, defensive in her posture, her tone. "And you don't need me, anyway."

Don't need…

Before I could manage a coherent thought, Shenka severed her connection to the family magic, stepping out of it almost like a second skin. It sighed its sorrow at her passing, returning to me, slinking up against me to shiver its sadness. I gaped at her as she pushed open the kitchen door.

"Be well, Syd," she said. Walked out of my life, closing the door behind her. Magic bloomed, she had a ride, obviously, set up and ready to take her back to her sister.

"Do something!" Sassafras prodded me with power, but I just hugged him, kissing his soft forehead, clenched myself against the inevitable tears while I did the hardest thing I could do at that moment.

I let my best friend go.

THIRTY-TWO

Could this giant, bubbling mess really get any worse? I hoped not.

Fortunately, when I traveled to Harvard to check in on my kids, Gabriel was perfectly fine. Smiling, no nightmares, so I could only trust him when he told me he was okay.

The problems didn't start until Max and I tried to convince him to open a new gateway for us, to find the next piece. As hard as he tried, Gabriel simply couldn't manage to do it. I could feel the underlying fear in my son, now tied directly to the power within him, and had a brand new worry to add to the pile. He might have been okay on the outside, but how much damage had Max and I done to his confidence?

That meant our plan to lure the other players in the search for the pieces was a go. We had no idea where the next part of Creator was hidden. Which meant we needed a different advantage and pinning down our competition seemed to be the best course of action.

The Empress's hints about the pieces made me wonder if she might be attached to enemies we had yet to encounter.

There was no news from Trill, her brothers keeping me updated as they searched for her. Their grandmother made it safe and sound to Wilding Springs, enjoying sitting out in the back yard in the peace and quiet, so I was happy that much of their family was together.

I turned over Trill's insistence in my head she wasn't my enemy time and again, trying to find a way to trust her, but just couldn't bring myself to do it. Maybe if she'd given me more information, some reason to believe what she was doing was the right way. I'd help her, even. But knowing how much she'd changed and that she was now involved with some shady people who tainted their creation magic on purpose just gave me the feeling she was lying to herself to make her feel better about the betrayal.

Regardless, when I got my hands on her finally, I'd have the full truth from her if she liked it or not. And trust me, she wouldn't like it one little bit.

The only bonus from the whole situation with the missing pieces was the fact Belaisle seemed as frustrated as Max and me when he went after the thief. The shock on his face and the fact he did nothing to attack us, simply abandoning the chance to take me out when I was clearly outnumbered to go after Trill, was all the evidence I needed. If she'd been working for him, he wouldn't have flipped out and taken off after her like his life depended on it. Trill having two of the pieces had to be tearing the Brotherhood leader to shreds with frustration. I hoped he choked on it.

Not a peep from Shenka, though I didn't expect there to be. I missed her like I'd lost something precious and couldn't put my finger on what, a gaping hole in my life. The coven felt her loss as powerfully as I did, coming to me with petty complaints, fears and worries I didn't know how to handle. Thank goodness Sassafras stepped in, though I knew—and he continually told me—I'd have to pick a new second sooner rather than later.

I just couldn't bring myself to do it.

Piers worried about Zoe, I could tell every time we talked. But I kept reassuring him anyway, though I'd been unable to locate her myself. I was sure she was fine and hoped the vision she'd seen when Gabriel opened the gateway was giving her the guidance she needed.

He grew grim quickly and I hoped Zoe would return to help temper him. The weight on his shoulders was a visible thing, at times, though Gram and Demetrius were fabulous at supporting him. He invited me to a few of his meetings, as a show of good faith and to stress our alliance, even including Femke from time to time so his people would grow used to the fact the Steam Union had been dragged into the present, now members of the World Paranormal Council.

Growing pains accompanied the inclusion of a large number of new members, but I knew Piers's plan to recruit more sorcerers, young and untainted by the Brotherhood, was an excellent one. And he was a strong enough leader to hold them all together.

Danilo had been forced, at last, to stand down, though from what Charlotte was willing to tell me— herself suddenly secretive and slinking about without Sage—I assumed her brother was planning something that the World Leader wouldn't like even a little bit. I asked Sage behind Charlotte's back to keep an eye on things, and he assured me he already was.

I'd just leave it at that, then. Sage loved Charlotte too much to let her get into something she couldn't handle without alerting me first.

I hoped.

My few attempts to talk to Quaid about our misunderstanding fell on quietness and sullen rejection. I had no idea what his real problem was, but honestly I was getting a little tired of the hurt boy act. He spent so much time away working with Femke these days it was like I was single all over again. The kids missed him, and I did, too. It felt like no matter what I did we were growing further apart and the girl who'd had her heart broken so many times desperately wanted to cling to him and pull him back. To return to the way things used to be, to seven years of bliss and love and happily ever after. But I was a big girl and understood Quaid needed to spread his own wings, no matter what that might mean for our relationship. He'd come home to me once he was comfortable with his new role. I had to believe it. And he deserved to find his own way, as much as I found mine. I just wished we could do it together instead of being so far apart.

I really had to find a way to get through to him before I was forced to pounce on him and wrangle him with magic.

That would go over well, I was sure.

Max had been quiet lately, too, something that worried me even more. I gave him his space, though. And when I needed him to discuss our plans, he was always there, if withdrawn and sad. He would just have to work through his guilt on his own time. We had a Universe to save.

Simon was settled in nicely with the Zornov boys, had even opened channels of communication with his parents again. I was surprised to find they'd stayed in Wilding Springs and was happy to hear my old friend had given up on a lot of the hurt and anger he carried after the disaster at Harvard that shattered him so badly.

Even better, he was hard at work restoring the fortunes of the various families targeted by the Brotherhood. I was a little miffed to find out he was doing so for free, that he'd only charged me an outrageous fee for his services. Not to mention racking up a massive bill on my credit card to replace his computers.

I guess I'd let him have his fun. I just hoped it helped him to feel like part of the family. I knew they adored and welcomed him for saving them as he did. In fact, he and the Zornov brothers were smothered in adoration on a regular basis by the young witches in the family, something Nona watched with iron fisted amusement. She was a hell of a chaperone.

Piers kindly agreed to allow his Steam Union members to train witch families in sorcery while accepting reciprocate help in tracking his mother. Eva Southway and her budding Sorcerer Guild had vanished after her appearance with Piotr Wilhelm and I could only imagine what she was up to now. I worried for Piers and his people, but knew I had to stay out of it. If anything happened to Eva, it had to be Piers who followed through. He'd never forgive me otherwise.

I attended Queen Yana's funeral, one of the saddest moments of my life. Danilo was despondent and refused to talk to me afterward, Charlotte protecting him from me. Oleksander swore to me he was watching them both along with Sage, but seeing the siblings plotting, cutting the rest of the world out, made me immensely anxious.

Sunny and I pressured the Empress to allow her to retake her throne after Piotr's arrest. I have no idea if Max's stern and unhappy presence was the deal sealer on that particular decision of hers, but the way he glared at her and how she shifted under the pinpoint gaze of his diamond eyes told me inviting him along as encouragement was the right decision.

The only problem with our victory showed its worrisome face when Sunny and I, Max in tow, returned to Castle Wilhelm and found it empty. Cold and dark as Sebastian's base of operations, the vampires gone, their power missing.

Sunny's grief at the loss of her family hit her hard and I sent her home with Uncle Frank when I returned to see the Empress and confronted her. Upon receiving the news, she turned away from us and refused to speak further, scary little Jiao firmly escorting us out.

Which told me things were far worse for her race than she'd led us to believe. I wondered how many others had vanished up to this point, but had no way of knowing.

The worst part was Piotr was also gone, vanished from his cell, never having faced justice. Danilo threw a fit, naturally, Femke's hands full dealing with the uproar. My hope Piotr's trial and execution would soften Danilo's hate backfired. When he found out about the loss of his primary target to some unknown force, I watched his hate transfer from Pitor to all vampires in a clear and aching shift in his magic.

Not good.

As for Femke, things were still tense between us, though I did my best to walk softly and not antagonize her. Our talk in the palace helped, but she was still touchy and so was I, especially over Quaid. Still, her willingness to try gave me more hope than anything else lately, that we'd be friends again.

I kept Mom religiously up to date on the shadow council's meetings, though, it turned out, they were mostly talk to reassure each other everything was okay. Which was fine by me.

Except, of course, for the fact Tallah wouldn't meet my eyes.

I guess I didn't blame her.

Like what you read? Find out more at
pattilarsen.com

Here's a look at the first chapter of
Book Three of the Hayle Coven Destinies

THE BROTHERHOOD

ONE

Normally the cushion of my favorite chair in my sunny living room felt soft, inviting me to curl up in it, flop to one side with my legs hooked over the arm while one or both of my children piled into my lap with a fluffy silver Persian perched on top for good measure.

As I sipped my coffee that tasted vaguely of ashes thanks to the burning in my veins, for the first time ever the seat felt more like a plank of concrete. Probably because my muscles were so tensed they vibrated.

The reason for my tension—both of them—sat delicately on the edge of the sofa across from me. Sonja O'Dane's smile screamed falsehood, as fake as the dyed-blonde of her hair and puff of her overly-plumped lips. My darling Liam's mother disappeared from my life shortly after Gabriel was born. And honestly, I hadn't thought anything of her since. She'd done enough to betray her son and husband in my books, pairing with the exiled Sidhe Lord Venner to use the Gate Liam guarded to gain access to the Sidhe realm. Almost dooming me and all of Wilding Springs in the process. I would never forgive her for the bullet that laid Liam's grandfather, Fergus, low, forcing him to retreat to the realm to save his life. Or for thrusting Liam into the position of Gatekeeper way before his time. I still wondered if perhaps things would have been different if Liam hadn't died at Ameline's hand.

I simply couldn't allow myself to think that way.

Considering the fact my son's first reaction to his grandmother had been uncharacteristic unhappiness, I had been more than willing to watch her walk away and never come back. So much for that dose of wishful thinking.

"Warm September we've been having." Sonja's voice shook ever so slightly as she glanced with wide eyes sideways toward her companion. I ignored the statement, not interested in small talk. At least the woman next to Sonja had the good grace not to try to pretend she was happy to see me. Hortense Spaft hadn't changed a bit since I first met her all those years ago. I had no idea my former vice-principal was part Sidhe and an Unseelie servant, or that she had it in for me, not until the night Fergus almost died and Liam was forced to take over as

Gatekeeper. Since then, she'd been an occasional pain in my backside, though not much since Venner got what he wanted and was allowed to return to the realm.

"The boy is well, I take it?" Spaft's black eyes held mine behind her horn rim glasses, beady and vaguely rodent-like.

The boy.

I wondered how much effort it would take to throttle her. Normally, Sashenka Hensley, my second, would be here to relieve the pressure, to give me the space I needed to rein in my temper. I'd gotten good at it over the years, but mostly, I was now realizing, thanks to her steady presence. But Shenka had left me, gone back to her sister, Tallah, only a few days ago, leaving me alone and unsure what to do.

Well, not entirely. Before I could decide on rude or ruder for my return comment, a busty redhead hurried into the room. Her entire being glowed with charisma, shining curls bouncing around her shoulders. Green eyes sparkling, Tippy Meeks flounced to the coffee table with a beaming smile and an almost physical wave of enthusiasm and set a plate of warm cookies on the surface.

"I hope you're hungry, ladies." She smiled all around, though when her gaze settled on mine, I caught the spark of emotion in her that had nothing to do with good nature. She perched next to me on the arm rest of my seat and I instantly relaxed.

Was I really that incapable of handling people on a normal level? Clearly. As Sonja helped herself to the chocolate chip wonders, I breathed an inward sigh of relief. About two days after Shenka left me in a panic over what to do, my old college buddies showed up at my door and hugged me into submission. All former Hensley witches, Tippy, Nicci Mortimer, Josie Ambrose and Donalda Pierce all expressed their distinct unhappiness with Shenka's decision to abandon me and bailed en masse from the vastly shrunken numbers of the Hensley coven.

To come help me.

So many tears that day. More than I was willing to admit to. Shenka's loss hit me hard, though I understood—or told myself I did—why she left. Since the Brotherhood attacks decimated over one third of the North American witch compliment, many covens were struggling. Tallah's had been hit especially hard. I thought I was doing the right thing, sending Shenka home to help her sister temporarily. I didn't intend for her to poach my second and best friend in the process.

But family was family, right? Except Shenka was supposed to be my family now.

I cleared my throat, surreptitiously squeezing Tippy's hand in thanks. She and the girls saved me from the daily tedium of the coven and I would be forever grateful to them. And guilty I had failed to check and see originally if they survived the attacks.

Bad friend, Syd.

Sonja helped herself to her third cookie until Spaft stared at her like doing so meant a death sentence. Not that I wasn't aware of the power dynamic, but it appeared the chilly stick woman hadn't lost her commanding presence.

"You didn't answer my question." Her thin lips pinched into a line, lipstick oozing into the cracks around her mouth. Her prim, black wool suit made me itch just looking at it, tight bun pulling her pale skin taut, collar tied tight around her neck in a precise bow of fabric that bobbed when she swallowed. As usual, she reminded me of a spider, all spindly and spooky, ready to attack at a moment's notice.

My temper rose at her tone, but I held it in, even managed a smile that might have passed for polite. Maybe. "Gabriel is doing very well," I said. No need to tell either of them about his power as a Gateway. I had no idea how much they knew about his early childhood, his capture by Ameline Benoit, his forced aging, the fact he almost destroyed our Universe by allowing through Creator's Dark Brother. Or his ties to the pieces of Creator herself. All because there had to be a reason for their appearance. No way Sonja showed up out of the blue after eight years looking to reconnect with her grandson.

I was just too cynical to believe it.

Say the word, boss lady, Tippy sent while continuing to radiate cheer and good nature. *And these two are out on their asses.*

As much as I would have enjoyed their exodus, my demon growling her agreement with Tippy's suggestion, my curiosity won out. Neither woman was a threat to me, and both had kept themselves out of trouble and under the radar for a long time now. At least, I hadn't heard of them stirring up anything. I'd be checking as soon as they left, mind you. But, for now, I was more interested in finding out what they really wanted.

Especially if Gabriel's safety and wellbeing were involved.

"Good to hear it." Spaft turned her head slowly toward Sonja. I could almost hear the creak of rusting metal as she did, picturing a hideous robot frame beneath the icy shell of her exterior. "Isn't it, Sonja." Not a question.

Sonja nodded quickly, nervously, swallowing her last bite of cookie. "That is, of course, why we're here, Sydlynn."

Of course. "You remember the last time you saw Gabriel," I said as coldly as I could. Maybe it was wrong of me to jab her as hard as I did with the memory, but my son's protection was all that mattered. No way I was letting her anywhere near him if she had an agenda.

Sonja actually flinched, triggering my empathy at last. Maybe she hadn't earned it with her past actions, but she was his grandmother. And family meant everything to me. It was possible she really was here just to see him.

Scratch that. She'd have come alone if she just wanted to see him. Spaft's presence changed everything.

The flush on Sonja's cheeks spread to a large blotch on her neck as she cleared her throat.

"I realize we didn't part under the best of circumstances," she said, fluttering her hands in her lap, white napkin rustling in her grip. "That cruel things were said on both sides." Um, yeah, whatever, lady. She smiled briefly before barging on. "I know I'm not welcome here. But Gabriel is Liam's son. And I deserve the right to get to know him."

Spaft didn't move or speak, simply watching me. I hated her silence and stillness. It made her hard to read, as did the shell she held over herself, the thick layer of Sidhe shielding. I could penetrate it and find her secrets no problem, but without provocation? Not a great idea.

Speak for yourself, my demon snarled.

I'm happy to do it for you, Shaylee sent, my Sidhe princess ego sniffing in royal arrogance in Spaft's direction.

Now, now, ladies, my vampire sent. *If Syd can keep her temper, you two should have no problem.*

Thanks for that. I shut them all down. Maybe there was a time we could have bent the rules. But with the creation of the new World Paranormal Council, I had to tread lightly. The last thing I wanted was to add to the pressure on Femke Svennson's shoulders. Bad enough she and I had almost lost our friendship over my suggestion she take the job as leader. She had a whole pile of stress to deal with thanks to the vampires and werewolves. Me purposely incurring Sidhe issues wasn't something I wanted to lay at her feet just now.

Though hasty, your alter egos have a point. A soft but heavy bundle landed in my lap, silver fur ruffling as Sassafras, my demon cat, finally made an appearance. He smelled of fresh air and grass, so I could only assume he'd been outside doing the elements knew what cat things he did to keep himself occupied. Relief he was here with me took me by surprise, though it shouldn't have. He'd been my rock my entire life, even when I didn't want to admit it. *I take it you're allowing these two to remain out of a need to understand their ultimate motives?*

Smartass. I almost hugged him.

"Perhaps," Sassafras said out loud, amber eyes narrowed as he curled his thick, fluffy tail around his paws, "it would be best to allow Gabriel to decide if he would like to see you, Sonja."

I hadn't thought of that. *He'll say yes*, I sent, knowing my son. His heart was Liam's heart, huge and kind.

He may, Sass sent. *But it will give us time to prepare him, rather than thrusting him into a meeting he might not be emotionally ready for.*

Sonja's lower lip trembled. "How do I know you'll ask him?" She seemed truly distraught. Compassion bloomed beside empathy, held hands and sang kumbaya. A large tear trickled from the corner of her eye and down her heavily made up cheek. She dabbed at it with her wrinkled napkin, a second drop landing on the curve of her chest, spreading a dark spot of moisture on the pocket of her green silk blouse.

Tricksy, Sass sent. *Spaft is probably thralling her.*

Maybe. She'd done so before, controlling those around her to do her bidding with the glamor of Sidhe magic. But Sonja's pain felt genuine to me. "I promise," I said, standing with Sass in my arms, ending the visit with that simple act. The pair on the sofa reluctantly stood to join me. "I'll ask him tonight and let you know what he says."

Spaft nodded stiffly to me, while Sonja came toward me, grasping my wrist, kissing my cheek. She smelled of perfume and desperation, her high heels digging holes in the thick carpet.

"Thank you," she whispered against my skin before leaning back and stepping away.

Okay then.

"We're staying at the Hilltop Hotel." Spaft handed me

a card, which Tippy swiftly intercepted.

"Wonderful!" She gestured toward the hall and the formal front door, still beaming. "We'll be in touch."

She guided our two guests out, leaving me to flop into my chair again, Sass hissing at me as he landed hard on my stomach.

"Am I really going to let him near her?" I shook my head at my oldest friend.

"Not without supervision," Sass said. "Or his permission. With both?" He sighed, leaned in and licked the tip of my nose. "We'll see."

The front door slammed firmly about a heartbeat before Tippy stormed into the room. Her happy-go-lucky charisma bubbled with irritation.

"Tell me," she said, "the next time that woman," I knew she was talking about Spaft, "shows up at this door," Tippy jabbed at the exit so hard her generous breasts bounced up and down like enthusiastic melons in a sack, "I get to tell her where she can take her freaking attitude."

I grinned at her. "You can," I said. "The minute one of you agrees to be my second."

Tippy grinned back, though with sadness. She sat down beside me one more time, touching my hair.

"Syd," she said. "The girls and I are here for you. But none of us are taking the damned job permanently." She snorted as she transferred her attention to Sassafras who rewarded her enthusiastic scratches with his deep, rumbling purr. "We love you, but none of us are that stupid."

I rolled my eyes at her, but smiled back. "I'm that hard to get along with, am I?"

Tippy kissed the top of Sass's head. "Should I be straight with her, my handsome prince?" He loved it when she called him that. His purr grew in volume. "Or kind?"

"Hit her with it." His amber eyes sparked before he settled into the scratching once again. Long, red nails dug into his mane as Tippy laughed.

"We love you," she said, going serious at last. "And the four of us are happy to take turns keeping you going. But Syd, Shenka is your second. And she'll come to her senses. I know it. You just have to have a little patience."

They'd all come from the very coven Shenka left me for and all of them said the same thing. I allowed hope to win.

"Thank you," I said. "For taking care of me."

Tippy winked, leaning forward so far I feared her ample bosom would burst out of the top of her low-cut t-shirt. "Someone has to," she said.

I didn't get a chance to comment. A surge of familiar magic pushed me to my feet, Sass dumped into Tippy's arms as I hurried to the kitchen to find out what kind of mood my husband was in now that he was finally home.

ABOUT THE AUTHOR

Everything you need to know about me is in this one statement: I've wanted to be a writer since I was a little girl, and now I'm doing it. How cool is that, being able to follow your dream and make it reality? I've tried everything from university to college, graduating the second with a journalism diploma (I sucked at telling real stories), am part of an all-girl improv troupe (if you've never tried it, I highly recommend making things up as you go along as often as possible). I've even been in a Celtic girl band (some of our stuff is on YouTube!) and was an independent film maker. My life has been one creative thing after another—all leading me here, to writing books for a living.

Now with multiple series in happy publication, I live on beautiful and magical Prince Edward Island (I know you've heard of Anne of Green Gables) with my very patient husband and multitude of pets.

I love-love-love hearing from you! You can reach me (and I promise I'll message back) at patti@pattilarsen.com. And if you're eager for your next dose of Patti Larsen books (usually about one release a month) come join my mailing list! All the best up and coming, giveaways, contests and, of course, my observations on the world (aren't you just dying to know what I think about everything?) all in one place: http://smarturl.it/PattiLarsenEmail.

Last—but not least!—I hope you enjoyed what you read! Your happiness is my happiness. And I'd love to hear just what you thought. A review where you found this book would mean the world to me—reviews feed writers more than you will ever know. So, loved it (or not so much), **your honest review would make my day**. Thank you!

www.ingramcontent.com/pod-product-compliance
Lightning Source LLC
Chambersburg PA
CBHW070833280626
47161CB00015B/494